GUILTY MIND

GUILTY MIND

Irene Marcuse

Walker & Company ❋ New York

First published in the United States of America in 2001 by
Walker Publishing Company, Inc.
Published simultaneously in Canada by Fitzhenry and Whiteside
Markham, Ontario L3R 4T8

Library of Congress Cataloging-in-Publication Data

Marcuse, Irene, 1953–
  Guilty mind / Irene Marcuse.
    p. cm.
  ISBN 0-8027-3354-9
  I. Title.

PS3563.A6433 G85 2001
813'.6—dc21   00-068629

Series design by M. J. DiMassi

Printed in the United States of America

2 4 6 8 10 9 7 5 3 1

This one's for Philip
for making everything possible, and me happy

Acknowledgments

Here come the thanks.

To my readers: Janet Jaffe, plot consultant; Philip Silver, always the man with the best lines; Kyra Cubucuoglo, ESL teacher, who introduced me to the Riverside Language Program; Leigh Henderson and Caroline Donnelly, for deadlines and Des Moines; Barbara Greenwald-Davis and Dean Brewington, the eyes of authenticity; Peter and Frances Marcuse, for support, suggestions, and space. To the lawyers: Douglas Reiniger, my favorite attorney, and Daniel Arshak, for the background information on arrest, arraignment, and grand jury proceedings.

I hear the stories, and I know how lucky I am to have Sandy Dijkstra for an agent and Walker for a publisher—all the people there have been wonderful to me, especially Michael Seidman, who edits with just the right touch, and Cassie Dendurent, publicist, without whom no one would know I'd written a word.

I couldn't do it without a computer, and computers don't do anything without screwing up—Jeff Rosnick and Leigh Henderson helped me climb through Windows, and my brothers and Web masters, Harold and Andrew, got me a spot in the brave new world.

Chris Shook, my partner in research, thank you for night court; and Katie, for seeing us through the tunnel and back into the light.

This book is also dedicated to the recent immigrants who study at the Riverside Language Program, and to the everyday courage they bring to starting a new life—not to mention learning a language as irrational as English. Joe Lihota and Moira Taylor, volunteer coordinators, thanks for putting up with my erratic cancellations!

Tabitha, being thirteen, you get the last word. I love you.

GUILTY MIND

Prologue

I was a happily married woman, necking on the stoop with my husband as we had on our first date. Then I'd gone in alone with the afterburn of Benno's one long kiss still making its way from my lips downward. Tonight we kept on kissing in the elevator.

When we got out on the twelfth floor, I wiped at the lipstick I'd left on his mouth, so the baby-sitter wouldn't see. Not that Ellen would have noticed; she'd fallen asleep to the lullaby of turned-down-low MTV. She sat up and rubbed her eyes.

"Everything okay?" I asked, pausing with my hand on the knob of Clea's door.

"You know she's always good, Anita," Ellen answered. "I hope you don't mind, she wanted me to do her hair. I took the cornrows out and put them back the same way, and I had some new beads from the Harlem market, so I let her choose some of those."

"You mean she wanted to watch some television," Benno said.

I didn't care about that; Ellen would have let her, anyway.

That's what baby-sitters are for, to let seven-year-olds watch when parents might not. But braiding Clea's hair had saved me two hours of my Sunday afternoon, and I appreciated it. "Did she hold still?"

"Still enough. My sister's squirmier. I liked doing your pattern, Anita. It's very unique."

Since I'm white—and didn't grow up doing cornrows—I don't have a repertoire of braid patterns to fall back on. I invent my own, overlapping diagonals that suit Clea's little head.

"The cornrows look so cute on Clea. I wanted to ask you— when my hair gets long enough, will you do me?" Ellen patted her short Afro and gave me a tentative smile.

Ellen was style-conscious enough to know that any African braider on 125th Street could do as good a job, if not a better one, than I could, but I read a peace offering in her request. "I'd be honored to do your hair, Ellen." I smiled back, glad that she was willing to let the recent tension between us go. "Whenever you're ready!"

I checked the clock—12:22, so we owed her for six hours. Benno took his wallet out, and I nodded yes to an extra ten. Doing Clea's hair took Ellen half the time it would have taken me.

Ellen shrugged on her backpack. Benno opened the door for her.

"Do we need anything besides the paper?" he asked. "Breakfast?"

"No, I've got that covered." Croissants, and fresh oranges to squeeze for mimosas—we were celebrating.

"See you Monday at six?" Ellen said.

"Yes, thanks again, Ellen." I blew Benno a kiss and locked the door behind them.

Ellen had graduated from Barnard two weeks ago and moved from her dorm to grad student housing. Although the stretch of Broadway between us on 111th and Ellen's new building on 113th was well populated, Benno always walked Ellen home if we got in after midnight. It would take him ten, maybe fifteen minutes with getting the Sunday *Times*.

Long enough for me to change into a pale green silk chemise, light a candle, put some Coltrane on the CD player, pour two Metaxas, and get into bed. We don't do this kind of romantic very often. When you're closing in on fifty and you've got a day job and a child in private school in New York City, it's hard to stay awake long enough.

As it turned out, that night I didn't. The last thing I remembered was waking up to check the time, 1:14, and thinking Benno should've been back by then. I tried to wonder what he was up to, but sleep pulled me down again.

When Benno slid in next to me and leaned over to blow out the candle, the red numbers had climbed to 1:56. I opened my mouth to ask where he'd been, but he covered my lips with his and ran his hand up inside my thigh with the kind of urgency that sent my conscious mind somewhere beyond time.

After that I slept like I was drugged, which in a way I was. I'm not a drinker, and I'd started the night with champagne and ended it with brandy. Somewhere along with the sun, Clea came in. I was vaguely aware of Benno discussing time with her in terms of how long until 9:00 A.M., when she was authorized to watch television.

The morning air was chilly, and I pulled the quilt up over my head. A cool hand slid up the curve of my hip, under my arm, and found a breast. I stretched onto my back so the hand could make its way down my stomach.

"Is the door locked?"

"Oh yeah," Benno breathed into my ear.

I kept my eyes closed. We hadn't done it in the morning in years. If this was Benno's idea of scratching the seven-year itch, I was in favor.

His breathing turned soft and even. I let him sleep and got up to squeeze oranges. Clea was ensconced on the couch with a bagel and her baby quilt, mesmerized by *Reading Rainbow.*

A huge bunch of lilacs spilled the scent of late May from my grandmother's cut-glass vase on the table; Benno must've made a trip down to the all-night Korean market on 103rd for flowers.

I put the orange juice in the fridge and got into the shower, counting myself a happy woman.

1

I was just hanging up the phone at three-thirty on Monday afternoon when Clea poked her head into my cubicle at work.

"Hey, Bopster." I opened my arms, and she climbed into my lap. "Where's Ellen?"

"I don't know. She didn't come get me, so Ms. Simms watched me walk over here by myself to tell you."

My job at Senior Services, on the grounds of the Cathedral of St. John the Divine, didn't pay all that well, but it had good fringe benefits. The one I appreciated most was the cathedral school, two buildings away from my office. It made me feel secure, knowing Clea was so close.

"Ellen said I could see her new room," Clea whined. "And I hurried up and finished this so she could have a place to keep her pencils!"

She held up a drinking glass that had been papered with scraps of rainbow-colored tissue glued down with a shiny glaze of some sort. I sighed. "Well, let me give her a call. Maybe she got tied up at work."

Actually, I was worried. Ellen had been picking Clea up on Mondays all year; it wasn't like her not to call if she'd be delayed. I dialed Ellen's new number and got her machine on the second ring, which meant she wasn't in her room and probably hadn't been for a while. I left a message.

"Tell you what," I said to Clea. "I have a little more to do here. You have homework?"

She nodded.

"I'll set you up in the conference room, and when I'm done, we can stop by Ellen's on the way home. Then you can leave your housewarming present for her if she's still not there."

May is New York at its best. The days are warm without the humidity of summer, and everything is in bloom. Clea held my hand, humming to herself as we walked past the canon's lawn with its wild border of columbine and tulips. The community garden on the corner of 111th and Amsterdam had beds of iris blooming purple and yellow.

"Dad said she has her own bathroom." Clea pulled my hand to make me walk faster. "And the bookcase they found is bigger than me!"

May is also graduation month, which means lots of students moving out, which makes it the best time for Dumpster diving, the traditional New York way to furnish a first apartment. When Benno had escorted Ellen home Saturday night, they'd found an abandoned bookcase on the street and carried it up to her room. The bookcase was a bit rickety, so Benno put the starter toolbox we'd given Ellen for graduation to good use and stabilized it for her.

Benno's a cabinetmaker by trade, and tools, in his opinion, are essential to every independent young woman. When Ellen moved from the dorm to her own room-with-bath in grad student housing, we'd given her the basics: hammer, crescent wrench, pliers, screwdrivers, tape measure, hand saw, drill, nails, screws, and other miscellaneous hardware. If she'd been a man, I would have seen that she had what every independent young man needs: a toilet brush, cleanser, sponges, broom and dustpan, detergent, an iron and ironing board.

We crossed Broadway at 113th Street and climbed the four steps to Ellen's new building. The front door was propped open while the Super, a Pakistani man in a blue Columbia uniform and matching turban, made conversation with the mailman in the lobby. I found Ellen's name and room number, 7D, on the directory. The elevator doors parted, and a skinny girl with fuchsia hair and two rings in her left eyebrow got out.

"Promise me you'll never pierce your face!" I whispered to Clea. "But if you want purple hair, I'll understand."

"Yuck," Clea said. "One time I saw a man with a safety pin in his cheek."

The seventh-floor hallway was shadowy and cool. The walls were a smooth, pale cream, the doors black enamel. A faint thump of bass vibrations rippled toward us. I knocked on Ellen's door. Clea added her knuckles. There was no response.

"Shall we leave the pencil jar in front of her door? I'll write her a note, and we can put it in the jar." I rummaged in my purse for a pen.

"If we leave it in the hall, Mama, someone might steal it," Clea objected. She kept on pounding at the door, a staccato rap, rap, rap, in time to the bass beat.

A door across the hall opened. The petite girl who came out reminded me of myself at a younger, slimmer age. She wore jeans and a baggy gray T-shirt with the neck cut out so it hung off one shoulder. Her hair was thick, curly, uncontrollable—but without the gray that so liberally streaked through mine.

"Hey, Clea," she said. "Are you looking for Ellen?"

Clea nodded and held up her creation for the girl to see. "I made this for Ellen to keep her pens and pencils in."

"I see you two know each other. I'm Anita Servi, Clea's mother." Because I'm white and Clea's black, people frequently don't connect us as mother and daughter. To avoid later awkwardness, I've gotten in the habit of announcing the relationship up front.

"It's nice to meet you. My name is Miranda Washburn." She stuck out a hand, and we shook.

"Do you by any chance know where Ellen is? I was expecting her to pick Clea up this afternoon after school."

Miranda frowned. "I think she went somewhere for the weekend. If she's not answering, she's probably not back yet."

"Are you sure? She baby-sat for us Saturday, and she didn't call to say she couldn't get Clea. I can't imagine that Ellen would have gone away without letting me know."

"I'm not positive, but I'm pretty sure she wasn't here yesterday or today. There's only one kitchen on the floor, and I haven't seen any sign of her being here since Saturday morning, so I figured she took off for the weekend again."

I told myself there were any number of logical reasons why Miranda hadn't seen her—Ellen spent Sunday night with her boyfriend, or overslept and ran out without breakfast. But forget about Clea? Something was not right.

Clea bumped my hip with her shoulder and held up the present for Ellen.

"We were just going to leave this in front of her door, but Clea's worried someone might take it. You don't think so, do you?" I appealed to Miranda.

"Wow, Clea, that's really nice! I see why you don't want to take any chances with it. I have her key if you'd like to go in and leave it on her desk."

"That's a good plan," Clea said, "and then we could see the bookcase Dad found!"

Miranda disappeared into her room. I might have stopped her to object that maybe she shouldn't be opening Ellen's door for whoever wanted in, harmless though we might seem, but in the circumstances I had to admit I'd be glad of the opportunity to check out Ellen's room.

In my job, when someone hasn't been heard from in several days—well, it's every elderly person's nightmare, dying in her apartment and not being found for days or weeks. More than once, I've unlocked a door and found a client on the floor. Of course, I didn't expect to find Ellen in her room, but I had a dread of not knowing. At least if she wasn't there and I didn't hear from her by evening, I could call her mother, report her missing.

"You know, it's a good thing we exchanged keys. The Super has extras, but he told everybody we should leave one with a neighbor because he has to charge us if we get locked out. And don't you know I did, last week? I mean, I was just going to the kitchen to get a soda, and I forgot that the door would lock behind me. Ellen having my key saved me ten dollars!" She held out a ring with a neon green alligator and a single key attached to it.

I unlocked Ellen's door and pushed it open. From the doorway I could see that the shades were drawn, leaving the room in semidarkness. The square silhouette of a computer monitor was visible on a desk in front of the window. Clea hung back, not wanting to go in until I'd turned on a light.

There was a funny smell in the room, sweat and stale air, the ammonia reek of urine and something like the sweetish odor of rotting food, a smell that made me draw back instead of going in.

I kept my hand on the door and turned to Miranda. She'd been willing to trust me; I'd have to do the same with her. "Would you take Clea to your room for a minute? I think Ellen might be sleeping. I'll just go in and see."

Miranda, God bless her, picked up on the tone in my voice and didn't ask questions. She took Clea's hand. "Come on, honey, I'll show you my virtual fish."

I stood in the doorway of Ellen's room, letting my eyes adjust to the dim light. A large wooden bookcase stood against the wall opposite the window, with a pile of cardboard cartons on the floor in front of it. The hall light cast my reflection in the mirror on the half-open bathroom door. I stepped into the room. The weight of the door swung it closed behind me.

A blinking red light on the bedside table indicated that Ellen had several messages. I switched on the lamp by the answering machine. In the halo of yellow light I could see that Ellen had the blankets pulled over her head. I had had enough experience with death to be afraid of the motionless shape in the bed.

I didn't want to touch her, but I held my breath and reached for a corner of the blanket. I gave a gentle tug and got more than I bargained for. Ellen's whole body rolled over with the covers, a rag doll with blood caked around her mouth, blood dried on her gray T-shirt, and the handle of a screwdriver sticking out of her chest.

I made it to the bathroom and sent my lunch down the drain. It was worse than my worst fears—in her own bed in her own room, stabbed to death with a screwdriver. I turned the cold-water tap on full, splashed my face, and rinsed out my mouth.

For all my worrying beforehand, I'm usually competent in a crisis. I turned the water off and glanced up. The eyes that looked back at me from the mirror over the basin knew what to do.

This is a crime scene. I held on to the words like they could ward off evil. I went back over to the bed, closed my eyes, and crossed myself, whispering the skewed version of a Hail Mary I learned from my lapsed-Catholic mother. "Hail Mary, Mother Goddess, pray for us now and at the hour of our death, Amen."

I made the 911 call from Miranda's room, with Clea on my lap. She and Miranda had taken the news with a stunned silence. I went for the phone without giving them time to ask questions; hearing the facts again would help it to sink in.

When I hung up, Clea said, "Mama, Ellen's not dead. She's not old enough to be dead."

For a seven-year-old, Clea's had quite a few encounters with death. I work with the elderly, and she's accompanied me to several memorial services and, once, an open-casket wake. Those experiences, however, were with death as it should be, the natural conclusion to a long life. This death was something else entirely, sudden, violent, unexpected; it had come to someone Clea saw almost every day, someone she loved. Acceptance would not be easy.

"Maybe you made a mistake?" Miranda chimed in.

Clea headed for the door. "I'm going to wake her up!"

"No, you're not." I grabbed her arm and pulled her back to my lap. Miranda started to cry. I had tears in my eyes, too, and I let them fall into Clea's hair as she struggled to get out of my embrace.

When I wouldn't let go, Clea went limp and started sobbing. "No, no, no, Mama, Ellen's not dead!"

Miranda joined us on the bed and handed me a tissue. I wiped my eyes. We exchanged a brief look over Clea's head. Miranda's face was white and pinched. When I put a hand on her knee, she grabbed it and held on.

One thing about children, they focus your mind. I forced my brain to register the objects in Miranda's room while I got a grip.

Miranda had her furniture situation more in hand than Ellen had. Metal shelving lined two walls, already filled with books. The double bed we were sitting on took up most of the floor space and appeared to function as an extension of the closet—half of it was covered with a mound of clothing that ran heavily to black. A virtual aquarium of tropical fish swam across the computer on the desk, their brilliant yellow stripes and rippling fins as unreal to me as Ellen's body in her bed.

I caught myself wondering if Miranda might need a part-time job. I know it sounds terrible, but baby-sitters are hard to find, and shock does funny things to your mind. I shook the thought away, appalled, and stroked Clea's back until she quieted.

When we heard voices in the hall, I lifted Clea gently from my lap and wiped her face. "I'd better go out and talk to the police. You stay here with Miranda, okay? I'll be right back."

Miranda slid over next to Clea on the bed and reached under her pillow to pull out a bedraggled stuffed leopard. "Would you like to meet Booney?" she asked.

I picked up the neon alligator with Ellen's key attached to it and went into the hall. Two uniform cops, a short white guy and a shorter Hispanic woman, were knocking on Ellen's door. I handed the key to the female officer, who unlocked the door and went in. She was back in seconds, on her radio, calling it in as a homicide.

I was telling my story to the white guy when I heard a voice behind me.

"Hey, Social Worker, long time no see." It was Michael Dougherty, the only cop I have a high opinion of. Michael's a good-looking man, in his late thirties, tall, what my grandmother used to call "black Irish"—fair skin, black hair, and green eyes that at the moment were full of concern. I took in the fact that rather than his uniform, Michael was wearing a gray suit with a wild blue, magenta, and black tie. It was an enormous relief to realize that his promotion to detective and his appearance on the scene meant he'd be in charge of the investigation.

"Anne told me you've come up in the world," I said. I've known Michael since he was on foot patrol, when I inadvertently introduced him to his current paramour, Anne Reisen, the administrative assistant at my agency.

"Hard to believe they actually rewarded brains for a change, huh?" Michael put an arm across my shoulders and gave a quick squeeze. "So, you want to tell me what's up?"

I went over it again, expecting Ellen to pick Clea up, finding her body, the last time I saw her.

"Tough luck," he muttered. "I hate it when young women get themselves killed."

"You sound like it was her fault!"

"Jesus, Mary, and Joseph, that's not what I meant. You and Anne, you carry this women's lib stuff a little too far." Michael shook his head, exasperated. "Before I talk to this kid across the hall, you mind taking a look at her again to see if she's still wearing the same things she had on Saturday night? She's been dead awhile, and we'll need all the info we can get to pinpoint time of death."

The last thing I wanted was to walk back into that room, but I did it. Someone had pulled up the shade and opened the window. It didn't do much to ease the smell. Ellen's body lay the way I'd left it, partially rolled over onto her back. Michael lifted a corner of the covers.

Besides the gray T-shirt, she had on navy sweatpants. The handle of the screwdriver was yellow plastic. This time my brain registered the fact that it was one of the set we'd given her for graduation, a tool intended to help her into a new stage of life.

I stood there with my hands pressed against my chest, trying to hold on to a time before this had happened. I couldn't bear to look at Ellen. I glanced up at the wall over her bed, at the tape scars where a former occupant's poster had hung, then across to the bookcase. It was about five feet tall, three feet wide, dark-stained wood with a solid back. Three shelves had already been filled with books. *Black Boy*, by Richard Wright; *Makes Me Want to Holler*, Nathan McCall; *Beloved*, and the rest of Toni Morrison. My eyes filled.

"Anita?" Michael said. "Anything?"

I was totally unable to conjure up an image of what Ellen had been wearing. "Maybe. She could have been. I don't know, I don't remember."

Michael put his hands on my shoulders, turned me around, and guided me out of the room. I leaned my forehead against the wall and let the tears run while I took long, slow breaths. The cops let me be, until a white handkerchief was pushed into my hands. I remembered where I was, that Clea was waiting for me. I blew my nose.

"It's okay, Anita. Since your husband actually saw her after you did, we'll get the information from him. I'll stop by your place later to talk to him."

"Can't you just call him at the shop instead? I don't want Clea to hear any more about this than she has to."

"We're gonna need to see him, but I guess a phone call'll do for starters. What's the number?" Michael wrote it down, then knocked on Miranda's door.

Booney the leopard was carrying on a conversation with a koala bear on the bed. I let Clea introduce me to the animals while Miranda told Michael she'd slept past noon on Saturday, spent the evening with friends in Brooklyn, and stayed overnight; got home around two on Sunday, went to the library, came home and cooked herself dinner, watched some TV, went to bed, got up this morning at eight for a nine o'clock class, and hadn't seen Ellen since Friday night.

Although she was way too big for me to carry, I hoisted Clea up, backpack and all, and settled her on my hip. Ellen's door was wide open. Clea took a quick peek, then buried her head in my shoulder.

"Take her home, Anita," Michael said. "I'll see you later."

I was only too glad to go.

We were waiting for the elevator when a young man's breezy voice came out of Ellen's room. "Ellen? Hey, I know you're sitting tonight, but if you want to grab a beer at Canon's afterward, I'll be there until about one."

Clea squirmed in my arms. "That's Jamie!"

I put her down and raised my eyebrows in a question. "He used to be Ellen's boyfriend, but she doesn't like him anymore."

Clea would have gone on, but I held a finger to my lips to shush her.

There was silence followed by a long beep—someone hanging up.

Then a woman's voice, low and urgent: "Ellen, I stopped by to see you this morning, but you weren't home. I'm free tonight, and we need to talk. Please call me."

"No, Bopster, that's just someone listening to the messages on Ellen's answering machine."

The clicks, followed by silence and the long beeps of two hang-ups.

The young man's voice again. "Ellen? Are you there? So you didn't want to have a beer last night, how about supper? I reserved a table at your favorite restaurant, Chez Chinese Delivered. Be there at eight, or the Moo Goo Gai Pan will be cold and congealed." Pause. Click, the machine disconnecting.

Another hang-up. A young woman's voice. "Ellen, this is Aisha. You want to catch a movie tonight? Call me."

The young man, worried this time, and trying to make light of it. "Ellen? It's ten-thirty, in case you forgot you have a day job now." There was a pause before the beep of the machine put an end to his message.

The next message was from me. I sounded like a stranger on the tape, a distracted woman with equal measures of irritation and concern in her voice. Three final beeps sounded after my voice.

The elevator doors opened, and we got in. "How come you think Ellen didn't like Jamie anymore?" I asked.

"I don't know, but I think he must have did something bad, because she wouldn't tell me. Her face got all mad when we saw him on the street, and she wouldn't talk to him."

"Must have *done* something bad." A mother is a mother. "Maybe they just had a fight." Clea could be pretty perceptive when it came to relationships. She had her finger on the shifting dynamics of her second-grade class—who were the teacher's favorites, who was a nerd, the "top boy" and "top girl." Although I'm the one in the family with a social work degree, my interests lie with changing the system rather than changing people through therapy. Benno's the one who dropped out of a master's program in psychology to work with wood, and the one who gets into long conversations with Clea, analyzing and examining why people behave the way they do.

"Also because Jamie's white, and Ellen says white men are the *oh*-presser." Clea stopped and stamped her foot for emphasis.

"Ellen said that?" I knew Ellen's views on race were evolving; in her senior year, she'd added a minor in pan-African studies to her economics major. But what a thing to say to Clea, when the father who was raising her was white!

"Mama, what's an *oh*-presser?" Clea tugged my hand.

"Oppressor. It's someone who uses power to take advantage of other people, someone who presses down on people, like back during slavery, the white slave owners were oppressors."

"Jamie doesn't have slaves."

How do you explain institutionalized racism to a seven-year-old?

"No one has slaves. Ellen meant that Jamie's part of a system that once benefited from the labor of slaves, and that as a white person he has certain advantages in the world just because of the color of his skin."

It's a fine line, talking about the history of race relations, protecting a child from what she has yet to encounter while preparing her for the time she inevitably will.

I was glad the walk home was so short.

Our apartment has always felt to me like a safe harbor, perched on the top floor of the building, with a view out over the Hudson. Unlocking the door this time, the place seemed empty, desolate.

The phone rang just as I was closing the door. It was Benno. Michael had asked him to stop by Ellen's building to get his version of what had happened Saturday night.

"Do we need anything?" Benno asked.

"Breakfast," I answered. "I didn't think about stopping at the store."

"Are you two okay?"

"We're all right, just come home."

"I'm leaving now. I'll be there as soon as I can."

I hung up the phone and sat on the couch. Clea climbed into my lap. I stroked her head, my hand lingering on the neat cornrows Ellen had done.

"Ellen did a good job on your hair," I said.

"I'm never taking these braids out," Clea said, fiercely.

I felt tears start up again. "You can keep them in as long as you want."

We sat there until the clock chimed six and nudged me back to reality.

In times of sorrow, I've found, the best you can do is cling to routine and wait for the sadness to lift. I got Clea to help me make meat loaf for supper. It was therapeutic for both of us. Under cover of chopping onions, I had a really good cry. Clea worked her feelings out by squeezing egg and bread crumbs into the chopped meat, then pounding it with her fists until it had the consistency of pureed baby food.

Grief has stages, and I was hoping Clea had moved from denial to anger. I didn't realize how long she'd stay mad before moving on.

Neither one of us was the least interested in the food when it came out of the oven. We were pushing sweet potatoes and mush drenched in ketchup around on our plates when the phone rang.

"Anita, it's Michael."

"Where's Benno?" I said.

"He just left, he'll be there in a few minutes."

The tightness in his voice reminded me that Michael was a cop before he was a friend. I put my guard up.

"Can you tell me what time he got back from seeing Ellen home Saturday night?"

The red numbers, 1:56, flashed a caution in my mind's eye. "We got in just after midnight, I'm sure of that because we paid Ellen for six hours. On the way to Ellen's, he said they found a bookcase on the street, and he helped her carry it in and got it set up for her. Then he went to 103rd for flowers—it was our seventh anniversary we were celebrating—then he bought a paper and came home. I was asleep when he got in."

"Did Ellen eat at your house? If she did, I need to know what she had and what time it was."

"I left out some cheese raviolis and sauce for Ellen to heat up. Hang on, I'll check with Clea." I held the phone to my chest and put a hand on Clea's arm. "Bopster, what time did you eat supper the night Ellen sat for you?"

Clea ducked her head and looked up at me apprehensively.

"It's okay, I won't be mad."

"She let me watch *Xena* while I ate."

I smiled and patted her arm reassuringly. I have no problem with Xena as a kick-ass female role model for Clea, but to Benno the show is dreck.

"They watched *Xena, Warrior Princess*, so that would make it eight o'clock," I told Michael.

"Thanks, Anita. One more question: Was Benno having an affair with Ellen?" Michael said it like he was asking where Benno worked, or what he'd eaten for breakfast.

I was stunned. The possibility had never crossed my mind, not once. I couldn't even begin to imagine that he would have, or Ellen, either. "No," I said. "Benno's not that kind of man, not to mention he's old enough to be her father!"

Of course, as soon as I said it, I realized how stupid it was. Michael pounced. "You hesitated before you answered. Are you sure he wasn't spicing things up with the baby-sitter?"

"I'm positive. Besides, what about Ellen's boyfriend? We

overheard you playing the messages on Ellen's machine, and Clea recognized his voice."

"Now you tell me! So what's this clown's name?"

"I was going to call you later. I can't for the life of me remember his last name, but his first is Jamie. He's a teacher in the ESL—English as a Second Language—Institute in Riverside Church, where Ellen worked. Clea said Ellen broke up with him, not that you could tell from the messages he left."

"Yeah, he sounded pretty friendly for a dumped lover. Thanks, Anita. We'll look into it. Now tell me again, what time exactly did Benno get home on Saturday night?"

This time I didn't miss a beat. "I don't know, exactly. I was too occupied with other things to be noticing the clock."

2

FTER we put Clea to bed, I kept waiting for one of us to bring up Benno's interview with the police—and my call from Michael. Neither of us did. We sat at the kitchen counter and discussed whether or not to keep Clea home from school for a day or two. In the end, we decided to send her and see how it went; if she had a hard time, I could always bring her home.

It's an old married trick, easing tension by focusing on the child rather than each other. I put the leftovers away while the air in the kitchen thickened with the unspoken.

Benno started on the dishes. I rested my elbows on the counter and studied him from behind. Benno's short, about three inches taller than my five-two, with wide shoulders and a great butt—firm, rounded, muscular. Even doing dishes, he had the graceful confidence of someone who works with his hands and body. When I first saw him at the Art Students League, what I noticed was his thick, curly black hair and the way he stood at his easel, feet planted solid on the floor, ready for anything. This is a man who carries his own load, I thought, a man who can be leaned on without breaking.

I usually prefer to ride things out without confrontation, but this time I couldn't. "Michael called me after he talked to you." I spoke to Benno's back. "He asked me if you were having an affair with Ellen."

"What did you tell him?" Benno scrubbed at the meat loaf pan with short, jabbing strokes.

I don't know what response I expected, but that wasn't it. Why wasn't he angry or indignant, why didn't he take me in his arms and deny it?

"I told him no."

Benno didn't turn around to look at me. "Did he ask you what time I got back after I took her home?"

"I told him I'd fallen asleep so I didn't remember, exactly. What did you tell him?"

Benno shifted bowls around in the dish drainer so he could add the pan to the pile. A wineglass jumped off the edge and shattered on the floor.

"Damn!"

I bent to pick up the pieces.

"Get out of here, Anita. I'll clean it up."

There was a savage tone to his voice. I backed away. It didn't seem like the right moment to ask again about what he'd told Michael.

After such a heavenly anniversary weekend, why was Benno so tense? And I'd just told him I'd more or less lied to the police for him.

I went into the living room and opened the paper. What I wanted was to be held, comforted. But Benno went to bed. I stared at the Op-Ed page of the *Times* and let enough time pass for him to fall asleep before I joined him.

It wasn't a restful night, but at least Clea slept through. She woke up subdued but more cheerful than I'd expected and didn't seem reluctant to go to school. There's a comfort to sticking to a routine, and I was glad of it. Drinking coffee, eating breakfast, Benno and I were quiet with each other. I felt like we'd taken a test with no right answers and were waiting for our grades.

When Clea and I hit the street, summer's balm was heavy in the late-May air. As we entered the narrow, shady road on the cathedral grounds, two peacocks with their tails spread circled and cried out in their ugly, shrieking voices. In the absence of peahens, we stopped and admired the stately prance and dip of their fans. The only sign of yesterday's tragedy was in the long hug Clea surrendered to, rather than the quick kiss I usually blew at her back as she darted into her classroom.

Between the school, which is a separate building at the back of the cathedral grounds, and the Senior Services office, located in the basement of St. John the Divine's stone hulk, there's a small garden planted with herbs mentioned in the Bible. I entered through the open gate in the low wall. The sage plants were waist-high and full of buds. At their feet, clusters of thyme spilled onto the flagstones. I followed the path around the inner edge, the sun warm on my arms, mentally preparing myself to go in to work.

Standing in the herb garden, I sent up a prayer that Ellen was at peace, wherever she was. I pinched off a sprig of lavender and headed for work.

"Well, will you look at us!" Anne Reisen turned from the answering machine to greet me. Her color of the day was green—long, broom-pleated skirt and forest green velvet vest over a sky blue silk blouse. Her waist-length blond hair was unbraided, caught in a clasp at the nape of her neck. "I was going to call you this morning to offer my sympathies, but I figured I'd see you soon enough. It looks like I should've called for a wardrobe check instead!"

I was wearing a sleeveless rayon dress, moss green with swirls of blue in a muted tie-dye pattern. Given Anne's penchant for color-coordinated outfits and mine for basic black, it wasn't often that our colors matched.

Anne's official job title was administrative assistant, but in a three-woman social services agency, she did everything except carry a caseload—although she knew our elderly clients as well as my boss and I did, and frequently used her common sense to solve their problems before they even got to one of us social workers. Anne's fifty, seven years older than I am, but she's been with Senior Services for twenty years, longer even than our executive director, Emma Symonds. There's no question who holds the most unofficial power in the office.

Anne's a passionate defender of the underdog, of society's misfits and outcasts. Since she's been seeing Michael Dougherty, she's used her pipeline into the Twenty-sixth Precinct to ensure that anyone over sixty-five who comes to the attention of the police—victims of crime, accident, scam—also gets referred to Senior Services.

"Did you see the coverage?" Anne waved her hand at the stack of newspapers on her desk. "Michael told me about Ellen's death last night. It must have been awful for you, and he said Clea was there too?"

I nodded.

She went right on. "I picked up all the papers this morning, I thought you might like to see what they had to say about it. Good old *Times*, they bury a murder in the B section. No sensationalism for the paper of record, but the tabloids did it up right."

"I haven't read anything about it," I said. Benno usually picked up the *Times* on his way to work; I didn't read it until he brought it home in the evening.

"They mention you by name, as the person who found her. The story says the police don't think it was a random break-in, that it looks like she was killed by someone who knew her and they're looking for a boyfriend."

Part of me wanted to read the articles, but another part was repulsed. I stood there, indecisive, waiting for Anne to finish chatting so I could head for my cubicle without being rude.

She swiveled her chair around and started straightening the piles of papers. "You know, if you live long enough, you get smart." This remark seemed to be addressed to the computer monitor on her desk.

"So, you're starting a new career writing fortune cookies?" Cryptic remarks are not Anne's style; she can be direct to the point of bluntness.

Anne swiveled back in my direction and turned her attention to sorting pens. "You live with a man long enough, you can tell." She left the pens alone and looked at me.

I sat on the folding chair next to her desk and narrowed my

eyes at her. "What's the deal, Anne? Did Michael ask you to pump me about whether Benno was having an affair with Ellen?"

"Michael would never. He asked me for my opinion, did I think Benno was the type? I told him he should know I'm the wrong person to ask. I think all men are the type, given the opportunity, and Ellen was a fox."

I came close to hauling her up out of her chair and shaking her. Instead I walked away. If my cubicle had had a door, I'd've slammed it.

Anne came after me. "I'm trying to help, Anita. You know Benno is one of my favorite men on the planet, but he's still a man. You have to protect yourself, and Clea."

"What are you talking about? How can you even think Benno was up to anything with Ellen?"

"The hardest thing is admitting it to yourself, because it makes you feel like shit. But believe me, Anita, it's always better to know than not know."

My professional radar kicked into gear, and I realized Anne's agitation had to have more to do with her than with me. No way she was this upset about my husband's theoretical unfaithfulness. Then I got it. I knew Anne had been married when she was younger, and it hadn't ended well. The rare times she referred to her ex-husband, she was either bitter or mockingly ironic.

"What's going on, Anne?" I said.

Anne plunked herself down in the client's chair next to my desk. "Okay, so maybe the police are wrong and Benno wasn't sleeping with her. But you need to know for sure, Anita, and maybe I can help you."

"Help me? By telling your boyfriend the detective that Benno's just another lying, cheating son of a bitch?" The red numbers flashed inside my head. Why didn't the damn phone ring and interrupt us?

"That's not what I said."

I waited, unwilling to ask.

"I've been there." She said it quietly, but I could feel the old hurt behind the bare statement and I realized she needed to talk about it for her sake more than for mine.

"Tell me about it." The social worker in me yielded to the pain in her eyes.

Anne stared at Clea's drawings on the back wall of my cubicle. "I got married when I was nineteen. My parents didn't like him, which of course was a large part of the attraction. He was training to be a physical therapist, so I dropped out of college and got a job waiting tables to support us. It was very romantic. I'd come home smelling like hamburger grease, he'd rub my feet—he had good hands, I'll give the man that. He knew exactly where to touch me." Anne allowed herself a smile. "Then he started having study dates, only it turned out the anatomy they were studying was each other's."

I reached across the desk and took her hand.

"I knew something was going on months before I found the evidence. God, I felt stupid, doing laundry for a man who couldn't even be bothered to empty his pants pockets before he dropped them on the floor! I thought if I didn't say anything, he'd stop on his own. We hadn't even been married a year, and I wanted so badly for it to work.

"You feel so ashamed, it's hard to remember you're not the one who did anything wrong. I'd be back in the kitchen at work, putting in an order, and I'd realize there were tears running down my face. I couldn't even admit it to myself, how could I have talked to anyone else about it? The person I trusted with my life, my happiness, was making me miserable. I don't know how long it would have gone on if I hadn't accidentally caught them in the act."

"Oh, Anne." I couldn't begin to imagine.

"Actually, it was a relief. At least when you face the facts, you know what to do. I cut my losses and got out of there. But you've got a lot more at stake than I do."

"Wait a minute. Just because it happened to you doesn't mean it's happening to me."

"Knowledge is power, Anita."

"You're back in the fortune cookie business?"

"I'm offering you the benefit of my experience. If you don't want it, fine, but sooner or later you're going to need it." Anne stood up.

She was like the serpent holding out forbidden fruit. When she threatened to withdraw her offer, the apple became impossible to resist. "So sit down and tell me, O woman of experience."

"The first sign is that you stop having sex."

I couldn't even remember the last time, before our anniversary. Weeks, if not a month or more.

"Although if you're with a real asshole, it increases his appetite for you. Then you notice he's adding new positions, that kind of thing."

That night, Benno had definitely been hungry. I got a tingle between my breasts, remembering. But that was the night Ellen had been killed, and . . . "What else?" I demanded. One bite wasn't enough.

"He comes home late, he works weekends, he's vague about what he's working on and why it's taking extra time."

Well, with Benno that was a constant. He worked long hours and most Saturdays—sometimes I felt I was competing with the shop for his attentions. Then there were the nights he'd stop on the way home for a drink, to go over blueprints and work up a bid somewhere outside the shop, somewhere he wouldn't be disturbed by his demanding family.

"So? I don't account for every minute of my time, either." Of course, I always had Clea with me.

"Unusual expenditures. Receipts for dinners you didn't eat with him. These days, it would be on his credit card. My ex had this thing he'd do with checks made out to cash, blaming the bank for errors that were really his withdrawals."

We had a joint bank account for household stuff, and Benno had a separate account for his business. We kept separate credit cards; I paid mine from the joint account, and Benno paid his out of the shop. He never saw the items on mine, only the total. I never saw his at all.

"But none of this is proof."

"That brings us to the intangibles. Any woman with half an ounce of awareness can always tell, no matter how good a job he does of covering his tracks. You add up all the obvious signs, you take into account changes in his behavior—is he suddenly critical of how you dress? Does he complain about your cooking? Or did he used to complain, and now he doesn't seem to care? Has he started taking walks in the evening, so he can call her from a pay phone? Does he encourage you to go out with your friends, or is he jealous and suspicious? It depends on the man. That's why I say, the wife always knows. She may pretend she doesn't, even to herself, but there comes a point—" Anne shrugged.

"But that's so subjective. People change all the time." Even I could hear the uncertainty that had crept into my voice.

"And don't fool yourself by thinking that he loves you or you have a happy marriage and things are fine. That's just your opinion; he may not see things the same way. There's no one way to tell."

I don't know why I'd listened to her this long. So anyone's husband was capable of cheating, but the idea of Benno stabbing Ellen and then coming home to make passionate love to me was beyond unimaginable.

"Don't believe me. Ask your friends. It happens in a lot more marriages than you think."

"Hello! Is anyone here?" It was our boss, Emma Symonds.

Anne leaned over and whispered in my ear. "Even Emma. She didn't find out until she went through Fred's things after he died."

"There you are!" Emma stood in the door to my cube. "Anne, do you have those budget projections printed out yet?"

Saved by the paperwork.

3

A tall, well-built man was pouring himself a cup of coffee from a large urn on a table in the foyer when Clea and I stepped out of the elevator on the fourth floor of Riverside Church. Clea tugged my hand. The man turned around and smiled at her.

"Miss Clea, it's very nice to see you again." He bent his six feet down to her height and extended his hand. She ducked her head from shyness but allowed her hand to be shaken.

"Ms. Servi?" He touched my shoulder lightly before taking my hand in both of his. "Thank you for coming." He held on for a little longer than I thought necessary, but what really got my attention was his eyes. They were hazel, green with a rim of brown, and they had a glitter to them, like a bit of light was caught there. Not to mention his extraordinarily curly eyelashes, and the contrast of light eyes to skin that was—well, in the New York scale of things, he definitely wasn't white. Neither was he black, although his hair was dark and kinky, cut to a tight Afro. His skin was that of a man with a deep, even, all-over tan, and he had an elegant nose, maybe a trace of Semitic, maybe north African, with high, arched nostrils. I couldn't place his country of origin, not from his face and not from the faint British in his accent; the closest I could get was somewhere in the far reaches of the Empire. An Indian Brahman? An Arabian prince? He was about my age, mid-forties, in a beige raw silk jacket over a black T-shirt and black jeans. I was predisposed to like Arthur Nessim, since I'd asked for and gotten permission to bring Clea along, but I hadn't expected Ellen's boss to be so handsome.

"I'm glad you were able to be early. Would you care for a cup of coffee?"

Riverside Church, like the Cathedral of St. John the Divine, where I work, is home to a multitude of social programs serving all manner of constituent communities. The ESLI—English as a Second Language Institute—which is funded through a patchwork of city, state, and federal government grants, benefits legal immigrants who have been in the United States for less than a year. Ellen's part-time job had turned into a full-time summer position while the ESLI's coordinator of volunteers was on maternity leave.

The students needed more opportunities to practice English conversation with native speakers; my elderly clients were lonely and needed people to talk to. Several months ago, Ellen and I had arranged for a few of the new immigrants to visit with the older people. I'd been scheduled to lead a discussion group to see how the half-dozen matches we'd set up were working out, but when I'd called Mr. Nessim earlier in the day to see if he wanted me to go ahead as planned, he'd asked me if I would do a bit of grief counseling with the students instead.

I wasn't looking forward to it; groups of this sort aren't really my thing. Every time there's a disaster, they send in the social workers on the heels of the National Guard. Not that people in extreme situations don't benefit from counseling, but as in all fields, a few visible incompetents give the profession a bad name by overemphasizing the importance of "venting" rather than dealing with concrete needs of people who've lost loved ones, homes, pets, cars.

My idea for the group was simple: to share memories of Ellen, as in a wake or sitting *shivah*—to tell stories about the departed and remember the good things.

I gave Mr. Nessim—"Please, call me Arthur. We are informal here"—a brief outline of what I had planned.

"That sounds fine." Again, the brief touch on my shoulder. "Please, follow me."

Clea scampered ahead of us, like she knew where she was going. Which she probably did, I realized, since she'd accompanied Ellen to the conversation group here during her spring vacation.

We walked down a corridor lined with classrooms and around a corner. Clea disappeared into a large, sunny room at the end of the hall. Arthur ushered me into his office, a small room with a big window, a beat-up green two-seater sofa, an old wooden desk, and a wall of books.

After gesturing me to the couch, he sat behind his desk and looked vaguely around its surface.

"Our students are rather upset. The police had one of our instructors in custody until a few hours ago."

"Do the police think he was involved in Ellen's death?" I asked.

"I think it was more a case of his being involved in her life. It seems that Jamie and Ellen had been seeing each other romantically. Relationships between staff members are not encouraged, but these things have been known to occur." Arthur frowned. "I understand from Jamie that he and Ellen were no longer a couple at the time of her death, although they remained on good terms. It was nothing that would have interfered with either of them performing their responsibilities here at the institute."

"Why did they suspect him?"

"As far as I can tell, simply because someone told them he was Ellen's boyfriend, and it's common practice to look first to the person closest to the victim. Fortunately, he had an alibi—although that is the source of much anxiety among our students." He paused.

"Apparently Jamie and two students from former Soviet countries were at a bar in the neighborhood on Saturday night, which brought the police here asking questions early this morning. You know, many of our students come from countries where the police serve to reinforce the powers that be rather than to protect individual rights. Even though they are legal residents of the United States, it is difficult for them not to be afraid."

I nodded in agreement.

"And now there is this terrible new anti-immigrant act, where people who run afoul of the law can be not only imprisoned but also deported back to their countries. It was not easy to get the people Jamie was with on Saturday to verify his story, but once they understood the situation, they were brave enough to speak up."

He held up a copy of the Columbia paper, the *Daily Spectator*. "You've seen this?" The headline read: "Graduate Student Slain in University Housing." The article was accompanied by a photograph of Ellen in cap and gown.

"No, but I read the piece in the *Times*."

"The story takes great pains to emphasize that Ellen appears to have been killed by someone whom she knew. Naturally, their concern is keeping the student community from panicking. A concern which I share." Arthur rested his chin on steepled hands. "I hope you don't object to having Jamie join your group? I think it would help him as well as the students to get back to normal."

"Will you also be joining us?" I seemed to have picked up his formal habit of speaking.

"No. I have other work to attend to, and I expect the students will speak more freely without me there." There was a wry, knowing twinkle in his eye before he brought his lids demurely down.

This was a man well aware of the effect he had on women, I thought.

There was a tap on the open door.

Arthur stood. "Is it time already? Jamie Westlake, Anita Servi."

I'd met Ellen's boyfriend once before, but I don't know as I would have recognized him if I'd passed him on the street. He was probably in his late twenties, with reddish blond hair already thinning on top, and round, gold-rimmed glasses. He wore jeans and a light blue work shirt with the sleeves rolled down and buttoned.

I stood up also and shook the hand he held out. "I'm sorry about Ellen," I said.

"Yes." He had a strong grip and a nervous look. He didn't seem to have the slightest recollection that we'd ever met before, or that I'd known Ellen personally.

I followed Jamie into the room where Clea had already gone. It was large, rectangular, with a cluster of card tables with chairs around them in the middle and a sort of conversation pit formed by a square of sofas at one end, where the students were waiting for me.

On the opposite side of the room, two armchairs flanked a low table holding messy piles of magazines. Clea was curled up in one of the armchairs, engrossed in reading. Under the guise of patting her head, I checked out what she had—*People* and *Time*; nice, educational material.

The group didn't go as I'd expected. Although a few of the eight students talked about Ellen, they were more upset about the possibility of being victims of crime in New York themselves than they were about Ellen's death, and the conversation got off track into the ready availability of guns in America.

Jamie wasn't what I expected, either. Ellen had been vibrant, outgoing, beautiful. Jamie was quiet and nondescript. He didn't contribute more than an occasional remark to help one student or another find the right word. The various accents were difficult for me to follow, and I let the group take its own course more than I might have otherwise. I found myself following Jamie's lead, concerned that everyone had the chance to speak.

I knew three of the students because Ellen and I had already matched them with elderly people. Talile Areya, an Ethiopian woman; Vlad, a young man from Russia; and a West African woman whose name and exact country of origin completely escaped me. I was aware of her paying close attention to me, as if she wanted to say something, but when I tried to draw her into the discussion, she answered in monosyllables.

It was a relief when Arthur came in to let us know it was time to wrap things up. I'd meant to speak to Jamie on the way out, but before I could say anything to stop him, he took off down the stairs on the heels of the West African woman.

On the way home, we took a shortcut across the Barnard campus, entering through a back door from Claremont Avenue. The azalea hedges were in full bloom, walls of white flowers lining the brick pathway. As we were going out the main gate, we passed the dorm where Ellen had lived as an undergraduate.

"Why did Ellen have to move, Mama? If she stayed in her old room, she would have been safe!" Clea's voice was fierce, and my explanation of student living arrangements did nothing to appease her. Still stage two: anger, blaming the victim.

We stopped at UFM, University Food Market, for a loaf of rye bread. I wasn't even up for reheating leftovers; it would be meat loaf sandwiches with pickles for supper.

It was still full daylight at six-thirty. The warm evening seemed to have brought everyone out on the streets. The West End had its sidewalk café set up, and all the tables were full. This was New York at its nicest, in a mood so good you could almost smell the cheeriness. Clea dragged at my hand, her head down. I felt weary to my bones. We made our way through the crowded sidewalks like we were in space suits, breathing our own sad air.

The message waiting for us from Benno—"Anita? Are you there? I'm going to be late"—did nothing to cheer us up. While I fixed the sandwiches, I let Clea do her homework at the high counter Benno had built to expand our tiny kitchen to the glorious status of "eat-in." Even with the crunch of half-sour pickle, the meat loaf tasted like mournful mush. Neither of us finished our sandwiches.

Benno'd been reading *The Secret Garden* to Clea in nightly installments. When he still wasn't home at eight-thirty, after her bath, I could see the disappointment on her face. I propped up a pile of pillows and bears and sat next to her on the bed.

"Why isn't Daddy home?" Before she could work up to a

good whine, I opened the book. "I don't want you to read it, Mama." She squirmed away and tried to push me off the bed with her feet. "I want Daddy!"

I was too worn out to argue. I closed the book and leaned back against Betty, the biggest bear. "Okay, then, we won't read. Shall I tell the day before I tuck you in?" "Telling the day" used to be my nightly ritual with Clea; it had fallen into disuse since Benno started reading to her.

Clea, thumb in mouth, shook her head.

"What, then?" I knew her regression to sulky two-year-old was fallout from Ellen's death, and I was irritated with Benno for not being sensitive enough to know that Clea would especially need both of us right now.

Clea wouldn't look at me. I pulled her gently into my lap and kissed the top of her head. "I know, Bops. But sometimes Daddy has to work late. Shall we start a chapter, and he can finish it when he gets home?"

Her head nodded up and down, up and down. I opened the book again and started reading. When I got to the end of chapter 9, I kept going. About midway through 10, I felt Clea's body relax against mine. Her breathing was soft and regular. I slid off the bed, tucked her under the covers, and turned out the light.

It was nine-thirty; where the hell was Benno? I added worry to annoyance. Late, sure, but this was a good hour later than late.

I made his sandwich and set it on the counter. Let it get stale, then. I wasn't an all-night diner. Then I thought better of it and put an upside-down bowl over the plate to keep the bread from drying out and the pickle from wilting.

I wished I'd picked up some ice cream at UFM. I needed something sweet, anything to make me feel better. I went for the TV instead. Ten minutes into an episode of *Inspector Morse* I'd seen at least twice, Benno came in.

I watched as he took the paper out of his shoulder bag and deposited it on the table. "Don't start, Anita," he said. "I don't need you to snap at me, too."

"Tough day at the office, dear?" I said it lightly, hoping for a smile.

What I got instead was "You knew Ellen was killed with a screwdriver," flat, with a hostile look.

"Yes. It looked like it was from the set we gave her." I went over to him for our usual greeting of a quick kiss.

Benno jerked his head away from me. "It had my fingerprints on it."

"Of course it had your prints on it, you gave it to her!" I was indignant.

"Yeah, and your friend the cop came all the way down to the shop to tell me about it. It seems the handle was wiped clean, but my prints were on the blade. Never mind that I used it to put the damn bookshelves back together, to them I was the last person they know about who saw her alive, so I'm the one who killed her."

"But that's crazy," I said. "What time did she die?"

Benno shot me a look. "Sometime between 1:00 and 2:00 A.M., based on when she left here and what you told them about when she ate her last meal."

The red numbers flashed, 1:56. I had nothing to say to that.

Benno walked over to the counter and lifted the bowl. "This is dinner?"

"I'm sorry, we got home late, and I wasn't up for cooking."

He got a beer out of the fridge.

"Clea missed you. I read her a chapter and a half before she fell asleep," I said to his back. "I think it would help her to have us both around and to stick to her routines right now. She's pretty upset about Ellen, you know."

"We're all upset, aren't we." He yanked the stool out and sat down at the counter.

I stood there a moment, waiting for Benno to apologize for his uncharacteristic outburst, but he just picked up his sandwich and took a bite.

I went back to *Inspector Morse*. We *were* all upset. I counted on him to be there for me, with me. Rather than drawing together to comfort each other, Benno was avoiding Clea and shutting me out. Feeling resentful, I let him go to bed first again while I numbed my brain by following *Morse* with a *Law and Order* rerun.

As I fell toward sleep, the seeds of doubt Anne had planted began to sprout. To the rhythm of Benno's breathing, I pulled them up one by one. Benno would never do that to me, Benno would never do that, Benno would never, Benno would . . .

4

LEA woke up with the first light and snuggled her little self down between us. We both rolled over to face her and, in the détente of sleep, linked arms across her belly. This, I thought, is exactly what she needs. What I needed, too.

But I couldn't get back to sleep. The worries that hadn't taken root overnight mutated into a different type of threat to our family unit than infidelity. We've had Clea since birth, delivered from the hospital directly to our living room by a social worker in a taxi, but she is still technically a foster child. Although the rights of her birth parents had finally been terminated this past March, we were waiting on the family court judge to issue the ruling in written form so we could complete the paperwork needed to file for adoption. In the meantime, we endured the monthly visits of an ever-changing stream of nice young social workers from Catholic Children's Charities, the foster care agency.

Thanks to a new law, the Adoption and Safe Families Act, fingerprints were required from all current and prospective foster parents, which Benno'd said was how the police had identified his prints on the screwdriver. The law included some kind of mandatory notification from Criminal Justice to Children and Family Services if the prints turned up a record for a wide range of felonies such as child abuse, sexual abuse, murder, rape . . . I had no idea whether fingerprints at a crime scene would trigger the police to inform Catholic Children's, but anything that might bring the foster care system down on our heads was a threat.

Clea rolled over, fitting her little butt to my belly like a spoon. I tried to put my concerns on hold until I'd had a chance to talk to our lawyer, but my brain wouldn't let go. What I should have done was head down to Riverside Park for a walk before work, to stretch my legs and silence my thoughts. Given Benno's mood of the night before, however, I didn't want to leave Clea alone with him. Whatever was eating him, Clea needed his undivided attention as well as mine.

We managed to avoid any direct conversation at breakfast. There seemed to be a minefield between Benno and me, a militarized zone where any casual remark could set off an explosion. As for Clea, I saw a sadness in her eyes, as if the world had let her down in some fundamental way and a deep wariness had set in.

On the way to school, Clea and I walked through the summer air in silence, holding hands, oblivious to the other people swirling around us on the sidewalks. When we got to the cathedral grounds, one of the fancy roosters who live in the Biblical Garden was crowing around the stone wall along the rear drive. He was so pleased with himself, his tiny, iridescent chest puffed out like a macho man's, that we had to laugh. The hug I gave Clea outside her classroom wasn't quite as long and tight as yesterday's.

I headed back to Amsterdam and got myself a cappuccino and croissant to go from the Hungarian Pastry Shop. I was a little reluctant to go in to work and see Anne. Up until yesterday, I'd thought her relationship with Michael was a good thing. Although he was almost ten years younger than she was, Michael was the first man who'd lasted more than a few months in Anne's life. But if being the lover of a police detective meant she was going to scrutinize my behavior and try to pump me for information, it made for a situation I didn't care to be in.

It was nine-fifteen when I walked in the door. Anne's glance up from her desk was more like a glare. The slender young West African woman—Nafissa, her name popped into my head as easily as if I hadn't spent the better part of two hours trying to remember it during the ESLI meeting yesterday—sat in the waiting area.

I turned to her instead of Anne. "Are you here to see me? Let me put my things down, and I'll be right with you."

Emma, whose sympathetic blue eyes, trained by forty years in the social work biz, didn't miss a trick, was waiting for me in my cubicle. She didn't say a word about my being late; for a three-woman agency, fifteen minutes was well within tolerance levels, and she knew how Ellen's death was affecting me. Nevertheless, between Anne's attitude, Nafissa having come to see me before I'd made it in myself, and Emma's concerned gaze, I felt like a heel.

I sat down and stowed my purse in the bottom drawer of my desk. I let the bag with my breakfast sit untouched next to the telephone and turned to Emma.

"I had a call this morning from Mr. Nessim at the ESL Institute," she said. "He was quite pleased with the results of your group session, and he asked if I might lend you to the institute for a series of small groups. I told him I would discuss it with you. Since they seem to be providing us with a rich source of reliable volunteers, I think it would be a good idea to work with them on this."

"What kind of groups?" I was cautious. Grief counseling sessions were not the kind of thing I felt were very effective.

"From what I gather, his primary interest is in providing opportunities for the students to practice conversational English. He dressed it up in fancy pedagogical language, but that's the gist of it. My interest is somewhat different. I'd like to foster a relationship with the institute, with the goal of connecting their students and our clients in a mutually beneficial arrangement. If they could expand from friendly visits to include running errands and doing escorts, it would be an enormous help to us."

This was basically what Ellen and I had already been doing, and it was clear from the urging in Emma's voice that she wanted me to go on with it. Myself, I didn't mind the idea of spending more time than usual out of the office. Recruiting volunteers had become a large part of my job, and I agreed with Emma that the institute could be a gold mine.

Emma stood up. "Think about it, Anita. Whatever you want to do is fine, just write it up for me, would you, so I can present it to the board?"

Ignoring my breakfast, I followed Emma out of my cube.

Anne was admiring the fabric of Nafissa's long skirt and matching vest, a swirling purple and blue batik print that Nafissa said her brother imported from Senegal. I noticed Nafissa staring at the photograph on Anne's desk, a shot of Michael in uniform, holding up his gold detective's shield. I'd been surprised when Anne had first put the picture up—it wasn't like her, hippie tendencies alive and well, to glorify Michael's career in law enforcement—but why did Nafissa seem so struck by it? Then I remembered that Michael had been to the school asking questions after Ellen's death; Nafissa probably hadn't expected to recognize him in this incongruous context.

I touched her elbow.

Nafissa started back and stammered, "I'm sorry, I have come not at a good time. I will come another time."

I had a hunch her problem would require more patience than I felt capable of at that moment, and I would've let her go, except as far as I could tell there wasn't going to be any better time in my foreseeable future.

Besides, Nafissa was the volunteer for my most difficult client, Mabel Johnson, a ninety-three-year-old who suffered from some indefinable complaint the main symptom of which was that she never went out unless she was in a wheelchair. She was bossy, demanding, manipulative; she complained so much about so little that no volunteer I'd ever found for her would push her wheelchair more than once—until Nafissa. So whatever she needed from me, I'd try to give it to her.

I put on a smile and made her welcome. "What did you want to talk to me about?"

"The lady I am assigned to help, Mrs. Johnson?"

I nodded encouragingly.

Nafissa seemed not to know what to say next. "I only wanted to say that I will continue with her."

"Was there a problem?"

"Yes, but now I have understood her better."

"What was it you didn't understand before?" And why did you come all the way over here to tell me about it if it's no longer a problem?

I studied Nafissa's face, her high cheekbones and eyes that tilted up at the corners. She looked down at my desk rather than at me. I knew she had to be at least seventeen to attend the institute, but with her smooth skin she looked about twelve. As we spoke, I revised my estimate of her age upward into her midtwenties at least.

I encouraged Nafissa through what amounted to a shopping list of Mabel's worst qualities. I'd thought it would help to vent her frustrations, but with each negative quality, Nafissa made understanding excuses for why Mabel was the way she was. Once I laid off Mabel myself, Nafissa was free to bring up the behavior that really bothered her.

"She tells me I am a hard worker, I push her chair better than anyone. She say all good things about me. Then we watch on the television and Mabel says about black people, they are lazy, they don't want to work, only live on welfare and buy big televisions. I tell her, I don't have welfare, I don't have big television. Then she says"—Nafissa paused and drew in a big breath —"she says I am not that kind of black person, I am from Africa so I appreciate in America I am living in a house and wearing clothes and shoes."

I opened my mouth, horrified that anyone in this day and age would be ignorant enough to think African people were naked savages living in grass huts, but Nafissa held up her hand to indicate she wasn't finished.

"I know Mabel, she says what she thinks. When I first come to her, she asks why I don't have long neck, why I don't have big earrings to make my ears long. I tell this to Ellen, and she says Mabel is racist, she can give me someone else to help. I say no, I keep with Mabel, she need help. But now I ask you, you are white American, if all American people think this about African people, or if it is only old American people, or only Mabel, because of who she is?"

It was as neatly as I'd ever seen racism sliced—is it all-pervasive, only in one strata of society, or individual? That Nafissa could look at the situation with such understanding said a lot about her comprehension not only of English but also of human nature. I reassured her that it was only Mabel, and reiterated Ellen's offer to match her with someone else. Once again she declined, thanked me for explaining it, and with an air of relief, took her leave.

But I wasn't satisfied. I didn't feel I'd helped her to deal with the situation, and even more, I had the distinct feeling that discussing Mabel's outdated stereotypes of Africans was not the reason Nafissa had come to see me.

I spent the next half hour on the phone with the lawyer who was helping us with the adoption. The upshot of the conversation was that the law was so new it was impossible to predict how it might apply to our situation. Before the Adoption and Safe Families Act, Clea couldn't be removed from our home without notice and a fair hearing; now the agency could pull her without warning and hold a hearing afterward.

I rested my elbows on the desk, my head in my hands. The thought of Clea being taken away—I'd known, logically, for the past seven years, nine months, and some-odd days, that as a foster child, Clea's position in our family might not be permanent, but you tend to ignore the risk when your day-to-day life is secure.

I grew up in earthquake country, Berkeley, California, within a few miles of the San Andreas Fault. Nothing might happen for weeks or months, but after enough tremors you get sensitized to the most subtle movements of the earth. The foundation of my family was built on a fault line of legal uncertainty, and the needles of my personal Richter scale were vibrating.

I felt Anne come into my cube and sit quietly in the chair by my desk. Working in an office with no door and partial walls, we tended to behave like members of a Japanese family living separated by shoji screens—privacy was granted by pretending not to listen. Anne was notorious for acting on what she overheard when it came to clients, but she'd never violated my personal sphere before.

I raised my head and glared at her.

"Don't tell me it's not my business." Anne glared right back at me, but her voice softened. "If there's anything I can do to help, Anita, you know I'm there."

"Like by getting me to figure out whether Benno was having an affair with Ellen, which would provide him with a motive for killing her? Whose side are you on, Anne?"

"Yours. And Clea's. Michael's been telling me more than he should about this case. He made me promise not to say anything to anyone, but I think he wants me to talk to you about it." Anne took a breath. "He said they already have enough to hold Benno, the only reason they haven't brought him in yet is that Michael wanted to be sure all the other possibilities were ruled out first. He knows you guys, he knows Benno, but his boss is breathing down his neck—there's a lot of pressure to close the case because Ellen was a student, and we can't have the university community worried about a killer on the loose, can we? Michael says it's just a matter of time before the DA will be after him to arrest Benno."

"How could he? Benno's never even lifted a finger to me or Clea. He works with tools, he uses tools to make things, not destroy them—he would never use a tool in a way it wasn't intended for!"

"Michael says none of that makes any difference; what matters is the evidence, and it all points to Benno. They've got means and opportunity—Benno was alone with Ellen at the time of her death, and his fingerprints are on the murder weapon." Anne stopped.

"What else?"

"They're looking for evidence that Benno and Ellen were having an affair."

I could see how they were putting it together. This is how it happens in a Kafka story; you go to work one morning, and all the evidence is stacked against you. Or against your husband.

"I'm sorry, Anita."

"Yeah, me too." I grabbed my purse out of the drawer and stood up. I had to get out of there. "Tell Emma I'm taking the rest of the day as personal time."

I didn't know where else to go, so I headed home. I was thinking I'd change my clothes and take that walk in Riverside Park after all. Coming down 111th, I saw Barbara Baker, the co-op apartment building's Superintendent, out front, washing down the sidewalk.

When she noticed me, Barbara turned the hose nozzle until the water slowed to a trickle and stopped. "Good morning," she greeted me.

"What's so good about it?" I shot back. It was our usual joke, but the words came out bitter.

"You don't have to bite my head off, Anita, all I said was good morning." She put her hands in her pockets and frowned at me.

I apologized. Barbara, a medium brown, medium tall woman two years and two days older than I am, is a good friend. She coiled the hose, heaved it over the railing to the areaway under the stairs, and wiped her hands on the green coverall she'd customized with collar and trim in orange, green, and yellow kente cloth to match the twist of fabric wrapped around her hair. The building's board of directors may have been able to make her wear a uniform, but they couldn't shut down her style.

She pulled a pack of Winstons out of her pocket and offered me one. I hadn't smoked in years, but I took it.

Barbara exhaled smoke. "So what's your trouble, Anita?"

Everything was so turned around, upside down, just plain wrong, I didn't know where to begin. My eyes filled with tears. I took a hit of the cigarette to keep from crying and choked instead.

Barbara pounded my back. "Hey, girlfriend, you need a cup of coffee. You home for lunch? Come on down, I just fixed some tuna."

Barbara made small talk about her grandson, Malik, while she spread tuna on rye bread and poured coffee. When it was all ready, rather than taking the long way around to the side door, I hoisted myself over the windowsill directly into the yard. Barbara handed the plates and mugs out, then followed me.

Along with the Super's basement apartment, Barbara has access to the cement area behind the building. Before he died, her husband George dug up a full row of the concrete squares across the back and turned it into a garden. It doesn't get a lot of direct sunlight, but over the years they refined their crops to what does best in the microclimate of a New York yard— impatiens, hot peppers, basil. The Cyclone fence serves as a grape arbor, with coils of razor wire along the top making a very effective bird deterrent.

The air back there was cool even in the heat of early summer, a relief from the hot streets and the tense atmosphere I'd created at work. At least in Barbara's world, I knew who my friends were.

We chewed peacefully while I tried to come up with a way of telling her what was going on. In the bright noon sun, it was impossible to form the words "my husband is about to be arrested for murdering his young mistress." Instead, I asked her, "Was George ever unfaithful to you, that you know of?"

Barbara sputtered coffee. "That I know of! Not for long, sister!"

If you'd asked me, I'd've said George and Barbara had a good marriage. They'd been married nineteen years when George had a fatal heart attack at the age of fifty-two. Two of their three girls had gone to college; the third, Malik's mother, lived with his father although they weren't married, and she was pursuing a career in hotel management.

"It's funny now, but back then, let me tell you, I was boiling mad. Twice, he tried it. After that, I told him if there was a next time he was gonna be cohosting a radio program with John Wayne Bobbitt."

"How did you know? Did he tell you?"

"Tell me?" Barbara thought that was funny too. "They never

come out and tell you! First time, I was seven months pregnant with Tabitha"—her youngest—"and all I thought, big as I was, was thank God he's leaving me alone. Then came telephone calls with no one on the other end. After one of those calls, George would go out for cigarettes and stay gone for an hour."

Barbara's voice went bitter. "George had the habit of washing his hands after we did it, you know, get up out of bed and go wash. So those times when he'd been at the store after a phone call, first thing he did when he came in was head for the sink. Yeah, I figured it out, and one night I put a deadbolt on the inside of the basement door, locked him out on the street. He didn't dare raise any sand, because the whole building would have heard. That put an end to it.

"A couple years later, he's always fixing a leak in 8B. Come to find there's a subtenant in there, and the plumbing problem is a little south of her navel. He came down for his dinner one night, and I put the plate on the floor, told him he could eat it on his hands and knees like the dog that he was!"

"Jeez, Barbara!"

"Three kids, you think I should have left him? Besides, men, they just want to see what they can get away with. We never had any problems after that." Barbara lit a cigarette. "You worried about Benno? I wouldn't pick him for the type, but he's a man, and you've been married about long enough for it to happen. You seeing the signs?"

"I don't know. I don't know how you can tell."

"All's I can say is, when you know, you know."

"Big help you are!" I felt like I was being inducted into a sisterhood I hadn't known existed, and I didn't want to join.

"You sure you want to know, Anita? Sometimes it's better to let it blow itself out. But if you want proof, my advice is start with his underwear drawer. Men don't stray too far when it comes to hiding places. Tabitha's bringing Malik by later. Why don't you bring Clea down after school? She can hang with Malik and me, give you some time to do what you need to."

✦

But if Benno had anything to hide, he'd do it at the shop. That was the center of his life, what came before me, what would continue on after me, should a time like that come. I just needed to be out of the apartment, to work on my escape plan if there was any threat to take Clea away from us.

Canada, that was the ticket. I hadn't fantasized about running away in years—not since the days when Catholic Children's Charities was pushing Clea's maternal grandmother to take her. Canada had been my backup plan; we could take the train to Montreal and be over the border before anyone knew, no passports necessary.

I mentally withdrew cash in $500 increments from the automatic teller machine and debated how best to carry it on my person while I changed into sweats and a T-shirt. I was doing warm-up stretches when the phone rang. If I hadn't been distracted by thinking about the merits of renting a car versus taking the train across the border, I would have let it go, but at that moment my instinctive reaction to the noise was to pick up the receiver.

"I know I'm not supposed to call, but honestly, Anita, this has been going on long enough. Thank goodness you're home. I've been having the strangest dreams for days now, and I just have to know that you're all right."

My mother never said hello; she'd just start in with whatever was on her mind, like we were continuing a conversation she'd been having in her head. I have to admit, the sound of her voice was a relief. We'd had a major falling-out three years ago, and I'd made it a rule that she wasn't to call me, I'd call her when I felt like it. Needless to say, this hasn't stopped her from picking up the phone and dialing my number if the impulse strikes. Benno, who likes my mother and whose own parents are both dead, insists I talk with her whenever she calls.

"I know something's going on, Anita. Don't shut me out if you need help."

I held on to the phone like it was a lifeline.

"Please, talk to me. Is Clea okay? Is it Benno? I've had the most awful feeling about Benno. Tell me, Anita, what can I do?"

As usual, she'd gone right to the heart of it. I don't know if it was intuition or a lucky guess or playing the odds and getting it right, but my mother always knew. I surrendered and told her the whole story—Ellen's death, Benno's possible arrest, my fear of losing Clea.

She punctuated my story with "Oh, honeys" and "Oh, dears," followed by a long silence when I finished. I let the tears come and waited like a six-year-old for my mother to make it better.

She did. "Benno loves you, and he loves Clea, and he would never do such a thing."

I felt a weight lift. I knew Benno wouldn't, I knew it in my bones, but after listening to Anne and Barbara . . . What I needed was someone to remind me that now was not the time to stop trusting my husband.

"What you need is a good lawyer," my mother went on. "I know just the man. What time is it there, two o'clock? I'll call you right back." She hung up without another word.

I listened to the dial tone in a daze. My mother was a force to be reckoned with. That I'd stood her off for three years was amazing. I put the phone down. Whoever her legal eagle was, I hoped he'd be good. Paying him was another matter, but one thing I've learned from my mother is that in an emergency you don't worry about the cost. Money is only paper, and it can be sorted out later.

5

MY mother's brand of irrefutable logic had a way of both reassuring me and putting me back into the mind-set of a rebellious teenager. She was always right, which put me always in the wrong. Just as I had at fifteen, I felt impelled to act out. The needle of my moral compass drew me north to Benno's bureau.

There was no point in rooting around in Benno's socks and underwear. We kept an envelope of cash in that drawer, and I was more than familiar with its other secrets: a plush jewelry box that held his father's army insignia, his mother's broken wristwatch, a champagne cork from after our marriage at City Hall; a few unopened packs of condoms left over from our early days together, before we'd learned that birth control was not going to be an issue for us.

No, I went for the bottom drawer, dead storage for Benno's favorite items that had gotten too small, like a French sailor's striped wool jersey, his catcher's mitt from high school, things with too much sentimental value to toss out. The drawer seemed fuller than I'd remembered. I lifted off the top layer of sweaters and found a shiny black rectangular box with a gold sticker from Renell, a ladies' shop on Broadway. A present he was saving for me, for a special occasion?

I felt like a louse, prying into what was intended to be a surprise, until it dawned on me that we'd just had a special occasion at which he had not presented me with this gift. I opened the box and folded back the tissue paper. It was some kind of undergarment, silvery blue silk with a narrow V-shaped band of matching lace at the neckline, size small. I stood and held it up to my chest. It was a chemise, short and clingy.

I stared at my reflection in the mirror, a short, middle-aged woman in baggy pink sweats with a ratty green T-shirt, her graying hair twisted up on her head in a scrunchy from which it was trying to escape, like electric wires after a storm. The chemise dangled in front of me, the shed skin of my illusions. It might have fit me ten pounds and five years ago, but now there was no way I could've gotten it past my hips.

I refolded it, put it back in the box, laid the box in the drawer, replaced the sweaters, and closed the drawer. See where being sneaky gets you? I thought, addressing myself as much as Benno. I felt sick to my stomach.

I left the apartment in a daze. I still had time for a quick turn in the park before I had to collect Clea from school. But when I got down the hill, walking was not what I wanted to do at all. I didn't have the energy to lift my feet, to keep up a pace. The midday light filtering through the new leaves was too bright; there were too many people in the park. A pair of young men in shorts, T-shirts off and tucked at their waists like tails, ran by, their footfalls jarring my nerves. Every baby stroller seemed to have a white child being pushed by a black woman, and all I could think was, Why do women have children and leave them to be raised by other women who probably have children of their own being raised by grandmothers? Two old homeless white men sat on a bench drinking from cans of beer wrapped in brown paper bags. A multicultural group of teenagers with a boom box blaring laughed and jostled each other as they walked.

I hated all of them.

But I managed to trudge north the half mile to my favorite place in the park, the Grave of the Amiable Child, a secluded spot where I knew I could be alone. As I approached the stone urn that marked the resting place of Saint Claire Pollock, the little boy who'd drowned off the Palisades in 1797, I searched my pockets for a stick of gum or a Lifesaver I could use to observe the local custom of leaving a sweet for him. I patted the granite marker in apology and plunked myself down on the steps, where I could stare out past the scrim of trees to the Hudson. In spite of the traffic flowing down Riverside Drive behind me, this place was as isolated and peaceful as the city ever got.

I leaned my head against the railing and closed my eyes. I hadn't been there two minutes when I heard a rustling noise that brought back the sounds of the tissue paper as I rewrapped the chemise. I stood up and stared into the bushes down the slope. I wasn't nervous, just curious; I was ten feet from the sidewalk of Riverside Drive, an easy escape route.

I craned my neck and saw a tall, black-haired man in gray sweats, about twenty yards away. He had his back to me and stood in the posture of a man taking a leak. No big deal; I was, in general, in favor of peeing in the woods, although at the moment I wished he were doing it somewhere else.

Then he turned around and looked right at me. It took a second or two for me to realize that his hands were still at his crotch, and moving up and down. Great, a pervert. This day seemed designed to rupture every bubble of serenity I reached for, not to mention what it was doing to my opinion of the male gender.

I got up and crossed the street to Grant's Tomb. The classical columns and the eagle with its wings spread above the pediment aren't my cup of tea, but I love the colorful tile mosaic benches, architectural anachronism though they may be, that surround it. I wished I could drift with the mermaid, breasts bare to the sun, with no need to take apart the past year of my marriage and search for signs that my husband had been getting it on with our baby-sitter. Which, now that I was in a spot disturbed only by the occasional passage of a pastel-clad tourist, I realized I did not want to think about at all, because if I did, all the signs were there.

Benno certainly had opportunity; being self-employed, he could leave the shop whenever he wanted to. He paid his credit cards from the shop account; I had no idea what the bottom line was, let alone an itemized account. He could have been spending two afternoons a week at the Royalton Hotel, and I never would have known.

And he liked Ellen. They'd get into these long philosophical discussions, the kind people have when they're getting to know each other, the kind we used to have when we were first together. After nine years, I knew Benno's point of view so well I could've done both sides of the conversation myself. I'd thought it was a good thing, for both of them; Benno kept his brain sharp, and Ellen got to test her ideas on a man who'd actually read Mao, Marx, and Marcuse. If they wanted to think globally, that was fine with me. I'm more the type to act locally; I believe in changing what I can see, the people whose lives touch mine.

Which got me thinking about Ellen herself. The oldest of three children, Ellen came from a solidly middle-class family; her mother was a supervisor with the phone company, her father a staff attorney at a cable television company. Her parents had separated last year. Ellen was a sophomore at Barnard when she first started taking care of Clea two afternoons a week. In those three years, we'd watched her change from being observant yet reserved to a sharp, challenging young woman unafraid to speak her mind.

We'd accepted Ellen as a part of our family. Looking back now, I could see how she'd also come to occupy a niche in our marriage. For Benno, she'd been an intellectual companion. I let the thought sit there, without taking it any further. If Ellen and Benno had, well—well—I couldn't go there yet. Ellen was dead; Benno was my husband.

My relationship with Ellen was more complex, harder to name. We were neither peers nor sisters, and the difference in our ages made friendship a lopsided affair. If I had to put a word on it, I'd say Ellen and I were mentors for each other; I shared my experiences as a professional woman, while Ellen, as a young black woman, shared hers. While Ellen's conversations with Benno were abstract, philosophical, the substance of what she and I came to talk about, over time, was race relations.

It wasn't lost on Ellen that as a white woman raising a black child, part of why I'd hired her was because she was black. It was also part of why she'd taken the job. There's a long history of black women raising white children. I'd stayed home with Clea when she was a baby rather than hiring a black woman to care for her, but once she was in school, it seemed to me that having a black college student for a baby-sitter was a good thing. Ellen provided Clea with a role model other than white parents, and helped me to understand some of the issues Clea would face as she grew up.

For Ellen's part, Clea assuaged the homesickness she felt for her family, left behind in the Bedford-Stuyvesant neighborhood of Brooklyn. Although it wasn't much more than an hour away by subway, Bed-Stuy was a different world. What we gave Ellen was a supportive place from which to weather the occasional slings and arrows of attending an Ivy League university.

Sitting in the sun behind Grant's Tomb, I thought back to spring break, when Ellen had returned from a week with her mother, her once-straightened hair cut into a short, shapely Afro. She'd been tense, confrontational almost to the point of hostility. Being a social worker, you might be able to leave your job behind in the evening, but you never get away from the profession. I knew Ellen well enough to realize that her mood had to do with something going on internally for her rather than with me, and I'd finally asked her directly about it.

It emerged that Ellen's father had left her mother for a white woman he was now living with and intended to marry. The woman was a coworker, someone his own age whom he'd known for years. Ellen's father wanted her approval for what he was doing, but in Ellen's opinion he was taking a trophy wife, a slap in the face to Ellen's mother. In my opinion, while Ellen's resentment might have been justified, taking it out on me wasn't.

"My dad is focused on status," Ellen complained. "This woman isn't half as pretty as my mom, and she wears these power suits. The thing he really likes about her is she's white, and what kind of example is that for my brother? She's got this big apartment in Lincoln Towers. My dad's always wanted to live in Manhattan, but my mother would never move out of Bed-Stuy."

"It's always hard when a parent remarries," I tried. "It's natural to feel that you're being disloyal to your mother by accepting your father's new wife." Not for the first time, I felt the inadequacy of general truths in handling specific feelings.

"A white mother? It's too weird."

"Some of my best friends have white mothers," I said, trying to get her to see the humorous side of it. Although I don't think I'm naive about race, Ellen had stressed that there were things I might be able to observe from outside but would never understand.

Ellen shrugged me off. "That's different. You've had Clea since she was born."

"You're making a racial issue out of what's a universal, human issue. Is your objection to her because she's a stepmother, or because she's white? Would it be any easier if your father were marrying a black woman? What if she were twenty years younger than him, and black? You've got to sort out what it is that's upsetting you, instead of blaming him."

"They're having a church wedding. He asked my brother to be his best man, and she wants Jackie to be the flower girl and me to be a bridesmaid," Ellen said bitterly. "When he married my mother, they had the minister come to the house. It's just not right!"

"It must be hard for your mother," I sympathized. "But from his point of view, they're trying to include you children. I think that's a good thing, Ellen, but I understand why you wouldn't want to do it. How do your brother and sister feel?"

"Jackie's all excited because she'd get to wear a fancy dress. Eddie would do anything to please my father, but I can't go along with it. Why would she even want me for a bridesmaid if she knows how I feel? She's just doing it to make my father happy!"

"Why don't you want your father to be happy, Ellen?" Clea, as usual asking the obvious question with the complicated answer, put an end to the conversation.

I smiled at the memory of what Ellen had said to me a few weeks later. "Your relationship with Clea is the only thing that gives me hope, Anita. When Clea looks at you, she doesn't see white, she sees mother." I missed Ellen. Suddenly I was bent over, sobbing. I missed Ellen for a lot more reasons than that I now had to pick Clea up from school.

I headed over to Broadway, thinking that I could atone for my suspicions about Benno by cooking dinner. A real meal always brought out Benno's good side, and got me on it. There was just enough time for me to stop at Mama Joy's deli on the way to the cathedral. I had a twenty in my pocket; I never leave home without a cash stash, for just this reason.

Pasta and salad, that would do. I'm not half the cook Benno is, so I keep it simple. I picked up bialys for breakfast, sharp cheddar for Clea's lunch, a head of romaine, half a pound of Canadian bacon, and two big onions for Amatriciana, a sauce I hadn't made in years. It had been one of Benno's favorites when we were first married.

When I'd thought we would be happy forever. Stray snapshots from the past few months kept flashing in at the edge of my consciousness: Benno being snide about a new dress, a green wool knit that he said made me look like an army tent; Benno carping about the pile of magazines that spilled off the end table on my side of the couch, the way I stacked dishes in the drainer, how often we ate carry-out. It seemed like every time I turned around, he was nagging me about some little thing I'd done, or hadn't.

Clea and I took the elevator down to the basement and walked around to the backyard. Barbara was on her knees, planting an early crop of lettuce, spinach, and radishes. She patted the damp earth over her seeds, then stood up and peeled off her gardening gloves to give Clea a hug.

Malik, a chubby two-year-old with a head of long, soft curls, was grubbing around with a trowel and a bucket of dirt. His diapered butt stuck up in the air, a clump of dirt matted into the blue corduroy of his overalls. Clea immediately made for the watering can and proceeded to drench the last of the spring bulbs—a cluster of parrot tulips, their pointed petals streaked red and yellow. It seemed like too much of an effort to make her go up and change out of her spring uniform. There was always Stain Stick and Tide with Bleach Alternative.

"Hey, Malik, cut that out!" Barbara yelled.

Malik had pulled up a tulip and brought it over to Clea, who accepted it graciously as her due. I made my exit.

When I got upstairs, there was a message on the machine.

"Aaron Wertheim," my mother's voice announced. "Write this number down, he's expecting you to call him tomorrow morning, at ten-forty-five sharp. It's an appointment, so be sure you call him on time."

Aaron Wertheim? Defender of New York's high-profile victims of police abuse? How in hell did my mother know Aaron Wertheim?

"My plane gets in at five-something, I know that's rush hour, so I'll take a cab in, don't even think about picking me up. I'll see you tomorrow."

Her plane? Shit. I should've known my mother wouldn't be able to stay away. As if things weren't tense enough without my mother on the couch!

On the other hand, if I hadn't been boycotting her, I might've asked her to come myself. Clea had a whole month of school left before summer camp. Finding another sitter, someone we liked and who was reliable, would not be easy. My job was flexible enough to give me a few afternoons off, but with only three of us in the office, it meant Emma and Anne would be picking up a lot of my slack. So maybe I could bury the hatchet for the moment and manage to be civil. I needed her, and my mother lived to be needed.

I sautéed bacon and chopped onion, added two cans of to-matoes, washed the lettuce, and put a salad together. The thing that worried me was that I had no idea how Benno would react. Telling him about my mother's visit would be easy, compared to breaking the news that she'd arranged for me to talk to Aaron Wertheim. Not to mention the substance of what the new foster care law might mean to us; I'd also have to tell Benno I'd spoken with the adoption lawyer.

Sometimes it's easier to tackle a delicate situation from a bit of a distance. I took the coward's way out and called Benno at the shop. Besides, rather than brood about it until after Clea was in bed when we could talk, I'd get it out of the way. That way, when he came home we'd have Clea to prevent us from dis-cussing things any further.

That he was the chief suspect was not news to Benno. Evi-dently Michael had questioned him again—"and the one piece of friendly advice he gave me was to get a lawyer," Benno said. So Aaron Wertheim turned out to be welcome news.

While we talked, I went around the apartment with the wa-tering can, tending the African violets I'd inherited, along with the apartment, from my grandmother.

I understood how Benno felt about the cops, and as long as he wasn't angry at me, he could vent all he needed to. But when Benno's tune switched to what an inconvenient time it was for my mother to visit, I resorted to a tactic I'd first perfected when she was on the other end of the line—holding the phone away from my ear.

When I'd moved to New York to live with my grandmother, reversing my mother's own trajectory of east to west but with the same net result of getting 3,000 miles away from a domineering mother, she would subject me to transcontinental harangues about not using my talents (I'd dropped out of art school to care for my grandmother). I didn't want to hang up on her and pre-cipitate outright war, but if I'd listened to every word, I would've been suicidal. So I held the receiver just far enough so I could tell when she paused and make the appropriate *um-hm*.

When Benno ran out of steam, I put the phone back to my

ear and pointed out that it might be good for Clea to have her grandmother around, and that I could use the help with child care after school.

Which brought me to Clea. I hung the watering can back on its hook over the sink and sat down on the bed. I stared out over the Hudson, and told Benno what Joel Rheingold, the lawyer who was representing us in Clea's case, had said.

When I finished, the line was quiet.

"Are you there?"

"God, Anita, why is this happening to us? I feel like I'm caught in a nightmare that just keeps getting worse."

"I know exactly what you mean," I said.

The silence that stretched along the phone wires between us was shared this time, and comforting. At least in concern for Clea we were united.

I left the sauce to simmer while I went downstairs to collect Clea.

"You know where the beer is," Barbara greeted me.

I climbed over the sill into the kitchen and got two Coronas out of the fridge. A few minutes sitting in the shade wouldn't kill me.

Clea appeared to be teaching Malik how to mold a meat loaf out of mud, with a side of baked potatoes, while Malik garnished her creations with an assortment of pebbles. It was as close to peace and normality as I'd been in days.

As soon as Benno walked in the door, it was as if that moment of shared emotion had never existed. First it was the Canadian bacon, an ingredient he insisted I'd never used before. His kosher mother would never put a pork product in a red sauce, and besides, why did I think anything that had pasta in it was a comfort food?

Clea had already eaten and was in the tub, so she missed

most of it—until Benno insisted that I call my mother and tell her not to come, and I lost it.

"If you don't want her to come, you call and tell her!"

Clea swept into the living room with the towel wrapped around her like a robe and ordered us to stop fighting.

Benno made nice to Clea, but I was pretty steamed. I did the dishes with enough splash and clatter that Clea asked Benno why I was so mad, and he came in and told me to cut it out.

When you live in less than seven hundred square feet, there's not much of a place to go to get away from the person you're arguing with. The kitchen's more like a hallway at the center of the apartment; Clea's room is her room; Benno was in the living room; our bedroom was mostly bed, and short of getting in it, there was no place to go. It was too early for bed and too hot for a bath, my winter retreat of choice.

Whatever tendril of tranquillity I'd managed to hold on to during the day was long gone. I had to either get a grip or get out of the house. I made the best of Benno's mood until around eight, when I gave it up. There was a place I could go to do the only kind of meditation that appeals to me, walking.

"I'm going over to Riverside Church," I told Benno. "I need to walk the labyrinth."

"You're going out dressed like that?" he objected.

I'd added a dark green flannel shirt for warmth, but I was still wearing my pink sweatpants. "Yeah."

"Is it something I said?" Benno tried to make a joke of it.

"Something like that." Well, it was. "I should be back by nine-thirty, ten o'clock."

The sky was just fading to twilight, and I took Riverside Drive instead of heading up to Broadway. I walked fast, fuming. Who the hell did he think he was, putting me in the wrong? I wasn't the one who had a silk chemise in my bottom drawer!

6

I know, I should have just asked Benno about it, even if it meant admitting I'd snooped in his bureau. I operate on the principle that if you're going to invade someone's privacy, you at least owe it to them to act as if you hadn't. If I were honest with myself, though, I'd have to admit I didn't ask because I was afraid of the answer. If Benno had been having an affair with Ellen, I wasn't ready to know about it.

I went in the revolving door to Riverside Church, hoping the labyrinth would work its magic, quiet my brain and return me to a time before my world had gotten tied up in knots.

The labyrinth, laid out in the downstairs auditorium, was basically a huge, flat canvas circle rolled out on the floor. The path was defined by a pattern of blue paint. Overhead hanging lights turned down low, along with fat candles in eight tall torchères around the canvas circle, illuminated the large room. Another ring of candles in lanterns on the floor surrounded the labyrinth. The smell of burning wax filled the air. There was some kind of sacred music playing, motets or chants, sweet voices floating up into the stone arches, drifting back down from the wooden beams, the gold-painted ceiling decorated with deep maroon fleurs-de-lis.

I sat on one of the folding chairs and took off my running shoes. Several women were walking the maze, taking three steps forward, two steps back, making slow progress toward the center. I paused between the two candles flanking the entrance, a short, straight strip leading into the curved paths. The way was narrow, just enough space to put one foot after another. I stepped in.

A large blond woman in leggings and a blue work shirt was walking at a quick, unmeditative pace, neglecting the two steps backward, in a hurry to get it over with. A black woman in linen pants walked with her hands held out, palms up in supplication. A young white woman sat cross-legged in the center. I noted their presence, then let it go.

The labyrinth led me in an arc around the outside, then in, almost to the center, before bending again to another outside arc. The pace felt awkward at first, lurching backward and forward, not making much progress. As I went on, it became a rhythm, and I felt my brain slide into neutral. The music washed over me, the Latin words meaningless, soothing. I came to the center, marked out in arcs of deep red like the petals of a flower. The woman who'd been sitting there had gone. The black woman stood with her head bowed, the candlelight glinting on the gold buckle of her belt.

I turned toward the entrance of the maze and registered a man about to enter. He put his palms together and bowed deeply before setting out. It was Jamie Westlake. I ducked my head and turned away, not wanting to be recognized. I didn't think about why; it just seemed like the proper thing to do. We were here for our own private reasons.

I followed the other woman back onto the path. We kept our eyes down, focused on our feet. My arms hung at my sides. I passed Jamie, his hands clasped behind his back, head down, without any acknowledgment on either side. The way wound in reverse, leading back to the world.

When I arrived back at the beginning, my conscious mind seemed to have drifted off with the voices and settled somewhere up above the flickering lights. I sat in the chair, retied my shoes, and watched Jamie pace the winding labyrinth. His body was as long and narrow as the path, his shoulder blades poking up under his dark T-shirt like wings.

The hurrying woman had taken a Walkman out of her bag and was unwinding the cord to the headpiece. A young black

woman in overalls with a kerchief around her hair spoke quietly
to a white woman in a long flowered skirt. They walked around
the outside of the canvas circle and passed between the lanterns
on the floor, into the maze.

I watched the woman in overalls as she paced the paths, reminded of Ellen, her long legs and the graceful sway of her walk.

In that flickering room, Jamie seemed heaven-sent: someone who knew Ellen. Only time can ease grief, time and sharing
memories of the deceased. I'd called Ellen's mother the day
after she died, and learned that there were no funeral plans yet.
I hadn't really known any of Ellen's friends. Benno had shut me
out.

I just wanted to talk, to remember the sound of Ellen's
laugh, to hear words she might have said, things she might have
done. I had stories I wanted to tell, like the time I'd come home
to find that Clea had turned the tables and done Ellen's hair,
using every barrette she owned, about fifty of them. Rather than
undo Clea's masterwork, Ellen had asked if she could return the
barrettes the next day and walked out looking like a Christmas
tree without lights. Clea had been thrilled.

So I waited for Jamie to find his way out of the labyrinth. As
I sat, the day I'd come here to get away from seeped back into
me. What could I say to Jamie? I'm sorry the police suspected
you, now they think it was my husband?

It might have been divine intervention that gave me the
idea, but the train of thought that followed was far from Christian. I wondered what Jamie had told the police about his possible replacement in Ellen's life. If they really had had an
amiable breakup, would she have confided in him? From the
sound of the messages he'd left on her machine, they were more
friendly than any exes in my experience.

What if Jamie and Ellen had been getting back together?
The police always look at the boyfriend, husband, lover, first.
Okay, Jamie had an alibi. He also had a good reason—diverting
suspicion away from himself—to offer information about there
being another man in Ellen's life. Well, *someone* must have said
something to them about Ellen and Benno; they wouldn't have

invented a relationship from whole cloth, would they? The chemise drifted lightly through my mind. I took a deep breath and blew it out of the picture.

Jamie walked past me, to the row of chairs one stone pillar over, and sat to put his running shoes on. I took a seat next to him and put a hand lightly on his knee.

He flinched at my touch, an involuntary, violent jerk. I removed my hand and shifted slightly away from him.

"I'm sorry, I didn't mean to startle you," I whispered. "I didn't want to disturb the mood." I waved my hand around the room.

Jamie's gaze followed my gesture into the deep corners, up to the high gilt ceilings, as if struggling to come back to himself. When he did, it was abrupt.

"I don't have anything to say to you." He leaned over to collect his shoes, leaving me faced with his bent back.

"I'm sorry," I said again. "I didn't have a chance to talk with you this afternoon, at the institute, and I just—Ellen baby-sat for my daughter, Clea, and I just wanted—" I made the mistake of reaching out to touch his back. I couldn't help it; I needed to make contact, somehow, any way I could.

It was like I'd hit him with a branding iron. He slid two seats away and lifted his head to glare at me. The light reflected off his glasses, turning his eyes to golden disks. "I know Clea, and I know your husband killed Ellen."

Sitting this close to him, I realized that although I'd taken him to be thin to the point of scrawny, he was actually quite muscular. Skinny, yes, not an ounce of fat to soften the contours of taut, ropy biceps. I noticed the edge of a tattoo poking out from under the sleeve of his shirt, blue letters I thought spelled out "GRUNT" and the bottom half of some kind of creature.

I kept my voice low, neutral. "What makes you think my husband had anything to do with Ellen's death?"

He stared at me like I was something alien, incredible. Then he shook himself, as if remembering where he was. His voice started out gentle and wound up dripping with pity. "They say the wife is always the last to know. It's not my business to tell you this, but I knew Ellen was seeing a married man. She told me she wanted to end it, but she had to see him almost every day, and he wouldn't let go."

"I'm sorry," I started yet again. I could've kicked myself for being apologetic; who was he to condescend to me like that? "I'm sorry, but you're wrong about my husband and Ellen."

This time the contempt radiated from his whole face, unmistakable. "Yeah, well, sorry doesn't help." He stalked off.

The clock over the door said it was five to ten, not enough time to thread the labyrinth again and regain my composure. When the attendant came around with a long-handled snuffer to put the candles out, I got up and left.

It was a full moon sky, and a line from the poet Bella Frye popped into my head. "The night's a domino / the moon dot number one."

My mind was in turmoil, but my feet still held to the slow, deliberative pace of the labyrinth. Ellen was having an affair. With a married man. A married man she saw almost every day. So Jamie said. Who else would know? Who were Ellen's friends? Aisha, the other voice on the answering machine. Okay, I could talk to Aisha. I had to know the truth.

Jamie's attitude had also brought the implications of Benno being a suspect in Ellen's death into focus. If her boyfriend was this upset, how would her family feel? I couldn't imagine not going to the funeral; for one thing, it would be essential to Clea's coming to terms with Ellen's death. But how could we face her mother?

A wisp of cloud blew across the moon and vanished. I wished it were that easy. I put one foot in front of the other and went home.

Benno was already in bed when I got in. He'd left Clea's door open a crack, in case she woke in the night. I tucked the covers up over her shoulders and kissed her soft cheek. When I stood up, I realized mine were wet with tears.

That night, I dreamed I was back in California, on Limantour Beach in thick fog, walking at the edge of the breaking surf, the interface of air, water, sand. The heavy fog stroked my arms, my back. I turned into it and returned the caresses. I came out of the dream to my body entwined with Benno's, our hands following the well-known contours of each other. We made a soundless, dreaming kind of love, gentle and sad, tender as if to spare each other from unbearable pain. When I went back to the beach, my feet left a glittering trail of phosphorus in the sand behind me.

At work the next morning, Anne and I barely spoke. When I came out to tell her I'd be using the phone in the conference room, the only room other than Emma's office that had a door that closed, and not to disturb me under any circumstances, I noticed she'd turned the picture of Michael with his gold shield facedown on its shelf. I had too much on my mind to wonder if it was a gesture of support or simply tact.

To my surprise, Aaron Wertheim answered his own phone. His voice sounded more ordinary than I'd expected, having heard it only in radio and television sound bites, a baritone deepened by outrage at the injustice of whatever his current client was accused of. It was a voice, I thought as we got the pleasantries over with, that you wanted to trust.

I was surprised again when Wertheim himself brought up the subject I felt most awkward about: his fees.

My mother's financial situation went up and down like a yo-yo. Benno, however, had grown up poor and was extremely conservative about saving money. He'd agreed to let me talk to Wertheim this once, with the aim of getting him to recommend someone less expensive; we would pay him for his time as a consultant. But Wertheim would have none of it.

"Your mother is a very astute woman, Ms. Servi. She anticipated your objections and asked me to inform you that she has made arrangements for my retainer. It may well be that no more than that is necessary. If, however, the case does go to trial, your mother tells me that Mr. Servi is a talented woodworker, and I'm sure we can come to a mutually beneficial arrangement."

"I don't mean to sound ungrateful, but does my mother putting down a retainer mean that you're her lawyer or mine?"

Wertheim cleared his throat. "Actually, I will be representing Mr. Servi. The agreement your mother will sign is very explicit on that point. In other words, should a situation arise where your husband's interests are not the same as yours, or your mother's for that matter, my obligation is to your husband. In fact, it's Mr. Servi to whom I should be speaking, but since I have you on the phone, why don't you tell me briefly what's going on?"

I felt lighter, as if a small weight had been lifted from my shoulders. Until that moment, I hadn't realized how badly I'd felt that Benno needed someone in his corner, to take his side. Ordinarily I would have been his chief defender, but he had closed me out so completely . . . and there were questions I didn't dare ask.

I'd just finished with finding Ellen's body when Anne burst into the room. "It's an emergency, Anita, or I wouldn't interrupt. Barbara Baker just called to say the police are about to search your apartment. They came with a warrant, and she had to let them in." Anne left as quickly as she'd come, closing the door behind her.

If ever there was an apropos moment to have a lawyer on the line, this was it.

7

'M sorry, Anita, they wouldn't wait until you got here."
Barbara pulled the elevator door open as soon as it hit the
twelfth floor. "I told them I didn't have a key, but they
threatened to drill out the lock, so I figured it was better to let
them in."

"It's okay," I said. Wertheim had told me to stay calm, watch
what the cops did, and be sure to get a receipt for whatever they
took. In the meantime, he'd be contacting Benno, since the
shop was likely to be searched as well.

I opened the door to my apartment. A uniformed cop, a
bulky white guy, stood in my living room, guarding a clear
plastic bag with some of Benno's clothes in it. Great, the raw silk
jacket, Benno's most au courant garment, crumpled in with the
khakis he'd worn Saturday night. His dress shoes had been
added to the bag for good measure.

It was hot and stuffy in the small apartment. I brushed past
the cop to open a window. The couch cushions were jumbled,
and the jackets from the hook by the door had been piled on one
of the armchairs.

"Nice," I said. "You guys are neatness personified." I headed
for the bedroom.

The cop stepped into my path.

"Get out of my way," I said. "This is my apartment!"

Michael Dougherty, trim in gray slacks with a darker gray
linen jacket and tie with splashy blue swirls, emerged from the
bedroom. I felt small and vulnerable next to the two men·

crowding my living room, six-footers armored in their male uniforms of shirt and tie, looming over my five-foot-two in a short-sleeved cotton dress. Michael nodded to the patrolman, who stepped back.

"I'm sorry about this, Anita. We're almost done. It'll be less upsetting if you wait in the hall until we're finished."

"Less upsetting for who?" I shot back. "You mean you'll be more comfortable if I don't watch you ransack my things?"

"It's awkward for everyone," Michael tried to soothe me. "It'll just be another minute."

"I want to see the warrant. It's my home, and I have a right to know what you're looking for."

Michael shrugged, took a piece of paper out of his inside pocket, and handed it to me.

I unfolded the warrant. "What are you looking for?"

For an answer, Michael held up the plastic bag with Benno's good clothes in it. "Is this what your husband was wearing Saturday night?"

The police, like my Jewish husband, had a tendency to answer a question with another question.

"Yes." No sense in lying about that.

Michael nodded. "What kind of shirt?"

"Light green silk."

"Yeah, that's what he said, but we haven't found the shirt."

I walked around him into the bedroom. The closet doors were open. The laundry basket sat in the center of the room, our dirty linen spread on the bed.

"It's at the cleaners. He spilled some wine on it, so we brought it in first thing Monday morning." I got a cold feeling in the pit of my stomach.

Michael glared at me. "Where's the ticket?"

Usually I took care of the dry cleaning, and kept the ticket in my wallet as a reminder to pick the stuff up. That Monday, however, Benno had said he'd take the shirt himself. "I don't know. Didn't you ask Benno? He probably has it."

"Convenient," Michael muttered. A cell phone chirped. Michael pulled it out of his jacket. "Dougherty." He listened, told it to look for a dry cleaning claim check, and folded the phone back into his pocket.

The bulky cop joined us in the bedroom, and Michael nodded him to Benno's chest of drawers. He started at the top, rummaging through Benno's socks and underwear.

"Yo, Detective!" He held up the opened box of condoms.

Michael took it and put it in a smaller evidence bag. "Anita, it would really be better for you to wait outside."

"Not on your life." I started putting the laundry back in its wicker basket, one eye on the cop.

When he got to the bottom drawer, my heart started thudding. He lifted out the top layer of sweaters and pawed his way to the bottom without finding anything that caught his interest. The black box from Renell wasn't there. My heart quieted, but my brain picked up the slack.

What had happened to the chemise?

"Why are you taking the condoms?" I asked Michael.

"You read the warrant. We're looking for anything that indicates your husband was having an extramarital affair with Ms. Chapman. No traces of semen were found in the autopsy, but we have to consider that she might have had consensual sex with someone using a condom. If she did, there's a chance the lab can match the latex residue."

"But she had all her clothes on!" I objected.

"She could have gotten dressed again afterward. There weren't any injuries to indicate that she fought off her attacker, so we assume it was someone she knew and trusted."

I had a flash of Ellen's body, the screwdriver protruding from her chest, the blood on her shirt.

The drawers where we keep our clothes are part of a unit that runs the length of the long wall in the bedroom. Another Benno design, it starts with a double row of drawers to chest height, then steps down to counter level with a long desktop and drawers underneath. Uniform finished a quick run through my side of the clothing drawers and started rifling through the desk.

It was all I could do not to jump him. "That's my personal

stuff, not Benno's," I said. "There's no earthly reason for you to poke around in there!"

The cop straightened and looked to Michael for instructions. Michael jerked his head at the door and told him, "Wait for me in the car, Martinez."

To me he said, "We already got your husband's credit card info from his shop. What I'm after here is bank statements. Show me where they are, and I'll leave the rest of it alone."

I yanked open the top left drawer. Michael nodded approvingly as he glanced over the orderly, folded ranks with canceled checks stapled inside. This was Benno's department, paying bills; the left side of the desk was his. Michael lifted out the past year's worth of statements.

"What did you find at the shop?" It killed me to ask, but damned if I was going to let him walk off knowing something about my husband that I didn't, so he could leak it to Anne and she could turn around and feed it to me.

"I won't really know until we go through his credit card bills and checkbook. Can we talk, Social Worker?" Michael's voice was gentle. "I like you. I like Benno. This situation stinks, but it's my job. No one's arresting anyone at this point. You got any coffee in this joint?"

"What, you didn't familiarize yourself with the contents of my kitchen cabinets?"

Michael blushed.

"You went through the kitchen?" I couldn't believe it. "You needed to know what kind of ice cream we eat?"

Memory hit, and I doubled up over the kitchen counter, my head on my arms. We always stocked vanilla, Ellen's favorite flavor, when she sat in the evening.

"What is it, Anita?" Michael's voice was concerned, but he didn't so much as touch me for comfort.

"I miss Ellen," I said. "I can't even believe she's dead, and you think Benno—"

"It may surprise you," Michael started, "but I don't actually think Benno is who we want for this one. We're supposed to go by evidence, leave the psychological stuff alone, but I don't know a cop who doesn't rely on his gut. My instincts tell me Benno's not the type, but I've had enough experience to know that anyone is capable of anything. So I don't know if what my gut says is because I know you, or because I'm picking up something about the case itself. But the real problem is, you should know this isn't my case anymore."

I gave him a look that said, So what the hell are you doing searching my apartment, then?

"They turned the case over to Northern Manhattan Homicide, the big boys. Remember Neville? He pulled some strings, got me assigned to assist so at least I'm still involved. Was up to this homicide jerk, Peretti, he'd've had Benno charged by now. The media is all over us on this one, which means the brass has their knickers in a twist. Good thing the DA's office has some sense for a change, made us wait on more evidence. You want to hear what we've got, see if you can explain any of it?"

"Okay." Might as well know the worst. I put up water, measured French roast into the filter, and tried to listen objectively, without getting my defenses up.

"The way it looks, the physical evidence points to Benno. Yeah, it's all circumstantial, that's why we're after motive. I know you don't even want to think it, but men *do* cheat. Say Ellen threatened to tell you, don't you think Benno would kill to protect his family?"

I took a firm hold on what I wanted to say and matched his even tone. "No, I don't. I mean, when you say 'to protect his family,' if someone threatened Clea, let me tell you, I'd kill to protect her. But that would be to save her from imminent danger, in the heat of the moment; it wouldn't mean murdering someone in cold blood to cover up an indiscretion." I heard myself say it, an indiscretion. Was that how insignificant it had become? Compared to murder, infidelity was nothing?

"Okay, look at Anne," Michael argued back. "When she caught her husband in bed with that woman, she wanted to kill him. You think if she'd had a weapon, she wouldn't have tried it? What would you do to Benno if you found out he was seeing another woman?"

I took a deep breath and exhaled. "What I would do to Benno has nothing to do with what happened to Ellen, unless you're saying I killed Ellen, and Benno's helping me cover it up?"

"Did you?" Michael reached across the counter and grabbed my hand.

"No." I stared him down.

Michael let go of my hand and sat back. "You said it, not me."

It was as close to an apology as I was going to get. "So what's your point?"

"My point is that when sex comes into the picture, people react in abnormal, unpredictable ways. You know why I never got married? I wasn't ready to confine myself to just one woman forever. Maybe now I am, but if I as much as mention the word *marriage*, Anne won't give me the time of day."

"You proposed to Anne?" I was startled.

The phone rang.

"Aren't you going to answer that?" Michael looked away.

"Not unless it's Benno." I knew it wouldn't be; I didn't have the frisson of foreknowledge I get when I sense he's on the other end of the line.

The machine clicked on. "Mrs. Servi? This is Dawn Mitchell at Catholic Children's. I'm calling to schedule a home visit. Please call me back as soon as possible."

I closed my eyes and stood still as a stone until the machine beeped three times. Calls from the foster care agency are the main reason I've gotten in the habit of screening messages; I have so little say in what happens with Clea's legal situation that when I talk to the caseworker, I want it to be on my schedule, not hers.

The kettle whistled. I turned my back to Michael and shut off the burner. "Did you notify Child Welfare about Benno being under suspicion?"

"No. It came up with Benno's prints, but we don't have to let them know there's a problem until there's actually an arrest. If they've heard anything, it's not from us."

If. I held on to that thought. Maybe this was just a regular home visit; we hadn't had one yet this month. I poured the first shot of water into the filter. The smell of coffee rose.

"Don't you guys have a lawyer for this?" Michael's tone was uncomfortable.

I nodded, but I wasn't about to discuss Clea's situation with him. "Have you even considered anyone other than Benno?"

He pulled out a stool and sat at the counter. "We brought the boyfriend in—according to him, ex-boyfriend, and it was a friendly parting of the ways. His alibi looks pretty good—says he was out with a couple students over there where he works. They weren't any too keen on talking to the police, but they did back him up. And you heard the messages on the tape. Would a killer call and invite the victim to lunch, knowing she was already dead?"

"He might, if he wanted to look innocent," I said. "Don't murderers have brains?"

"Mostly they're dumb as dirt, apart from the ones Sherlock Holmes uncovered."

"Do you know which students he was with?"

Michael just looked at me. "I'm not telling you this so you can go off investigating on your own again, Social Worker. This is murder."

It had also been murder several years ago, when a woman died in the stairwell of my building, but the cops hadn't thought so until I'd "gone off investigating" and proved it. I kept my mouth shut; Michael's memory was as good as mine.

"They were young, a man and a woman, she was from Russia, and he was from one of those former Russian countries, one of those –stan places, you know, Afghanistan, Mongoliastan."

"Michael!" I was appalled. "Afghanistan was never a Soviet country, they fought a war against a Soviet invasion! And Mongolia is not a –stan, it's—"

Michael cut me off with a laugh. "Yeah, I know, I was just testing your geography skills. Relax, you passed."

"What about the other messages on Ellen's answering machine?" I was not amused.

"Well, there's the victim's future stepmother. Marsha Ginsberg. Seems Ellen was upset about her father's remarriage, and Ms. Ginsberg went over Sunday morning to 'hash things out,' as she put it. Someone let her into the building. She maintains that she knocked, got no answer, and split, which knowing what we know makes sense; then she called Ellen later in the day, not knowing she was dead, and left a message."

"There's a motive for you—Ellen was going to wreck her wedding." I was only half serious. "Maybe she was really there the night before and had a big fight with Ellen."

"You ever heard the theory that the simplest explanation is usually the correct one? Besides, Ginsberg really freaked when we broke the news and she realized she'd been knocking on a door with a dead woman on the other side."

I put a carton of milk and my grandmother's china sugar bowl on the counter. Michael helped himself liberally from both. If I'd been feeling more friendly, I would've offered him a chocolate chip cookie, but as it was, he'd have to make do with what my grandmother called a "dry" cup of coffee—nothing to nibble.

"But does she have an alibi for Saturday night?" I pushed. "Why don't you go poke into *her* life?"

"Listen, Anita, about those messages. One was from a friend of Ellen's, Aisha, I think it was. We got a story from her that backs up something the boyfriend told us, which is why we're all over Benno. They both said Ellen was getting it on with someone she wouldn't talk about. Aisha had the idea the man was married, or someone Ellen worked with, but Ellen never told her details. Jamie claimed Ellen wanted to break it off with this mystery man and get back together with him."

"He said, she said—that's proof?" I was incredulous, but at the same time it made a kind of sense. Ellen had been moody, preoccupied, for the past few months; I'd attributed it to her father's pending marriage, not to mention leaving Barnard and starting grad school right away in the fall.

Michael avoided looking at me. "Proof is what we're looking for with the search warrant."

Something cold got a grip on my heart. What if they found—what was there to find? I didn't know, that was the problem; I didn't really know what Benno might have been doing behind my back.

I cast around for some way to derail this train of conversation.

"You know, given how Ellen felt about her father marrying a white woman, and that she broke up with her boyfriend because he's white, don't you think it's unlikely she'd have an affair with a white man? A married man she worked with—I met her boss at the ESL Institute yesterday, Arthur Nessim?" I knew I was going to get Michael's back up, insinuating he'd missed an obvious possibility.

"You're a piece of work, Anita. I should just turn all my cases over to you. You see things we idiots don't even think of."

I met his disgusted look with hope in my heart. "What *about* Arthur Nessim?"

He sighed. "Of course we looked at Nessim. Home with the wife and kids, sound asleep."

What I thought was, Like a wife never lied for her husband? but it cut too close to home for me to say it out loud.

It was well past noon by the time Michael left. I figured I might as well take a long lunch break and straighten up the apartment, get rid of the violated feeling in my home, clean up a little for my mother's impending visit. First I called Benno at the shop.

It was a careful conversation, neither of us wanting to provoke a fight. I told him what they'd taken from the house, and he told me that along with his credit card bills and checkbook, the cops had taken a photo from his bulletin board—a picture of Clea in the playground, on top of the monkey bars, that happened to have Ellen in it. I reminded him that my mother was due in around suppertime, and he promised to be home early.

Then I got busy and channeled my frustration through the vacuum cleaner. One virtue of a small apartment is that it can be cleaned in an hour. I dusted, running a rag soaked in lemon oil over the wall unit, the arms of the couch, the black walnut headboard Benno had made for our bed. With my hands following the traces of his hands across the furniture he'd built, I felt like I was reconnecting with Benno. He was a good man. He had hands that created, not destroyed. Even when he tore out the old kitchen cabinets, Benno didn't go at them with a crowbar; he dismantled them, board by board, with a screwdriver.

Whatever disloyal thoughts I might be having, I put them aside. Benno deserved from me at least what the law gave him. Until he was found guilty beyond a reasonable doubt, I would believe he was innocent. Not only that, I'd do everything I could to find out the truth of what had happened to Ellen, and prove it.

I finished off my housework by smudging the place with a sage stick. I lit the wrapped bundle of herbs and held it up to the four corners of each room, to the sky and to the earth, smoking out the evil spirits.

8

EY, Sis, can you help me out?" The tall, dark-skinned man with wide shoulders and narrow waist, his hair in grown-out cornrows, held out a callused palm.

Oy, Leon. He seemed to live on the corner in front of Mama Joy's delicatessen, hustling for spare change, selling things he'd scavenged from the local Dumpsters. We gave him money so often that Benno joked we should take him as a deduction on our income tax. But he'd taken a shine to Clea, and saved children's books for her whenever he found them. I handed him a dollar.

"How you doin', Miss Clea?" He nodded a thank-you to me. "Terrible thing, terrible thing about that girl that got killed."

"She was my baby-sitter," Clea said.

"Was she now?" Leon's head snapped back. "That pretty girl I see walkin' you home all the time?"

"Someone stabbed her." Clea's voice was fierce.

"Did they now? That's a shame, a real shame." Leon's attention wandered off to the next group of people passing by. We were costing him money, taking up his time so he couldn't approach anyone else.

"Clea, go on ahead in Mama Joy's and pick out a treat. I'll be right in."

She scampered off. "Leon, what was Ellen doing the last time you saw her?" There was no point asking about a particular time or date; days flowed by Leon, unanchored to the calendar.

"Saw her with some guy, draggin' home a big bookcase. Late at night."

"My husband, was he the guy she was with?"

Leon cast a nervous glance up at the sky. There were gray clouds rolling in from the south. He shook his head. "I don't want to start no trouble, now."

"It's okay, I know about it. Did you see her after that? Later that night?"

"Hey, Leon!" The guy who sold used books on long tables set up across the sidewalk in front of Mama Joy's waved at Leon. "Gimme a hand!" The sky was getting dark fast. Thunder grumbled from the south. Leon shrugged his shoulders at me and went to help the bookseller load up his wares.

I went into Mama Joy's, where Clea conned me into a big bag of Twizzlers. I bought oil-cured olives, a chunk of feta, hummus, and taramasalata for a Greek supper. As a treat for my mother, I picked up whitefish salad and onion bagels for breakfast.

When we came out, the wind had picked up. The bookseller, a short Jewish guy with a frizzy gray beard, was loading milk cartons of books into his van. Leon grabbed a book out of the box he was filling and held it out to Clea.

"Hey, little Sis, here's something for you."

It was an old Scholastic book with yellowed pages. The title was *Vampires, Real and Imagined.* Just what she needed, nice peaceful bedtime reading.

"Thank you," Clea said dutifully. She turned the book over to read the back cover.

Leon looked over Clea's head and said, "This other guy she used to hang with, he got himself a new lady, they were around that night."

"What's he look like, Leon?"

"Skinny white boy with glasses, carries himself like he did time for Uncle Sam. He got a taste for brown sugar, 'cuz the new lady is too. Fine-looking African woman."

A few drops splatted down with the next gust of wind. Leon picked up another box and handed it into the van. I slipped him an extra piece of green paper—I figured Benno could just plump up his IRS deduction.

Jamie was with an African woman, not a couple from the former Soviet Union? I put that one away to think about later.

At West Side Market, I got a tomato, red pepper, a head of romaine, lemons, red onions, pita bread, and a can of stuffed grape leaves. This meal I knew Benno liked; it was a summer standby for days when it was too hot to cook.

The storm broke just before we hit the street. We stood under the awning with a small cluster of people, watching it pour down.

Summer in the city. The day starts out clear blue—an umbrella is the farthest thing from your mind—then around three or four in the afternoon you look up, and the sky's gone dark. Next thing you know, you're caught. People just wait it out, collecting under store awnings and in doorways.

"Now, this is what I call a real frog choker," said an elderly black woman in a navy blue straw hat. A diminutive white woman leaning on a shopping cart next to her agreed. Lightning cracked overhead, thunder hard on its heels, and set off a chorus of car alarms from 110th Street.

"Mama, how long do we have to stand here?" Clea pulled at my arm until I leaned over closer to her. "I have to pee," she whispered.

"How bad?" I asked. The thunder had rumbled on, but rain was still coming down hard. From the look of it, we were in for a good twenty minutes at least. The twisted look on her face told me she wasn't going to make it that long.

"Okay, here's the plan." I bent over and slipped out of my sandals. "Take your sneakers and socks off—we're going to make a run for it."

Clea looked at me like I'd lost my mind.

"So, we'll get soaked," I reassured her. "We can change our clothes, but there's no point in getting our shoes wet." Maybe it was my mother's imminent arrival making me frisky; maybe I just needed to cut loose. All we had to do was cross Broadway, then a block over and half a block down. The sidewalks were being washed clean, clear of anything like broken glass that could hurt us. Why not?

I added our shoes to Clea's backpack. When we got the Walk signal, I took Clea's hand and we darted across the street.

We tumbled into the building, totally drenched, laughing like maniacs. After Clea peed, we put on our nightgowns and curled up in bed together, watching the rain taper off and the sky clear.

We were still there when Benno came home, Clea asleep in my arms. Benno lay down, curled like a spoon around me. We watched Clea breathe until, sensing our watchful presence, she woke up.

Benno sliced vegetables, and I arranged them on the big Mexican platter. He sprinkled capers and oregano over the whole thing, then drizzled it with olive oil and vinegar. I poured us two glasses of wine, and juice for Clea. We were just about to sit down when the buzzer rang.

My mother never traveled light. She struggled out of the elevator with a huge tapestry suitcase on wheels, a leather carry-on, and a canvas shopping bag with two loaves of San Francisco sourdough bread sticking up out of it. Benno went to help her, planting a kiss on her offered cheek. Clea hung back, suddenly shy, but my mother bent down, opened her arms, and hauled Clea in.

It was the greeting I knew she wanted to give me, but I allowed her no more than the same kind of cheek she'd offered Benno to kiss. In spite of how happy I was to see her, I wanted to remind her that my unanswered questions about my father were still alive and well and on my mind.

For most of my life, I'd accepted her story—that she'd enlisted in the army to be a nurse in Korea, gotten pregnant by a GI who'd been killed before he even knew I was on the way, and been dishonorably discharged when her condition became obvious.

A few years ago, I'd gotten curious and went so far as to contact the army—and found that there was no record of her ever having served, in Korea or anywhere else, dishonorably or not.

Armed with that lack of proof, I'd confronted my mother and been met with a stone wall. After that I figured I'd fight silence with silence, and basically cut off all but the bare minimum of communication between us.

I had to admit, she looked good, my mother. In her sixties, she'd let her long hair revert to its natural, snowy white. She wore it up in a twist, held in place with a silver clip I'd given her years ago. Whatever tall genes there were in the family, she'd kept for herself; to my chagrin, I never got as tall as her five-foot-four. Nor was I as slender, although I noticed she had put on a bit of weight in the past year. It looked good on her, filling out some of the lines on her face.

"Your timing is perfect, Rosemarie." Benno gestured at the table. "Can I get you a glass of wine?"

"That would be lovely." My mother settled herself on the couch and started emptying her shopping bag. "These are for Anita, the one thing you really can't get in New York!" She handed me the loaves of sourdough, double-bagged in paper sleeves rather than plastic, which would have turned the crisp crusts soggy. The bread was from Il Fornaio, the best bakery in the city. There I was, back in Berkeley habits—"the city" meant San Francisco, just as in the outer boroughs, the city meant Manhattan.

Then came two bottles swathed in bubble wrap. "Now, Benno, I know you prefer Italian wine, but I've found a California zinfandel that I think will change your mind."

Benno accepted the wine with a tolerant grin. "Shall I open one of these, or will you try what I've got first?"

"Oh, whatever's already open! Let's not waste a good bottle."

Clea peered into the bag. "What else is in there?"

"You mean didn't I bring anything for my favorite grand-child?"

"Gamma Rho!" Clea protested. "I'm your only grandchild!"

The Greek nickname was a Benno invention, a formalized version of Clea's baby attempts to say Grandma Rose. It suited my mother, who maintained she'd rather be a Greek goddess than a grandmother.

"Of course you are, but you'd be my favorite even if I had fifty!"

I rolled my eyes. Benno handed my mother a glass of wine. I took a swig from my own glass. Go Mom, I thought. But Benno's smile was wide and genuine for the first time in days, and it was good to hear Clea laugh.

"Now, let me see, what else is in here? Ah yes, there it is!"

I knew as well as Clea did what was coming: a Ghirardelli chocolate cable car. It had been my childhood treat, a reward for everything from good grades to a volleyball victory, and Gamma Rho always brought one for Clea.

"After dinner, Bops," I reminded her. "Mom, are you hungry? We were just about to start."

"Famished. The food they give you on those planes, I wouldn't feed it to a slug!"

I cut chunks of sourdough instead of the pita bread. For the next few hours we seemed like a happy family, except that my mother's occasional scrutiny of Benno and me served to underline the fact that he and I never looked directly at each other.

After we tucked Clea into bed with the promise that Gamma Rho would pick her up after school tomorrow, Benno brought up the subject of Aaron Wertheim, and paying his retainer ourselves.

"Don't be silly." My mother shrugged him off. "Didn't he tell you he'd be interested in bartering cabinetry for his fee? Besides, I used the money I've saved on plane tickets these past few years since I haven't been allowed to fly back here."

That little gibe was aimed at me. I deflected it. "How do you know Wertheim well enough for him to take on plebeians such as ourselves?"

"Aaron Wertheim specializes in plebeians! Defending the wrongfully accused is his meat and potatoes." My mother faked a yawn. "You know, in spite of the time zones, I'm beat."

"How *do* you know him, Rosemarie?" Benno asked.

"Actually, it's his mother I know. I did some private-duty nursing for the family when her husband was dying. Aaron was just a teenager then, but his mother and I stayed in touch, and of course I've followed his career in the news."

"Was that before or after you joined the army?" I asked.

She ignored my sarcastic tone. "Before. It was a live-in position, which got me out of my parents' apartment." My mother looked around the apartment where she'd spent her childhood and shuddered. The place looked nothing like it had fifty years ago, when Clea's room had been hers, but I had no idea what ghosts lurked in the walls, waiting to pounce on her.

"How come you never talked about knowing Aaron before?"

"It wasn't relevant before. Benno, could I have another glass of wine, please? The way my daughter is looking at me, I can see I'm in for the third degree."

Which shut me right up, as she'd intended.

I let it go and made up the sofa bed, after which my mother insisted I turn in with Benno instead of sitting up for the mother-daughter talk I was half hoping we'd have.

9

MY mother was still sleeping when Clea and I left the apartment the next morning, but some of her calm, competent vibrations must have emanated from behind the closed French doors of the living room and permeated my psyche. Ensconced in my cube at work, I felt ready to tackle the paperwork and phone messages that I'd let accumulate in the turbulent wake of Ellen's death.

On the more practical level, my mother's presence meant that I could get in a full day of work; she'd pick Clea up, and with any luck, even take care of supper. The first thing I did was to schedule a three o'clock meeting with the ESLI students. That left me the better part of the day to catch up.

Anne and I mended fences, but not to the point where I felt ready to broach the subject of Michael wanting to marry her. I noticed his photo was nowhere in sight, which I guessed was not a good sign. It was too bad; they'd been together three years, and I thought they suited each other well, for all how different they were.

Pondering Anne's love life made a nice change from worrying over mine, but what really took my mind off my troubles was my clients. By one o'clock my ear hurt from being pressed to the phone and I was starving. Anne and Emma had gone for lunch together, leaving me with a quiet office and the leftovers from last night's meal.

I made it a working lunch, taking a yellow pad to Anne's desk so I could write out an agenda for the ESLI meeting while I kept an eye on the door in case anyone dropped in.

Nafissa's visit had provided me with a germ of inspiration on how to proceed with the students. I knew from working with home health aides for the elderly, many of whom were immigrant women from the islands, that there were vast cultural and generational gaps between the aides and the clients. What I wanted to do was prepare the students for some of the attitudes they might encounter in the older people they'd be assigned to help.

Mindful that Arthur Nessim's agenda included providing plenty of opportunities for conversing, I thought I'd start by asking about their own grandparents. Along with today's meeting, I'd set up two for next week, so there'd be ample time to insert the information I wanted them to have. And with any luck, I'd be building on a base of respect for old people that the immigrants brought with them from their countries.

Yesterday's rain, rather than clearing the air, had brought on a summer bout of humidity. People on the sidewalks seemed sunstruck, pale in the heat, moving slowly. Even in a loose rayon dress and sandals, I was sweating by the time I'd walked the ten blocks to Riverside Church. It was cooler inside, but not by much. On the fourth floor, the heat was palpable again.

I stopped into Arthur Nessim's office and was surprised to find Jamie at Arthur's desk. He stood up when I stuck my head in.

"Excuse me, I was looking for Arthur?"

"He's with a class right now. Can I help you?"

I told him I was there to meet with the students who were volunteering to work with the old people, and added, "I'm sorry about the other night, I—"

"Please don't apologize again, Ms. Servi. I'm the one who owes you an apology. I go to the labyrinth to meditate, not to talk. It wasn't fair of me to sound off at you like that, about your husband. I was startled, but that's no excuse for my rudeness. I know what it's like to be wrongly accused."

"There's no need to apologize, I understand," I said, but what I thought was, If you know what it feels like, why are you falsely accusing my husband? Then I decided, what the hell. "If you don't mind my asking, did Ellen ever tell you in so many words that she was having a thing with my husband?"

"Not in so many words." He didn't meet my eyes. "But it seemed pretty clear to me from the context of what she did say. I didn't want to know about it, and I told her so. Married people are trouble." This time he looked right at me, and the implication was clear: You're trouble. Leave me alone.

I stepped back to more neutral ground. "I didn't mean to upset you. It's just, I still can't believe Ellen's gone. I keep wanting to talk to her, or at least to someone else who knew her, to figure out how this could be happening."

Jamie pushed his glasses up with a pinch of thumb and forefinger and rubbed the bridge of his nose. I noticed the fine lines beginning to cross his forehead. He let the glasses drop back in place and shuffled a pile of papers together. "Well, you'll have a chance tomorrow. I'm organizing a memorial service, and you and"—he paused, like a polite man swallowing something he didn't like the taste of—"your family would be welcome to come. It'll be at three o'clock, in the Chapel of the Cross, on this floor."

"Will Ellen's family be there?" I wanted to see her mother, especially, and her younger brother and sister.

"Arthur called to tell them about it, but I don't think anyone's going to show. They'll have her funeral at their church in Brooklyn, as soon as they can." He came around the desk. "I'll walk over to the Resource Room with you now."

All the windows in the big room were open, and a floor fan had been set up in one corner to blow the heavy air around. Three students were waiting for me at one of the card tables.

We made introductions. I was surprised that Nafissa wasn't one of them, but glad to see Talile Areya was there.

Talile, whose personality was as lilting as her name, had really taken to Septima Hall, the client I'd paired her with. Septima, a former music teacher, was ninety-eight years old;

Talile told the group about the grand piano that hogged all the space in her living room, and how Septima bragged about crossing the Atlantic Ocean seventeen times and the Pacific Ocean seven times—including one trip when she'd gone clear around the world, which accounted for the odd numbers of her crossings. The match had been Ellen's idea, and I was glad it was working. Ellen had thought it would be good for Talile to meet a woman who'd led a very different life than what people often think of as the typical black experience in America.

We moved around the table. Vlad, in his twenties, was from Azerbaijan. He'd learned woodworking from his grandfather, who made birdhouses in a small village where Vlad spent his summers. Vlad lived near Brighton Beach, in Brooklyn, and drove a cab at night.

The third person at the table was also from a former Soviet country, Ukraine. She was older, looked to be in her mid-sixties but was probably ten years younger. It can be hard to judge ages with people from the former Soviet countries; most women color their hair, but Olga wore hers gray and cut short and curly around her face. Also, she was a grandmother herself, living with her daughter and three-year-old granddaughter. Both of her own grandmothers were still alive, left behind in Ukraine, at 99 and 103. Ellen and I had planned to pair her with a ninety-eight-year-old former Russian, Reva Epstein.

It was what I'd hoped for, that the volunteers were comfortable with older people. American society has gotten so stratified, with children moving far from their parents, grandchildren not having the kind of daily, ongoing relationships that a less mobile society still maintained.

I asked if any of them knew why Nafissa wasn't there, and was met with an awkward silence. Finally Talile spoke up.

"She has stopped school."

It took me a second. "You mean she's not a student here anymore?" I was surprised. Nafissa had seemed so responsible, it was hard to imagine that she'd quit without letting me know. And if she had, wasn't it odd that Jamie hadn't said anything about it?

Three heads nodded Yes.

It was Vlad who spoke. "No, she is not in school anymore."

"We don't know why," Olga added.

"Yes, we do," Vlad said. "She is afraid."

"Afraid of what?" I asked.

This time they answered in unison. "Militsia. Police. Poleez."

Talile explained. "The police tell us, if we don't answer questions, we be sent back to our countries."

"You know, the police can't deport you if you haven't done anything."

They let my words sit in polite silence until Talile spoke up. "Nafissa's country is Senegal, near to the country of the man who was shot in his house. He didn't do anything. Forty-one shots they gave him."

"Amadou Diallo?" She was right. Giuliani time, when innocence was no guarantee of protection.

"Nafissa has a brother, very angry about police. He goes to protest with that big man." She made a smooth, wavy gesture above the top of her head.

"Reverend Sharpton?" The man with the James Brown pompadour. I was beginning to catch on to this pantomime language.

Talile nodded.

"So why did the police want to talk to Nafissa?" I was puzzled.

Olga frowned at Vlad. "Police, they are asking everybody, where was you Saturday night? Two peoples was with Jamie, but everyone must answer to police."

"Okay, I was together with Jamie when Ellen, she buy the white shoes. I tell police this." Vlad dismissed Olga's accusation.

Now I was totally lost. "White shoes?"

"Is idioma, we say in my country when a person—" He drew a hand across his throat, pantomiming a life being cut off. "Is more polite to say he wears white shoes."

"White shoes, like the dead person is with the angels?"

Vlad grinned at me. "Yes, yes. On the night Ellen she buys the white shoes, we was with Jamie. Myself and Natalya." He gestured across the room at a slender young woman with light brown hair. She was watching a movie on television with the aid of big blue earphones. "Police, they ask many, many questions about Jamie, about Ellen. We tell them no way Jamie is killing Ellen, Jamie is drinking beer with us.

"Police in New York is crazy. In my country, you know what police want. They stop your car, say you go too fast. No ticket, you give money." Vlad held his left hand out, palm up, and stroked it with the fingertips of his right hand, the universal gesture for bribery: greasing the palm. "In my country, is simple: militsia ask, you give. In New York, my brother tells me never give money to police, they will arrest you."

An innocent mistake by someone who doesn't know the unwritten rules, or speak the language that well—who knew how the cops would respond?

"Police look in everybody's business," Olga chimed in. "One week ago, my daughter, the daughter of her wanted ice cream in cone. Only I am in apartment and I cannot go out. She cry and cry. I tell her, when mother come home she take you to ice cream. My daughter comes, she is tired, don't want to go. Child is crying. Soon police come, knock on door." She rapped on the table three times, hard. "They say, child is crying, what you do to her?"

So of course they had to come in and look at the child. Fortunately, they read the situation for what it was—a neighbor, bothered by a crying child, dialed 911 and got instant results—rather than calling in Child Welfare and bringing the weight of the system down on them. In this country, even false accusations can ruin a life. I had only to look at my own situation.

Vlad lingered by the table after the women had gone. "You don't be worry for Nafissa. She come back to school soon. Jamie, he take care of her."

"Jamie?" I asked, deliberately naive. "Why? Is he Nafissa's boyfriend?"

He laid a hand on my arm and put his face close to mine. His breath smelled metallic, anxious.

"I don't say this. Jamie tell us, Nafissa be back in school, one week, two week maybe, her brother is letting her come back."

Damn the language barrier. What exactly did he mean?

"Why doesn't Nafissa's brother want her to talk to the police?"

Vlad backed his head away and nodded, relieved. "We tell you before. Police treat black peoples very bad."

I'd asked the wrong question, let him off the hook. Then it dawned on me. Vlad and Natalya and Jamie? Three's a crowd, but four is a double date. And hadn't Leon said he'd seen Jamie with an African woman?

"Nafissa was with you that night, wasn't she? When Ellen died?"

"No, I don't say this," Vlad repeated, but he wouldn't meet my eyes. "Is enough, police know I and Natalya was there."

A middle-aged man got up from a chair in the corner of the room and asked Vlad a question in Russian. His answer, in Russian, sounded like it was going to be long and complicated.

I walked over to the windows, lingering until Vlad finished with his conversation. I stared across the street at Union Theological Seminary. My thoughts were as convoluted as the stone tracery on the windows.

Nafissa's brother had pulled her out of the institute so she wouldn't have to talk to the police, but he didn't know—wasn't supposed to know—that she'd been in the neighborhood the night Ellen was killed. The others had lied for her. I puzzled over it.

What did I know about the fears of immigrants, especially West African immigrants? I had no idea what experiences Nafissa might have had with the cops. White, middle-class, who was I to think the fears of a black woman were groundless?

Nafissa's purported fear of her brother I found easier to understand. A Muslim woman, out on a date with a nonbeliever? So maybe the explanation was simple: She didn't want her brother to find out, the others knew this, and as Vlad said, he and Natalya were enough of an alibi. No need to drag Nafissa into it.

I realized the flow of Russian gutturals had stopped. When I turned, the room was empty. So much for clarification from Vlad.

I walked down the long hall, past Arthur's office. His door was closed. I knocked on it. There was no answer. I tried the handle, figuring I'd leave a note asking about Nafissa on his desk; if she'd really dropped out of the program, I'd have to find someone new for Mabel Johnson. The door was locked.

Talile was waiting for the elevator. She bubbled on about Septima as we rode down and walked toward the exit. When we got outside, I interrupted.

"Do you know Nafissa, where she lives? I'd like to talk to her."

"No." Talile's face said how sorry she was that she couldn't help me. "Ellen was good friend to Nafissa. She talked with Nafissa and put it on a tape recorder, about all Nafissa's life, then she write about it for her school."

"I didn't know that." I was surprised. Ellen often talked about her course work, particularly special projects, but she hadn't mentioned doing an oral history of anyone. Well, it had been a busy time. Or had she told a different member of my family about her project? I batted the thought away.

"Did Nafissa's brother know they were friends?"

I must have hit a tender area, because for the first time Talile's words came reluctantly. "When he knows, he tells Nafissa she must stop. American woman put ideas in her head."

"It's hard sometimes, coming from different countries and religions. Especially for women and children, America is a land of opportunity."

Talile's laugh was back. "Oh, yes! Ellen teach us an American expression. 'You don't keep them down on the farm once they see big city.'"

I could just hear Ellen's voice as Talile recited the words. It was so like her, rabble-rousing with these immigrant women!

We stopped to wait for the Walk light on 120th Street.

"Talile, do you know if Nafissa was out with Vlad and Natalya and Jamie the night Ellen died?" I was fishing.

I got the same noncommittal shrug as Vlad had given me.

"It's okay, I won't say anything. I know, if Nafissa's brother was upset about her being friends with Ellen, I can imagine how angry he'd be about her going out with Jamie."

"About that thing, Nafissa's brother and Ellen see the same." Talile made a vertical, chopping motion with her hand. "Ellen cut with Nafissa. Because of Jamie."

"Because of Jamie?" I repeated, not quite following.

"He like Nafissa. Then Ellen"—she made the chopping gesture again, indicating something cut off, ended—"no more friends with her. Man come in between women, not friends anymore. This is also American?"

"Well, yes. It depends on the situation, I mean, it's complicated." I felt compelled to defend my culture, but I had to stop and think about how to explain it. What we take for granted can seem barbaric to others; that a man should break up the friendship between two women? But it happens, it definitely happens.

Talile helped me out. "Everything in America is love, man and woman love. This is not bad! Man is good to woman in America! Brings her flowers and diamonds."

I nodded, in over my head. This was not the moment I wanted to get into a discussion of American mating customs.

"Ellen stopped being friends with Nafissa, because Nafissa was seeing Jamie?" What with language and culture, I wanted to be positive I had it right.

Talile nodded. The light changed. I was trying to come up with the next question when she waved good-bye and headed toward Broadway.

I spent the rest of the walk home worrying about where Nafissa was. I'd had the sense when she came to my office that more was bothering her than Mabel Johnson's stereotyping. And I was annoyed that Jamie hadn't told me about Nafissa dropping out of the program, and that Arthur hadn't called with the information, either. The more I thought about Arthur Nessim, the more I liked him as the mystery man Ellen had been having the

affair with. He was older, married, the kind of handsome that
needs to see itself reflected in the adoring eyes of women.

My mother practically flung the door open at the sound of my
key in the lock.

"Thank goodness you're home!" She pulled me in by the arm
and locked the door behind me, then bent to whisper in my ear.
"Benno's been arrested!"

"What? Where's Clea?" First things first.

"In her room. I set her up with the Walkman and a tape so
she wouldn't hear me on the phone. I've been calling all over
creation trying to find you." I got the same accusing look she'd
specialized in when I got home late from school.

I had more important things on my mind than excuses. "Tell
me what happened."

"Aaron called about an hour ago. Benno's down at Central
Booking, wherever that is. Aaron said they'll arraign him some-
time late tonight, and he'll try to get the charges dropped. The
DA has nothing but circumstantial evidence and speculation."

"Did you talk to Benno? Is he okay?"

My mother sat me down on the couch. "Stay calm now,
Anita. No, of course I couldn't speak with Benno. He did the
right thing and used his phone call for Aaron. Benno's a smart
man, he can take care of himself."

I had visions of a cell full of drug dealers, wife beaters, father rapers. Without thought, I sent a prayer to Mary for his
safety. I got up. "I'm going to call Mr. Wertheim. I have to know
what's happening."

"He gave me his cell phone number. He's somewhere downtown, and he said to tell you that you could go down to the arraignment. It's Friday, so they go all night. He said he'd let you
know closer to the time when Benno's case will be called so you
don't have to sit down there for hours." She handed me the pad
with Wertheim's number on it.

My hands were shaking when I picked up the phone. How
could this be happening to us? We were a nice, normal, nuclear

family; okay, maybe a little quirky, but not the kind of people whose baby-sitter died a violent death—let alone the kind of people who caused it. I just didn't believe it could happen.

I went into the bedroom and closed the door in my mother's face. I needed to hear it from the source. I sat on the bed and closed my eyes. What I needed most of all, simply to hear Benno's voice, was the one thing I knew I wasn't going to get.

Aaron Wertheim's baritone was the closest thing, a lifeline to my husband. He said the same things my mother had, with a dash of reassurance on conditions in the holding cells, and gave me the address of the courthouse on Centre Street.

"But really, Ms. Servi, there's no need to go down yet. It will be six or seven hours at least before your husband is transported from Central Booking to the arraignment. I'll see him at the courthouse, and I may be able to arrange for you to see him briefly at that time. Please, let me call you later. Night court is not a place you want to spend more time than necessary."

As soon as I hung up the phone, my mother opened the bedroom door. The tears on my face stopped her before she could get a word out. She sat next to me, held me in her arms, and whispered soothing words. I let myself be rocked while I wept.

But despair is an emotion the mothers of young children are not allowed to wallow in for very long. I sat up.

"What am I going to tell Clea?"

"I'd suggest that we don't say anything until we know what's going on." When that "we" came out of my mother's mouth, I felt a vast sense of relief. I wasn't alone; I had the most powerful woman I knew on my side.

"That's a good idea." I nodded. "I'll just say Dad had to work late, that's not unusual. Then if he's home in the morning, we'll just deal with whatever we have to when she's not around." I had not the slightest idea how optimistic that thought was.

We muddled through Chinese delivered for supper, keeping up the appearance of normality. After tucking Clea into bed and telling the day, she stopped me.

"You know what I like about Gamma Rho?"

"She brings you chocolate cable cars."

"Be serious, Mama."

"Okay, tell me."

"I like it that when she's here, I don't have to eat by myself."

I was taken aback. Eat by herself? Okay, so I usually fixed Clea's dinner first and waited to eat mine with Benno most weeknights, but I was always there while Clea ate. I pointed this out to her.

"No, Mama, I mean when Gamma Rho is here, we eat *together*."

Clea lay still for a moment. I switched off the light and bent to kiss her forehead.

"Ellen didn't eat with me neither." Her voice was small.

I sat up with a jerk. "What do you mean?"

Clea curled into my lap. "She did like you do, only she let me watch television. Ellen didn't ever eat her supper until I was in bed."

"The last time she baby-sat you, she didn't eat tortellinis with you while you watched Xena?" The implications of Ellen's last meal being several hours later than we'd thought went zinging through my brain. If she hadn't died between one and two in the morning, it would go a long way toward clearing Benno. Then the red numbers flashed, 1:14, 1:56; what had Benno been doing all that time?

"Uh-uhh. She was talking on the telephone the whole time."

"Do you know who she was talking to, Bops?" I didn't want Clea to clam up or get any wrong ideas, so I tried to keep my voice casual.

Clea shook her head, no.

"Did the person call her, or did Ellen make a call?"

"The phone rang, and Ellen answered it. Then she went in your room and closed the door. Is that how come she got stabbed?"

"No. Absolutely not." The linear thinking of a child. I hadn't intended to get Clea started on a chain of thought that would produce such a question. "I was just curious." I tucked the covers around her shoulders and gave them a squeeze. "Sweet dreams, Bopster."

10

IT was almost midnight by the time Wertheim called. In preparation, I'd already changed into slacks, put a book in my purse, and taken my Swiss army knife out—I knew from the security guards and metal detectors in family court that they'd take the knife away from me. Given the way family court scrambled my emotions, I figured night court would put me well beyond the point of remembering to reclaim my knife—it was better to leave it at home.

Leaving the house after eleven was so rare an event in my married life as to be nonexistent. My mother tried to convince me to take a cab, but the subway was cheaper and, even at that hour, faster. I tried to summon up the mood of going on an adventure, exploring a part of the infinite city that I'd never ventured into before, but my heart was too heavy.

I swiped my card through the turnstile just as a train was opening its doors. Seeing me on the run, a pair of black youths stood in the doors and held them open against the warning chime. I took it as a good omen for the smooth flow of the evening's events and for the kindness of the strangers I'd be putting myself among. I thanked the boys and found a seat, crushed between an overflowing Hispanic woman and a slender white man with his face buried in a book. The air-conditioning, as usual on all but the hottest summer days, made the car too cold for comfort. I leaned forward to put on the sweater I'd brought with me. The woman shifted slightly, making the narrow slot I'd occupied even more confining.

My stomach started churning as soon as I got off the train at Franklin Street, the same stop as for family court. I'd watched this station go from grimy to under construction to the soothing terra-cotta and green of historic renovation, but it did nothing to ease my nerves.

Nor did walking across to Centre Street. I had to go past the sheer, polished black granite monolith of the family court building, which the curved steel sculpture of a mother-shape wrapped around a child-shape did nothing to soften. I thought of family court as one circle of hell. The spaces inside were cut at odd angles, sharp-cornered rooms in weird shapes clustered around a central wall of windows yellowed from years of not being washed. The waiting rooms were always crowded with parents, social workers, an occasional frightened child, and lawyers, their arms full of file folders, calling the names of clients they'd never met before.

At least criminal court occupied an imposing, old-style building, with stairs up to a columned entry, lined with chiseled inscriptions like Justice Is Denied No One—yeah, right—and Good Faith Is the Foundation of Justice. A pair of white men in jeans smoked cigarettes by the entrance.

I circled through the revolving door and was spit out into a short line for the metal detectors. New York, you show up someplace at midnight, and there's a line.

The security officers were in no hurry. A well-padded white woman in uniform was running a handheld wand over a Hispanic woman in jeans too tight to hide anything. I laid my bag on the counter. A uniformed black woman with short, straightened hair pawed through it, even opening the tube of lipstick and rolling it out to be sure it wasn't a concealed weapon, I supposed.

The whole time she was inspecting my bag, she never paused in her conversation with a fellow court officer. I tried not to stare at him, but his white shirt, navy pants, clip-on tie, and hip-holstered gun made an incongruous contrast to the personality inside them. His head was shaved except for a short, braided ponytail of black hair high on the back of his head; he had heavy silver and turquoise rings on three of his fingers, and two gold hoops in each ear. They allowed court officers to accessorize themselves like that? Then I noticed the wide gold band on his left ring finger. This man was married? To a man or a woman? I wondered.

Aaron Wertheim had told me to go directly to the court-room. Either Benno would be let go, or bail would be so high we'd need time to figure out how to raise it.

He'd also said I wouldn't have any trouble recognizing him, or he me—no one else in the courtroom would have the same demographics as we did—but just in case all lawyers looked alike to me, he'd be wearing a tie with overlapping circles of red, teal, cream, and black.

I went through two sets of swinging doors and into what was surely another of the outer rings of hell.

The room itself was a whole lot better than the misshapen warrens across the street—high ceilings, wood-paneled walls lined with windows starting about six feet up. In the daytime, it might even be pleasant; at night, the fluorescents hanging in long rows cast a light that was not quite bright enough but appropriate for this otherworldly hour. There were a dozen rows of wooden benches, divided into three sections, for the friends and families of the defendants. Then a low wooden wall across the front of the room, penning in the judge, the lawyers, clerks, cops, miscreants. The judge sat up high, facing the room; the minions of law and order, backs to the anxious spectators, kept themselves busy at several long tables piled with papers, computers, a scattering of phones.

To the left of the judge was a double row of dark heads facing the wall. It didn't take a guidebook to identify them as the people waiting to be arraigned.

I didn't see anyone who looked like Wertheim. No one paid the slightest attention to me, so I took a seat in the fourth row on the left side and tried to get my bearings.

The judge, no surprise, was an elderly white man, with a round balding head, a round body under his black robe, and round steely glasses framing round blue eyes. The main action seemed to be in the hands of the court clerk, a tall black man with gold aviator glasses, who called names and read charges in a rapid staccato that was almost impossible to follow. As I sat there, the room sorted itself out into coherent components. The defendants came and went; when the bench emptied, a court officer brought in more. The table directly in front of me seemed to house a pool of Legal Aid attorneys, who took turns standing up for three or four defendants in a row. In front of the judge was a man I assumed to be the assistant district attorney, a youngish white guy with small ears and a jutting jaw, assisted by a blond woman in a gray pants suit with a zippered jacket, who occasionally disagreed with him. A clerk of some sort sat next to them and passed folders of papers.

Then there was the court stenographer, a massive black woman in a red dress with a bosom that sloped so steeply it could have been an Olympic ski jump. She kept her eyes on the clerk while her fingers flew over the small keypad of a machine that emitted a long curl of paper.

As I listened, it seemed clear that most people were in for petty offenses—DUI, possession, violating orders of protection. The DA usually favored five days' jail time, and the judge made the defendant allocute—say what he'd done. And they were all men, all minorities—black, Hispanic, an occasional token Asian.

It was grim. A few times, one of the defense attorneys gestured toward the spectators, informing the judge what a good family man he had standing before him. My company on the free side of the room was an indecipherable assortment. One bench held five young whites, boys and girls with notepads on their knees, probably college students observing justice in action. A young Hispanic woman with a ponytail and big gold hoops in her ears was biting her nails. A boy, maybe eight or nine, sat quietly next to her. A middle-aged black man napped with his head on his wife's shoulder. Her face was ancient, sad.

Wertheim was right: there was no one else like me in the room—a middle-aged white woman, alone. And right again —when he came in from the back of the room, I would have known him without the tie. He was easily the most prosperous, best-dressed, most well-fed individual in the room, as well as one of the shortest.

Maybe he was five-five, but no more. His suit was charcoal with a fine pinstripe, the double-breasted jacket buttoned over a substantial but not ostentatious belly. His silver hair was brushed straight back; his beard was trimmed close and shaved under the chin. The briefcase he carried was smooth black leather, scuffed with wear.

You might think he'd look out of place, uncomfortable, but somehow he seemed to fit right in with the nocturnal environment. There were nods and smiles among the court officers and Legal Aid attorneys. Wertheim's presence lightened the air in the room, as if his vigilance opened the eyes of justice a little wider, made the cut of her sword a little more precise. This was a man you wanted on your side.

When he turned to me, his smile was warm and genuine. I took the hand he extended. "Ms. Servi?" His hand was warm and dry, his grip solid. I trusted him implicitly, even though the facts of the case against Benno, as he proceeded to outline it to me, were all bad.

"What the police have, along with Mr. Servi's prints on the murder weapon and the fact that he is the last person known to have seen her before she was killed, are three items they found in the search of his workshop: a photograph of Ms. Chapman, a negligee, and a frame he was evidently making for Ms. Chapman's college diploma."

Wertheim grimaced. "The photograph was of your daughter as well as Ms. Chapman. The negligee was found in his bag; he told them he'd bought it for your anniversary and, realizing that it was the wrong size, was going to return it. They did not believe that he would have mistaken his wife's size. As to the frame, that gets a bit complicated. I won't go into details now, other than to say that your husband claimed Ms. Chapman's father's fiancée hired him to make the frame. It's all circumstantial, all with an innocent explanation.

"They are also attempting to retrieve the shirt he wore that night from the dry cleaner. Assuming there is no evidence of blood, that won't be a problem. What we're really up against here is, I believe, primarily political. Columbia University carries a lot of weight in the community. Their interest is in seeing someone apprehended, ideally a person who is neither a fellow student nor an outsider who managed to get past the lax security and enter a university residence. Their need is to reassure the academic community as to the safety of its members. Our need is to prove the police have made a mistake and there is still a killer at large."

I nodded, trying to take it all in, but my mind was spinning. Benno had said nothing to me about framing Ellen's diploma—not that he always discussed small commissions, but in this case, since I knew who it was for . . . And then his story about the chemise, not negligee as the police misidentified it—I wanted to believe it was a mistake, that Benno'd realized I was no longer a size small, but—

"Can you confirm your husband's story about either the negligee or the diploma?" Wertheim asked me.

I couldn't, but under his direct brown gaze, I tried. "Of course. I've forgotten the woman's name, but he told me about the frame last week. And the chemise, if it was supposed to be a surprise, I didn't know about it."

Wertheim checked his watch. "Let me see if they're ready to bring him in." He put a hand on my knee. "I should warn you, your husband will be in handcuffs. I was able to have them transport him separately from those accused of lesser crimes, but the cuffs were unavoidable. The escort will remove them once he enters the courtroom, and I'll be able to talk with him over there." He nodded at a narrow, glass-enclosed space on the left side of the courtroom. It had two doors and a table separating the sides. I'd watched a lawyer enter from one end, the client from the other, presumably so they could confer privately yet still be under observation by the court officers.

"So do you think the charges will be dropped?" It seemed impossibly hopeful, in these surroundings, that Benno would simply be let go.

"Of course, that's what I'll ask for. I think, however, that it's highly unlikely. The district attorney's office will want to present the evidence to a grand jury, and the judge is likely to agree to hold Mr. Servi in custody pending an indictment. Bail is rarely granted when there's a charge of murder."

"How long does it take for the grand jury?"

"By law, the district attorney must present his case within 144 hours from the time of the arrest. Basically, that gives him six days. Now, Benno was picked up Friday morning, but wasn't officially arrested until early afternoon. So it would have to be done by Thursday morning at the latest."

It just kept getting worse. "Will I be able to talk to Benno tonight?"

Wertheim sighed. "Probably not. I can request a rail visit, which means that you would be seated in the front row on this side, and your husband in a chair about five feet back on the other side of the rail. If the judge allows it, which I must warn you I think is unlikely, you'll have perhaps two minutes to talk across a distance of approximately ten feet. It's not much, and unless there's something extremely urgent you need to say, which does not require privacy . . . well, it might be better to wait until tomorrow, when you can visit with him, either at Rikers Island or, if we're fortunate, here in the Tombs."

I reached for my sweater. The stuffy room seemed to have gotten colder.

Wertheim put a hand on my arm. "The Tombs are actually not so bad these days. If, as I expect, the judge refuses a rail visit, he may bend enough to order that Benno be remanded there rather than Rikers. It's closer, and it will be easier on you both." He reached for his briefcase.

"There's one other thing," I said. "I told you before that our daughter is still a foster child?" I sketched out the situation, and confided my worries about the impact of the Adoption and Safe Families Act.

Wertheim nodded as I spoke. "It's not my area of expertise, but I'll speak with your family law attorney tomorrow. Offhand I'd say that given the situation, it's actually for the best if Mr.

Servi is not granted bail. With him out of the home, there's a solid argument to be made for not removing the little girl from your custody. The agency may, of course, impose restrictions on his return, but that can wait until after we see what happens with the grand jury."

It was cold comfort. Wertheim went out the door at the rear of the room.

The Legal Aid lawyer, a blond man who seemed to feel the world owed him a round of applause just for being here, added a stick of Juicy Fruit to the wad he already had going. In family court, the judges would kick out anyone chewing anything; I'd almost been ejected for not swallowing a bite of muffin I'd taken just before we were called in. The Legal Aid guy bent over and whispered a joke of some sort to the female lawyer, a shapely blond in a fitted dress with one side bright red, the other side black, that buttoned across her waist with a big red button on the black side. She tossed her hair and laughed, then stood as her name was called.

I tried to focus on what I'd say to Benno if I got the chance, but I almost hoped I wouldn't. What I had were questions I didn't want to ask, answers I wanted him to volunteer. My attention kept returning to the lawyer in the red and black dress. She reminded me of someone. When I heard the click of her heels as she returned to the Legal Aid area, I got it: the social work supervisor at Catholic Charities.

Which brought my thoughts back to Clea. I realized I was focusing on Benno's situation rather than facing a fear that ran much deeper. I didn't care if Benno had to spend the weekend in jail, as long as it meant Clea would be allowed to stay with me.

There are women who put their husbands before their children, but in that moment I realized I wasn't one of them. If Benno had killed Ellen, I didn't care what happened to him as long as I could hold on to my daughter. It was a hard, sober truth. I closed my eyes and prayed that I would never have to make such a choice.

I rubbed my eyes, massaged my temples, as if I could wipe away my dark thoughts. I reminded myself that this was the dangerous hour of the night, the hour when molehills became mountains. I held on to the thought that while it seemed all was lost at three A.M., solutions could be found in the light of morning.

I felt a wave of charged air pass by my right side. When I opened my eyes, Benno was being escorted through a gate in the rail by a uniformed cop who paused to unlock his handcuffs before ushering him into the glass-walled enclosure where Aaron Wertheim was waiting.

After what seemed like another hour had passed, Benno's name was called. On his way to the table, he glanced out over the waiting room. I raised my hand in greeting and put everything I could into my smile. Benno turned away, as if he couldn't bear to acknowledge that I was seeing him in this place.

I sat up straight and held on to the back of the oak bench in front of me. The clerk read out the charges in a rapid monotone of penal code violation numbers. I had no idea what they meant. The judge looked up as Aaron Wertheim stated his name for the record.

"Mr. Wertheim, I wish I could say it's a pleasure to see you here at such a late hour. I hope your client is compensating you well for this disruption of your sleep." The judge's voice was snide, sarcastic.

Wertheim answered back with a touch of levity. "The pleasure is mutual, Your Honor. As to compensation, seeing that an innocent man's name is cleared will be compensation enough."

The judge snorted, and the group around the ADA snickered like a chorus of bullfrogs. The judge banged his gavel.

"How do you plead?"

"Not guilty, Your Honor."

"Mr. Gallo?"

"Your Honor, the people file notice of intent to present to the grand jury."

Then they dickered over bail, which as Wertheim had expected was denied. Wertheim whispered something to Benno, who nodded.

"Your Honor, may we approach?"

The judge lowered his head to signal that permission was granted. It was impossible to hear what was going on, but it seemed to take forever. Benno never once turned to look at me. I willed love and support to his back. Eventually the judge banged his gavel, and Wertheim and Gallo returned to their places.

"For the record," the judge intoned, "defendant's request for a rail visit with his wife is denied. Many people here have family members with whom I'm sure they'd like to speak. The court cannot grant all of these requests, and sees no reason to make an exception in this case."

Without a backward glance, Benno let himself be led through the door to the left of the judge's bench.

Wertheim came through the low gate in the partition and stopped next to me. "May I offer you a lift, Ms. Servi? I have a car and driver waiting outside."

Benno had come and gone so quickly, it took me a moment to realize he really wasn't going to be coming home with me. I felt tears pile up.

"We can talk in the car." Wertheim placed a gentle hand under my elbow and urged me to stand. "There's nothing more we can do here tonight, but I'll need your help to prepare for the next stage, and I'm sure you have questions for me as well."

Riding in the backseat of the big, quiet car, I felt like I was floating up the West Side Highway in a dark bubble. The lights slid past, a tunnel of white. I sat back and closed my eyes, feeling only the speed flowing me home. When I looked up, Wertheim was watching me.

"You look very like your mother," he observed.

"Most people don't think so," I said.

"Don't they? I believe you resemble her as a young woman. Of course, it's been quite some time since I've seen Rosemarie."

"Did you know her very well?" My curiosity about my mother's life before me woke up.

"Not as well as I might have liked," he said, dryly. "Rosemarie made quite an impression on me." He stared out at the green and pink neon bars outlining some sanitation facility on the Hudson. "I'd never known anyone like her."

The impression I got right then was that he'd had a crush on her.

Wertheim turned his gaze back to me. "You appear to have inherited something of her directness as well as her looks."

I felt a flush on my cheeks I hoped he couldn't see in the darkness of the car.

As if he sensed my embarrassment, Wertheim changed the subject. "May I call you Anita? And please, call me Aaron. We'll be doing a lot of work together in order to clear your husband. What can you tell me about Ellen Chapman? She was your baby-sitter?"

I nodded, not knowing quite what he wanted.

"Start at the beginning, Anita. How did you come to employ her?"

So I explained about the Barnard baby-sitting service, how you paid $15 a year for the privilege of having your requests for a sitter posted in their offices. The official hourly rate had climbed from $4.50 when Clea was small to its current $6.50. We'd been paying Ellen $7 for the past year, and would have raised her to $8 in the fall.

I remembered the first time Ellen had come to the house, wary and quiet. Her handshake was firm and she met my eyes, qualities the first two girls I'd interviewed had lacked. Her manner was guarded, as if she was sizing me up as much as I was her. I had the sense that she wouldn't work for just anyone.

When Clea came into the room, Ellen's face relaxed into a smile that seemed to surprise her as much as it did me. I've gotten used to the variety of facial reactions from people seeing us together as mother and daughter for the first time, and delight is not among the most common responses. It was in that moment I decided to hire her, if she'd have us.

"I can see you were quite fond of her," Wertheim murmured.

"Fond?" I was startled. "You make it sound like she was a

pet. I liked her right away, but Ellen was a complex person and it took time to get to know her. I suppose I thought of her as somewhere between a daughter and a friend. I learned a lot from Ellen."

It was my turn to stare out the window. We were past the elevated part of the highway, coming up through the seventies, where Riverside Park bordered the road. The trees here were in full flower, blossoms that in the bright night of the city were visible in color, clouds of pink and white reaching down to the ground.

"How long did she work for you?"

He followed this with a string of short, factual, easy-to-answer questions, which reminded me of what Clea had said about Ellen not having eaten supper with her on the night before Ellen died. When I told Wertheim, his eyes lit up.

"Tell the detectives. You know one of them personally? By all means, tell him. Better the DA gets this information from one of his people than through us."

The car turned off the highway and stopped for the light at Ninety-fifth.

"I know this is an awkward subject. I will only ask you once, Anita, but I do need to know. Please be absolutely honest with me. To your knowledge, was your husband having an affair with Ms. Chapman?"

Lawyers. "To my knowledge"—the answer to that was easy. "No." I said it emphatically and immediately.

We looked directly at each other for a few seconds. I had a sense that Wertheim knew I was holding something back, or maybe it was my own guilty awareness that I was—those red numbers, 1:57, and my own doubts. Then the light changed, and Aaron bent to make a note on the yellow legal pad in his lap.

I felt myself for the first time thinking as close to objectively as I could about the whole situation, weighing the bits and scraps of evidence, the "signs" my women friends had warned me to look for, against what I knew of Benno—not only his feelings for me but also for Clea; his sense of responsibility, the way he cared for us, his family. I also factored in Ellen, her intelligence and beauty, her sense of justice.

The car curved along Riverside Drive.

Ellen and I had grown close over the time she'd been with us; Benno and Ellen, on the other hand—the word I'd use to describe how they got along is *simpatico*; they seemed to understand each other spontaneously, without effort. It's rare to meet someone you get along with so easily. Compared to the tensions and irritations of even a good marriage . . . although I didn't want to admit it, in my heart of hearts, I could see how it might have been tempting to Benno. I didn't want to believe it. Not of Benno, and not of Ellen either, but it might just have been possible.

It was an anguishing thought. I tried to bury it deep, but the words were out before I could stop them. "What did Benno say about it?"

"I didn't ask him. I never ask my clients whether they've actually done what they're accused of. Benno volunteered a denial." Wertheim cleared his throat. "People often lie to their attorneys. My job is to see that evidence is gathered legally, that people are treated fairly by the law. Guilt or innocence is a matter for the jury."

So why had he asked me?

The driver turned up 110th to Broadway, turned left, then left again on 111th, and stopped in front of my building.

I was too tired to start an argument.

"When can I see Benno?"

"Well." Aaron sighed. "The Department of Corrections has a rather convoluted method of scheduling visits. It varies from week to week, depending on the letter of the alphabet of the inmate's last name. As it applies right now, you could visit tomorrow—or rather, today, Saturday, between Seven A.M. and Two P.M., although it would be difficult to arrange on such short notice. No visits are allowed on Mondays or Tuesdays, which means the next scheduled time would not be until Wednesday afternoon."

I stared at him, not quite comprehending. "Before two today?"

"Your husband asked me to tell you that he felt it was more important for you to continue with your usual routine over the weekend rather than making an effort to see him."

I knew Benno didn't like attention when he was feeling down, or when he was sick; he would retreat into himself, like an animal hiding in its cave, until he felt better. No soup, no ginger ale, no cough syrup, just leave him alone to suffer in peace. But not visit him in jail?

"I believe his concern was for your daughter, that she be protected as much as possible from the situation."

"Not until Wednesday?" I put my hand over my mouth and tried not to cry. We were caught by the system, caught but good. Heartless as family court was, it did occasionally bend to human needs. Nothing could have prepared me for how it felt to be in the inexorable grip of the criminal justice system—nothing.

Aaron laid a warm hand on my knee. "He'll be all right. The Manhattan House of Detention has improved greatly; he may even have a room to himself. Please, don't worry."

Don't worry, be happy? Might as well ask the sun not to rise. I wiped my eyes with the back of my hand.

"Please tell Rosemarie that I will telephone her later this morning. I'd like to invite her for brunch with my mother on Sunday. Also, I will see your husband on Monday, and I'd be happy to bring a change of clothing for him at that time, if you'd like to send it along with Rosemarie."

"He's allowed to wear his own clothes?"

"Yes. He can have underwear, socks, a few shirts, and a pair of pants, provided they're not dark blue—which would resemble a police uniform—or any gang colors, such as red or black."

Going up in the elevator alone brought home the absoluteness of Benno's absence. He should have been with me. Ellen should have been asleep on the couch, waiting for us. Instead it was my mother, the bed pulled out. She didn't wake when I pulled the sheet up over her shoulders. In spite of the day's heat, there was a predawn chill to the air.

I went into Clea's room. She was jumbled up in her covers, lying with her legs exposed. I straightened her out and tucked her in again. She didn't wake either, just sighed a soft exhalation of sweet child breath. I sat there in the dark with my hand on her little butt. What was I going to tell her? What could I possibly say or do to make her world all right again?

I kissed her cheek, closed her door, and went to bed myself.

As tired as I was, it took me a while to get to sleep. When my eyes closed, I was back in the high-ceilinged courtroom. The murmuring voices of lawyers and clerks, the court officers and the waiting family members, swirled around in my head. I saw Benno in handcuffs. How could things have gone so terribly wrong, for me, for us, all of us here in this place, waiting for judgment from a system that I no longer had faith was just, reasonable, protective?

11

CLEA opened the bedroom door and dragged in, thumb in mouth, bear in one arm. "Where's Dad?" she demanded. My breath caught in the base of my throat before I could answer, thinking of where Benno was, wondering how he'd passed the night. I opened my arms, lifted the covers for Clea to climb in, and rocked her gently. I was her anchor, keeping her safe.

"Dad had to work today, so it looks like it's you and me, kid, going to dance class."

"Do I have to?" Clea whined.

I thought about it. Given what had been going on all week, I felt it was better for Clea to stick to our usual schedule when we could. To a child, structure is safety—as long as it's not too rigid a routine. Besides, there was something I wanted to do while she was in class. Ellen's father, Carl Chapman, and his fiancée Marsha Ginsberg lived in Lincoln Towers, a few blocks from the Alvin Ailey studios. I was feeling like a condolence call might be in order, along with finding out what the deal was with the frame for Ellen's diploma.

"Yes, Bopster. The recital's in two weeks, and you have to rehearse, or they won't let you dance." They're strict at Ailey; recitals are not just for the parents of the little kids like Clea, but also a chance for the older students, in the preprofessional program, to strut their stuff to the public.

"I don't care." Clea struggled out of my embrace and sat up. "Ellen won't be there to watch me, and I'm not going!"

God bless the strong-minded child. I stroked her hair, still in the neat, tight cornrows Ellen had braided. "No, Ellen won't be there, but remember how she loved to see you dance? Wherever her spirit is, a piece of it will be in your feet, slapping out those dance steps."

Clea scowled at me, then ducked her head and squirmed back under the covers. The thumb went back in her mouth, and I felt her head bob with the fury of her sucking. I didn't make an issue of it; regression had its purposes, and comfort was comfort. I let her stay in my bed while I took a quick shower.

Part of Clea and Benno's Saturday routine is breakfast at Tom's. We had barely enough time, but I sent Clea in to wake Gamma Rho so I could tell her we were leaving and give her the message from Aaron Wertheim.

When we got outside, the day felt bright and new and full of promise. I was glad to be out and up and with a plan of action in my mind. I picked up a *Times* from the newsstand on the corner. Might as well see if Benno's arrest had made the news.

We got a booth, and the waitress actually stopped to take our order; I hadn't been there in a while, and she seemed to have forgotten me. Clea ordered her usual, a short stack with sausage. I had a scrambled egg with bacon. Clea got busy with the little plastic creamers, drinking one and building a tower with the rest. I scanned the front page, then flipped through the Metro section. There was a longish piece rehashing Ellen's murder, with a bit more detail on her life, but nothing about an arrest.

On the subway, I made a stab at the crossword puzzle, but I couldn't concentrate. Benno and I both looked forward to the challenge of the Saturday puzzle; it was the day we each bought separate papers. The thought of where he was froze my brain.

Clea had brought her Jacob's ladder, and she kept flipping it open and closed, showing off for the two little boys sitting across from us. One of them wanted a closer look; he came over and stood with an arm wrapped around the pole. Clea held it out like she was going to let him touch it, but then pulled it back, made it climb the colored ribbons and flip back down. I frowned at her, but she ignored me.

Then it was Sixty-sixth Street, our stop. I started a lecture on not teasing as we walked under Lincoln Center, but she skipped ahead of me.

Regression to defiance; well, better she act out with me than in class. I let her get it out of her system, claiming her hand to cross Amsterdam, then letting her run ahead to catch a friend from class and speed up the stairs while I waited for the elevator with the girl's mother.

One of the things I like about Clea taking dance at Alvin Ailey, besides its being a convenient answer to the question What are you doing to promote the child's cultural heritage? for our yearly recertification as foster parents, is that it's one of the situations where I find myself, as a white person, in the minority.

There's a sense of camaraderie among the dance mothers; I think of us as the urban version of soccer moms. We may not have station wagons and SUVs, but we *schlep* our kids around on weekends, after school; sit on benches and watch them perform, practice; talk among ourselves, neutral subjects like school and homework and television; thumb through magazines. I usually had one or two buddies in the group, but Benno wasn't in the habit of gossiping; he'd bury his face in the paper or pass an occasional word with the one or two other dads who got roped into Saturday-morning escort duty.

I nodded hello to a few of the women I recognized, but the mother I was closest to wasn't among them this morning. Today I didn't hang around to chat after I picked up Clea's clothes as she shed them, down to her black leotard, and disappeared into the dance studio. I turned around and went down the stairs, back out into the sunny day.

My first order of business was to call Michael and tell him what Clea had said about when Ellen had eaten her supper. I should have done it from the apartment, but I didn't want Clea or my mother to overhear. I turned my face to the sun and closed my eyes. In the red world my eyelids made, I saw Benno lying on the top bunk in a small gray room. I sent him the beam of sunlight I was standing in, and I thought he turned his head and smiled.

Okay, Michael. But maybe I needed more coffee before I butted heads with law enforcement. I headed over to the Olympic Circles coffee shop and took a stool at the counter. While the caffeine made its way through my system and the Miami Beach color scheme did its aqua-and-peach best to soothe my soul, I got a pad out of my bag and listed what I knew about Ellen's last night. I wanted to be sure I had my thoughts in order before I talked to Michael; no point in looking like a fool.

First, Ellen hadn't eaten dinner until ten or eleven, at least two hours later than we'd thought. That right there might be enough to clear Benno, if the time of death was well after he'd come home.

What really bothered me was how many things Benno hadn't told me. Starting with the chemise, of course. Could he really not have known my size? I suppose it was flattering if you looked at it in the right light—that he still saw me as the sylph he'd married, not the middle-aged frau I'd become.

Then there was the commission from Ellen's stepmother-to-be, to make a frame for Ellen's diploma—he had to know I'd be interested in his impression of the woman we'd heard so much about from Ellen.

The more I thought about her, the more curious I got. What kind of person was Marsha Ginsberg? How was she taking the death of her fiancée's daughter? What impact would it have on her wedding plans? I couldn't begin to imagine how Ellen's father would feel. I'd met him twice, once at his house—back when he and Ellen's mother, Muriel, were still together. They had the lower two floors of a brownstone, and we'd been invited over for a barbecue. The second time was at Ellen's graduation, when he'd been subdued and clearly on his best behavior.

According to what Ellen'd said, the date wasn't until late August. Was three months a decent enough interval to go ahead, or would they postpone it?

Or might Ellen's death smooth the path to the altar for Ms. Ginsberg?

She'd been to visit Ellen, so she claimed, the morning after she was killed. But what did that prove? She could've come the night before, then made up the Sunday visit as a cover in case anyone remembered seeing her in the building. It was totally possible to call and knowingly leave a message on the answering machine of a dead woman. As for what had happened, it was no secret that Ellen had remained opposed to the marriage. What if Ellen put her father in the position of choosing between her and Marsha? What if Marsha had gone to talk with Ellen, they'd argued . . .

One thing I did know—I wanted to talk with Ms. Ginsberg myself. I left $1.50 on the counter and used the pay phone by the rest rooms to call the Twenty-sixth Precinct. The man who answered said Michael was out in the field, did I want him paged? I said no, and left a message that I'd be at the memorial service for Ellen Chapman in the afternoon.

Going up Amsterdam past the housing project and onto the grounds of Lincoln Towers was one of those only-in-New-York transitions. Both housing complexes were high-rises, but that was about all they had in common. The projects were red brick, faced the street, had uniformed security guards only at night, and no balconies. The buildings of Lincoln Towers, made of higher-class white brick, had balconies and terraces. They stood around inner courtyards, small oases of magnolias and ornamental fruit trees in full pink blossom, with circular drives around islands of parked cars, including a few low sporty models covered in canvas against the weather.

The magnolias were past their prime, bruised pink blooms littering the ground below. A playground with a low fence and a gate with rules prominently posted was already occupied by squealing toddlers and doting parental units. This is how the other half lives, in a private compound cheek-by-jowl with public housing.

Dropping in on people unannounced is definitely not a New York thing to do. Etiquette required that I call first to be sure this was a convenient time, then have the doorman call up to announce my arrival. I hadn't done either.

I wanted to see Carl and Marsha in person; calling would have given them the opportunity to put me off. It wouldn't be the first time I'd claimed a Californian's ignorance of local customs, and saying I happened to be in the neighborhood was the literal truth. I'd brought along two books Ellen had lent me, which gave me an added pretext for showing up in person.

Getting in at Lincoln Towers was no problem. I've perfected my technique of avoiding doormen and security guards while visiting clients in the hospital. A middle-aged, middle-class white woman with a purposeful stride: if you walk straight in, looking like you belong, nine of ten will let you pass without question.

I gave myself the added camouflage, this Saturday morning when all around me were casual strollers, of tagging along behind three women, two of them just coming in from a run, the third with a baby in a stroller, who obviously all lived in the building. I held the side door open for the stroller woman while the others used the revolving door. All the brass was polished to a bright shine.

The doorman came out from behind the huge navy-blue marble desk to accept a load of dry cleaning on hangers from a deliveryman who followed us in. No way was he going to single me out and ask where I was going; what if I was a new tenant, someone who expected to be recognized, and I complained about him?

The lobby was immense, carpeted in dark blue wall-to-wall, with huge columns covered in smoky mirrors from the floor to ten feet up. There was an arrangement of comfortable sofas upholstered in easy-to-clean blue Naugahyde and matching armchairs with enormous urns of silk flowers artfully placed among them. Several elderly women sat together, passing the morning, watching the scene. I couldn't help contrasting how well dressed, coiffed, and healthy they looked, compared to the majority of my clients. These were people who could afford all the help they needed, from weekly housecleaning to regular visits to the beauty parlor.

We entered the elevator, also carpeted, walls a shiny dark blue Formica with little flecks of white to make it look like marble, and I squatted down to coo at the infant. It was a new one, maybe only a month or two. I kept my hands on my knees, not reaching in to stroke the feather-soft, sleeping cheek. The mother's nervous eyes didn't relax even when I stood up. "They seem so fragile when they're small, don't they?" I smiled at her.

That got me a twitch of the lips and a slight ease of the line between her eyebrows. New motherhood is tough. Start with sleep deprivation, add an overpowering feeling of love mixed with the impossible burden of responsibility. My heart thunked in my chest.

I lived every day with the fear of losing Clea. Over time I'd learned to compartmentalize, to keep it shut away. She'd been with us for all but the first week of her seven years; we were hers and she was ours; surely the system wouldn't take her away from us. But according to the law, they could.

In the days before a visit to the agency, or a social worker coming to our home, I would be irritable and tense. Nights before a court date were the worst. I used to sit up until three, four, five in the morning in the dark living room, not reading, not thinking, not doing anything except maybe praying. Benno had finally insisted I talk to the doctor about it, which had resulted in a prescription for Ambian to help me sleep. I could not even begin to contemplate losing a child to death.

The elevator door bonged open on 16. The hallway was also carpeted in navy blue, here with a twisted basket motif in tan and brown. This is how we measure status in New York: if the building is postwar (meaning low ceilings, modern plumbing, and rooms with normal shapes and proportions), wall-to-wall in the public areas means upscale. The walls were papered in a beige vinyl, textured to imitate grasscloth.

I ran my fingers along the ridged surface as I dawdled down the hallway. I genuinely dreaded the visit I was about to make.

What could I say to Ellen's father? Here I was, ostensibly paying a condolence call while surreptitiously on the lookout for any indication that the fiancée of the father of the deceased was actually responsible for the death. Nice, unmixed motives.

I might be making jokes about it, but my grief at Ellen's passing was genuine. What else can you say other than "I'm sorry for your loss"? I believe that death is the one area where platitudes are not only accepted, they're also appropriate. Nothing can make the death of a child any easier to bear.

There was a newspaper on the mat in front of the door to 16G. I rang the bell under the small nameplate with CHAPMAN / GINSBERG squeezed onto it in those plastic punch-out letters. It made a faint chime. I put my ear to the crack and thought I heard movement somewhere deep in the apartment. Working with old people, I've gotten used to long waits at locked doors, and keeping my senses tuned to pick up the slightest vibration from inside. I rang the bell again and followed it with a knock. After all, they weren't expecting me; and expecting a sound is half of hearing it.

I knocked again, harder. Maybe they were still sleeping? I picked up the *Times*, then slid my wedding ring up between my first and second knuckle and added its metallic power to a final knock. When trying to rouse a hard-of-hearing senior citizen, I often used my keys to knock with. New York apartment doors are steel, for fire safety, and the metal-on-metal sound carries well.

A voice called, "Carl? Wait! I'm coming!"

The door flew open so fast it banged against the inner wall. I stepped back reflexively. The woman who stood there looked as surprised to see me as I was at the sight of her, and a lot more disappointed. Her eyes had had a hopeful, joyous look in them, her arms had been ready to fly open and embrace the person she expected to see on her doorstep. Whoever it was, I wasn't it.

"Ms. Ginsberg?"

"Go away." She tried to close the door, but I'd stepped over the threshold and had my shoulder against the gaping door. I held out the paper.

"Give me that. If you're collecting, now is not a good time." She tried to push the door shut.

As she stepped back, however, she left enough space for me to enter the apartment, and she wound up slamming the door closed with me on her side of it.

I almost laughed. Okay, I was wearing jeans and a gray V-necked T-shirt, but I was a little old for a paper route. "My name is Anita Servi. I'm the woman Ellen baby-sat for?" I paused to see if she'd know who I was.

I wouldn't have recognized her from Ellen's catty description, either: "She goes in for the Liddy Dole look, pastel suits with fitted jackets and buttons the same color as the fabric. Or else they're gold. She's got a whole long rod in her bedroom just to hold her silk scarves, like a man would have for ties. And her shoes always match, too—can you imagine owning *aqua* pumps? I guess she's got a good figure, if you go for the emaciated look. Not quite Nancy Reagan, but not enough meat on her bones, if you know what I mean."

I'd raised my eyebrows at that one. Ellen, at five-eight, weighed all of 120 herself.

"Well, I don't need a personal trainer to look like this, it's just how my body is!" Ellen had defended herself. "Ol' Marsha works out three times a week and eats two lettuce leaves with dressing on the side for lunch. She used to be a dancer, and she claims she just 'never got in the habit of eating big meals,' " Ellen said, mocking a woman's high-pitched voice.

I'd laughed then, but I felt sorry for the woman in front of me now. Her hair, cut to just below her ears, was a silvery ash-blond that looked expensive and professionally done, but after she'd finished running her hands through it, it could have been used to dust-mop the parquet floor. She was wearing a satin robe, dusty rose, over a pale pink gown that matched the pink polish on her manicured toenails.

"I'm sorry to drop in without calling. I was in the neighborhood—my daughter takes dance classes at Alvin Ailey—and I just wanted to extend my condolences." The words sounded awkward, too formal for the palpable grief on Marsha Ginsberg's face.

She had the kind of porcelain skin that mottles red from crying, which she looked like she'd been doing. I followed her into the living room. The blinds were drawn, giving the room a gray tinge. Marsha took a wad of pink tissue out of her robe pocket and blew her nose.

I took the books out of my bag, two first editions of mysteries by Chester Himes, and held them out. "These belonged to Ellen. I thought her father might like to have them back."

"He's not here." Her voice was bitter. "That little snip was looking for a reason to stop our wedding, and I guess she found it. Carl's moved back in with the first Mrs. Chapman."

"I'm sorry." It was all I could think of to say.

Marsha gave me a sharp look. "No, you're shocked. You're the white woman who can do no wrong just because you took in a poor little black baby, and I'm speaking ill of the dead."

Now I *was* shocked. I put the newspaper down on the coffee table.

She sank down onto the sofa, which was upholstered in a fabric with cabbage roses in the same dark pink as her robe.

I stared down at her. I'm not often at a loss for words, but with this woman I just didn't know where to begin.

"Never mind," she said. "I don't expect you to understand. You probably thought Ellen was above reproach. It's how she acted, and it's how Carl treated her."

Jealousy. Now that I had a name for what she was feeling, I knew where to start. In my training as a social worker, I was taught to separate the deed from the doer in order to empathize with the human being. Sort of like the Christian philosophy of "hate the sin, love the sinner."

I helped myself to a seat in an armchair across from the sofa and let Marsha's comment about Clea pass unanswered. "I know Ellen was opposed to your marriage, but I thought she'd come around to accepting it. The last time she talked about it, she sounded like she was genuinely happy for her father." I made my voice tentative, questioning, to leave room for her to set me straight.

"Happy." The word sat on her tongue like a stone. "I thought I'd finally found a man who cared about my happiness."

"It looks like you were happy here." I gestured at the room, obviously decorated by a woman with a good sense of color, if a little too fond of floral prints for my taste. The masculine touches—the recliner in one corner, done in brown leather; the massive dining table with matching wood chairs; a sleek credenza—gave the room a balanced feel.

Marsha's expression was tragic. "I should have known better. Everyone told me not to get involved with a married man. I thought Carl was different—he really did divorce his wife. . . ." I followed her gaze across the room to a desk that held a computer, a laser printer, and piles of cream-colored envelopes. "Those are the wedding invitations. We were doing the addresses on the computer."

"What happened?" I asked.

She leaned over with her elbows on her knees, her head in her hands. "I don't even know. I told Carl I didn't mind if he wanted to postpone the wedding, but he just—he just—" She doubled over and started sobbing.

Well, that answered the question about the impact of Ellen's death on her wedding plans. I went over and sat next to her on the couch, put a hand on her shoulder.

"Grief affects people in funny ways sometimes, and a sudden death like this . . . I'm sure you'll work it out, if you just give Carl some time." Back to clichés.

Marsha sat up and plucked a tissue from a box on the glass-topped coffee table. There was a pair of mules trimmed in pink marabou feathers under the table. She looked not much older than I was, maybe late forties, but we were definitely from different worlds.

"I don't think so." She blew her nose again. "Ellen did her best to turn him against me while she was alive, and now he feels like he's being punished for wanting to marry up. Going back to Bed-Stuy is his penance for trying to have a better life."

I blinked at that one. Marrying up? I'd thought she was a midlevel executive in the office where he'd worked for twenty years. Up, because she was white? I was beginning to share Ellen's dim view of Marsha Ginsberg.

But I wasn't here to pass judgment on the woman; what I needed was her help. "From what Ellen had been saying about the wedding recently, I thought you and she were getting along?"

Marsha didn't answer, so I kept on. "And having her diploma framed, that was a very gracious thing to do."

Her eyes filled again. "You might think so, but that's what started it all. The framing was supposed to be a surprise, but one of those detectives asked Carl about it, and of course he didn't know anything about it." She swabbed at her face with the pink tissue.

"I took the diploma out of her room when Carl and I helped her move in. Last Friday, Carl asked Ellen for it, because he was going to have it framed himself, and she couldn't find it. That's what I wanted to talk to her about, to tell her I had it, and your husband was making the frame. I wanted her not to tell Carl."

"What time exactly did you go over there on Sunday?" I was thinking about the fact that, if time of death is not an exact science, especially after a couple of days have passed, and if Ellen had eaten several hours later than we'd originally thought, maybe she'd still been alive when Marsha went to her room that morning.

"Eight o'clock? Maybe nine? Early, because I wanted to catch her. Why?"

I shrugged it off. "I was just wondering. Why didn't you want Carl to know you'd taken the diploma?"

"It was supposed to be a surprise for him, too. You know, that I was trying to do something nice for Ellen. To be friendly." She blew her nose. "Some surprise! When the detective told Carl why he was asking about the diploma, Carl said Benno must have stolen it. Then, when he told me about it, I tried to explain what I'd done.

"Carl was furious. I still don't understand it. First he accused me of trying to make him look ridiculous to the police, then he said I had no right to interfere, and how could I have done such an underhanded thing. It didn't matter what I said, he didn't listen. He said if it wasn't for me, Ellen would still be alive, because if he hadn't left his wife, Ellen wouldn't have left that nice young man she was seeing, who just happened to be white, and she wouldn't have taken up with—" She stopped herself before blurting out Benno's name and shrugged apologetically at me. "Who also happens to be white. Then he packed a suitcase and left." She leaned back against the flowered couch cushions and stared at the darkened windows.

"You know, that's just the reason I don't think my husband was the person Ellen got involved with after she broke up with Jamie."

"What is?"

"Because he was white. I mean, if that was the problem with Jamie, why would she leave him for another white man?"

"Why didn't I think of that when Carl was shouting at me?" Marsha Ginsberg looked at me with interest. "I knew Ellen since she was fifteen. She came into the office with Carl occasionally, and we used to have some good talks. She was smart. She had principles, but she wasn't race-conscious then. Did you know Ellen chose Barnard over Spellman, because its program suited her interests? And when she first got involved in the African studies program, she didn't romanticize Africa as the motherland—she saw it as a collection of individual countries, backward maybe, but with great promise. There was a woman from one of the French-speaking countries, a Muslim, whom Ellen befriended. She used to talk about the difference between real Islam and the American version, how Farrakhan had corrupted the religious teachings." She sighed. "You know, I liked Ellen. I thought she liked me, too, until Carl and I—"

It was the first glimpse I'd gotten of an intelligent woman, a woman capable of catching the attention of Carl Chapman, or any man.

"Do you know if Ellen was seeing anyone after she broke up with Jamie?" I asked hopefully.

Marsha sat up. "I'd be the last person she'd have confided in! Although I know she thought highly of her boss at that English program, what was his name? Something Egyptian, I think. She had a picture of him on her desk. A very handsome man."

"Arthur Nessim?"

"That sounds right. I thought she had a crush on him, you know, hero-worship. The attraction a powerful older man might have for a younger woman. A mentor, but platonic."

Sort of like the relationship I'd thought Benno had with Ellen, only without the crush. What if it had gone beyond that with Nessim?

"I'm sorry to have poured out my troubles like this. You must think I'm really a basket case." Marsha gave a self-deprecating laugh. "Can I offer you some coffee? Atone for my rudeness?"

I looked at my watch. Clea would be done in ten minutes. "No, thank you, and there's no need to apologize. I was the one who intruded on you. I hope things work out for the best with Carl."

"Yes, well, I should have known better. You can't compete with a daughter, not when her father thinks she walks on water."

She walked me to the door. I squeezed her hand before I left. Whatever opinion I might have of her, she was a woman in pain.

Jealousy might be a powerful motive, but I couldn't see Ellen letting Marsha Ginsberg get close enough to stab her. And if Ellen had fought back, my money was on Marsha to be the one who ended up with a screwdriver in her heart.

12

I was not looking forward to the service. Much as I needed to share my grief and mourn for Ellen, I was worried that, as the wife of the accused killer, I'd be ostracized. Benno's arrest might not have made the morning papers, but it would have been on the news on the radio, and word could well have gotten around at the institute and on the street.

Clea and I got back to the apartment with just enough time for a quick bite and to change into more appropriate clothes. I put on a black rayon dress; Clea's was white with large black polka dots. My mother—well, if nothing else, she was unique: charcoal silk pants with a dark purple silk tunic and a scarf in wild pink, purple, crimson, and neon green. It worked.

Clea wanted to know why Benno wasn't joining us. I could have stretched out the work excuse; he spent more time in the shop than anywhere else, including sleeping time. If I didn't put my foot down, he'd have worked weekends. As it was, he often went in on Saturdays when he had a big job under way. Clea might have accepted that as an answer, but at seven years old, she's starting to have her own opinions, and express them. I could hear her argue: "If he went to her graduation, how come he's not going to her memorial? This is more important!" And she'd be right at that.

Besides, I was afraid she'd overhear something, or worse yet, someone would say something directly to me, or to her, at the service. I've always felt it's better to tell children the truth, even if it's bad, but how do you tell a child her father's in jail for killing her baby-sitter?

We walked along Riverside Drive, under the canopy of trees where we could admire the tulips blooming. I explained as best I could that the police were not always right, that sometimes they made mistakes, things weren't always how they appeared, of course Benno would never hurt Ellen. . . . My mother chimed in, but Clea's steps got slower and slower, and her hand dragged at mine.

Finally I paused and sat on the steps leading up to the church. I pulled her close to me, looked her in the eye, and overrode my doubts. "You listen to me now, Clea Servi. Your father had nothing to do with Ellen's death. We have a good lawyer who's helping us to find out the truth, and Daddy will be home before you know it."

Clea stared back at me, confused, wanting to believe, not knowing even what to ask. I held her gaze, willing a certainty I didn't feel into her soul. My mother crouched down behind Clea, and we folded her into our arms. Her little body gave a convulsive shudder, but she didn't cry—which was more than I could say for myself.

My mother cleared her throat. "Now, ladies, we have a service to attend. Remember, this is for Ellen. She would want you to be brave and to think of her with love."

We all three straightened up. My mother glared at me, and I wiped my face on my sleeve. "You remember what I said now, Bopster. Daddy didn't do anything wrong. He loved Ellen, we all loved Ellen, and we're here to honor her, so hold your head up."

"Are you going to cry at the service?" Clea had Benno's accusing tone. I'm a well-known weeper; they tease me unmercifully when I cry over *Seventh Heaven* on TV.

My mother came to my rescue. "It's all right to cry when you feel really sad, honey, and I'll bet you'll see tears on more people than your mother today. So you go ahead and cry, too, if you want."

"C'mon, Mama, we'll be late." Clea tugged me up.

✦

We climbed the stairs and went through the revolving door into the vaulted entryway to Riverside Church. The service wasn't being held in the nave, to our left; it was in a smaller chapel on the fourth floor, next to the ESL Institute's classrooms. We rode up in the elevator, holding hands. I read the look my mother turned on me as, Keep it together, Anita, you have a child to think about. So I did.

We walked down the empty hallway, past the closed door to Arthur Nessim's office, and turned the far corner away from the Resource Room. A pile of folded programs lay on a small table in the anteroom outside the chapel. We each picked one up and paused in the doorway; the seats up front were already filled, so we made our way to the back. The chapel held maybe sixty people; I was surprised to see so many there, but listening to the muted Babel of languages, I realized almost a third of the institute's two hundred students must have turned out.

Music started up from a small organ to our right. I could just see the top of the organist's head, bathed in a soft lavender light from the stained-glass windows. It was an interesting little chapel, more modern than the nave, but with a fifties feel. As I examined the stained-glass windows, I realized that they were not only geometric abstracts but also had painted panes with scenes of everyday life—a man in a red shirt laid bricks with a trowel; another man in a blue suit peered through a microscope. Each section of stained glass had a different dominant color, sort of like Anne's outfits—to our right, it was lavender, deep blue behind us, and the section toward the front was pale greens. In all the sections there were panels with etched glass, flowers, waves, stars, on a yellow background. Just above the organ, written on vivid blue panes, were the words *The light / is still / shining in / the darkness.* The words slanted down at an angle, set amid textured rays of yellow and white.

The altar was a long table that held a plastic window box of silk daisies under a brass-filigree crucifix set against a mosaic tile wall. The pattern looked like the swirl of an angel's wing, set with a scattering of gold tiles that glinted in the sunlight, surrounded by semicircles of red, blue, green. Although the ceiling was low and made of concrete, it went up a full story above the altar, giving it a feel of holiness.

I glanced at the program while a few voices soared above the organ—"on eagle's wings / and bear you on the breath of dawn / and hold you in the palm of his hand." Although this was a memorial rather than a full service, it was presided over by one of the half-dozen different pastors who served at Riverside Church. If Ellen had been elderly, it would have fallen to the pastor of the Senior Ministry; I wondered what rationale had put her under the auspices of the Social Justice Ministry rather than the Youth Ministry.

Arthur Nessim would be speaking, as would several students and most of the teachers, one of them Jamie. I looked over the people seated in front of us and located his close-cropped blond head. I searched for Nafissa but couldn't tell if she was there or not.

The reverend gave a brief, generic eulogy about the tragedy of losing someone in the prime of her life, potential to do good lost, et cetera. Clea squirmed and tried to see past the person in front of her. My mother had placed a warning hand on her leg to keep her still, but it wasn't working. When Nessim got up to talk, I lifted Clea onto my lap so she could see.

Nessim stood at the smaller, wooden pulpit to the right of the larger, stone pulpit the pastor had used. The paper trembled in his hands. He set it down in front of him and closed his eyes for a brief moment. I thought I saw the shine of tears on his cheek. Clea leaned back against my shoulder, and I felt her arm go up, thumb in mouth. My mother and I glanced at each other, but I let the thumb be.

When Nessim opened his eyes and began to speak, his voice was strong and rich. He talked about Ellen's accomplishments, how proud her family was of her—at which point I tried to see if any of them were there, but no one in the front row was dressed formally enough to be Ellen's parents. When he got to Ellen's role at the school, Nessim seemed to stumble over his words.

As if sensing his disorientation, the organist played a few chords. Nessim gave an involuntary shiver, as a man might waking from a bad dream, and looked out over the room. Finally he located Jamie, gave a nod in his direction, and waited while Jamie made his way to the front. Was this the behavior of a mentor who'd lost a prize devotee, or did Arthur Nessim's grief signify something more?

Jamie stood at the pulpit, waiting for the organist to finish, and scanned the audience. His gaze stopped briefly on a woman, her head wrapped in a turban of purple-and-gold African cloth, in the aisle seat in the last row of the front section. She was with an older man in a dark suit and a crocheted skullcap, his arm protectively across the back of her chair.

The organ fell silent. In the pause Jamie allowed before he began to speak, the sound of a truck downshifting filtered in through the open window. Then the sharp flash of a siren wailed and faded.

Jamie took his time, and from the moment he opened his mouth, the room was his. Although he had a sheet of paper in front of him, he did no more than glance at it. It wasn't what he said that mattered, anyway; it was the way the words flowed into the room, the cadences of his voice, that seemed to touch each one of us.

His eyes looked directly into the eyes of each person listening to him. I noticed his gaze kept returning to settle on the woman with the turban. When she looked sideways at her companion, I recognized Nafissa.

Clea trembled in my arms. I bent to whisper in her ear, "It's okay, Bopster, it's okay."

My mother handed me a tissue, and I dabbed at Clea's face. "It's okay to cry."

But my own eyes were dry. As the organ started up again, Michael Dougherty walked quickly into the room and crossed to the last row. I stared over my shoulder at him, and he smiled in acknowledgment. Then Jamie was introducing someone else and returning to his seat. When I looked again at Nafissa, she was gone, along with the man in the suit. Damn.

Jamie's head had also swiveled back to find her, and I saw a flash of panic in his eyes when he realized she was no longer there. So was it true, Jamie had taken up with Nafissa after Ellen broke things off with him? Jamie started to do what I would have if I hadn't had Clea on my lap, get up and go after Nafissa. But the woman sitting next to him put a hand on his arm and pulled him back into his seat. For a second I thought he was going to lash out at her the way he had at me when I touched him at the labyrinth, but he got a grip and sat. The woman, with pale skin and black hair, whispered something in his ear. Jamie nodded.

I tried to concentrate on what the next speaker was saying, but she was already leaving the pulpit. Next up was an older man, Russian or from one of the former Soviet countries, to judge by his accent. I shifted Clea around so I could check the program. She didn't like my moving and slid herself over to Gamma Rho's lap.

There were seven more speakers to go, followed by another hymn. I decided to follow my impulse to find Nafissa.

"I'll be right back," I whispered to my mother. She scowled at my behavior, but there was nothing she could say.

Naturally, the hall was deserted, and no one was waiting for the elevators. I debated running down the stairs and trying to catch Nafissa, but I had no way of knowing which floor she'd chosen to exit from, and I didn't want to be gone that long. Besides, now that I was standing alone in the quiet hall, I realized that more than anything, I'd needed to get away from the service.

The whole situation was unbearable. Ellen's death was too much to accept, let alone that it had been a violent one. And Benno being in jail, arrested for killing Ellen, accused of having had an affair with her . . .

I stared around at the little foyer, the coffee machine, the signs offering summer programs for children, the blank gray elevator doors, the red exit sign over the stairs. There was no way out. I closed my eyes, but nothing disappeared.

I turned back toward the chapel. At least there were people I loved waiting for me there. But not Benno. I collapsed into one of the chairs scattered in the hall. It was too much. I couldn't face anyone, not even for Clea. I let myself cry. The closed classroom doors in front of me offered no comfort.

I wiped my face on my sleeve. Get a grip, Anita, a voice in my head whispered. This isn't the time or the place to give up.

I stood and started again for the chapel. On my left, I noticed a half-open door. It was Arthur Nessim's office. I paused in front of it, put my hand on the brass knob, and pushed it open.

Particles of dust shone in the sunlight coming through the window. Get a grip, get a grip, the words came again. If it wasn't Benno, was it Nessim?

I wiped at my eyes with the back of my hand. As I looked blankly around Nessim's office, my training took over. A lot of social work, at least the agency-based, service-oriented type of social work I did, was targeted at finding solutions. With the elderly, who often would not come right out and ask for what they needed, I made home visits and did assessments based on what I observed. An empty refrigerator might indicate a need for Meals-on-Wheels. Piles of papers might mean assistance with bill paying was in order.

I realized that, without consciously planning to, I'd been conducting the same kind of interviews with people who'd known Ellen as I did with neighbors and friends of my clients—not with any particular goal in mind, other than gathering information so I could develop the most complete picture of the situation as possible.

So what I was looking for in this room was any indication that Arthur Nessim had more than a professional interest in Ellen Chapman. The walls were covered by bookshelves, except over the couch, where he'd hung a museum poster, a reproduction of a Matisse woman in a flowing dress, sitting next to a table that held a vase of flowers. The edges of the shelves held a collection of different objects, a few small metal toy cars, a line of ebony elephants with ivory tusks marching past the spines of books with titles in an Arabic script, a few framed photographs.

Most of the photos were of a blond woman and two honey-skinned children who grew from toddler to preteen. There were several group photos, evidently of classes from the institute; I recognized one or two other teachers, as well as Arthur and Jamie. Ellen's face did not appear anywhere among them.

I glanced at the pile of books and magazines on a low table next to the couch. *Newsweek, Time,* two volumes of the trilogy by Naguib Mafouz, an empty coffee mug. I walked behind the desk and studied its surface. Telephone; a photo of the blonde with the two children, almost hidden behind a clock radio; a spike impaling dozens of pink message slips; manila file folders in a rickety pile. I scanned the tabs; they seemed to be course outlines for the current semester. There was a desk calendar, the kind with pages that lie open to show two days at a time. I ruffled back through them for the past month; the only mention of Ellen was a start date the Monday after she'd graduated.

Two lined yellow pads occupied the place of honor, front and center. The top one had pages turned back and a blank sheet showing. I picked it up and flipped the sheets back. They appeared to be drafts of what he'd said at the service. The man had a lovely handwriting, delicately formed letters in small, slanted script, and he used a fountain pen. I looked more carefully at the desktop; there it was, in a wooden tray next to a bottle of black ink.

I picked up the second pad and saw that it had been covering a sheaf of papers stapled together in the top corner. The title of the paper was *The Middle Passage: A Modern Journey by Choice,* subtitled *A Muslim Woman's Flight to Freedom?* Ellen's name was typed in the lower right corner. So this was what she'd written about Nafissa. I wondered about the question mark in the second line. Had Nafissa not found freedom here? Was it due to the conflict between American culture and her religion, or to the protectiveness of her brother?

I remembered Nafissa's visit to Senior Services the other morning, and the feeling that she'd changed her mind about the real reason for coming to see me. I badly wanted Ellen's essay, but I'd left my bag in the chapel, and I had no way of carrying the paper without being seen. I took it anyway, rolled it up to be inconspicuous, and slipped out of the office.

Back in the hall, I could hear the organ starting up again. This time I walked quickly, pausing only to pick up another program and roll it around Ellen's paper. When I entered, everyone was standing, and they were on the second verse of Ellen's favorite hymn, "It's me, it's me, it's me, O lord, standing in the need of prayer." I joined my voice to the chorus. With all my heart and soul, I felt in need.

As the music died away, I sat back down and pulled Clea onto my lap. I wrapped my arms around her, rested my cheek on the top of her head. My mother slid into Clea's empty chair and hugged us both. I'm not into organized religion, but it has its uses. Transforming sorrow to hope for redemption is one of them. My mother's second-favorite quote from Karl Marx is "Religion is the heart of a heartless world."

When we finally lifted our teary faces, the room was almost empty.

Except for Michael, examining the figures painted on the stained glass, half-turned toward us, waiting.

Under cover of getting a tissue, I stuffed the rolled-up paper into my purse. I used the tissue on Clea's face, held it for her to blow her nose like a toddler. We all three let out a little tension-breaking laugh at the sound. My mother sat back.

"Well, I don't know about the two of you, but I believe I'm hungry. What kind of food do you think they've got at this shindig?" She fanned her face with the program. "What do you say we go find out?"

"You go ahead, I'll join you in a minute."

I gestured over at Michael. My mother scowled at him, but stood.

Clea squirmed off my lap and took Gamma Rho's hand to lead her into the Resource Room, where the reception was being held.

"Nice service," Michael said.

I nodded. Small talk was not what I wanted. "Clea said Ellen didn't eat with her Saturday night; she said Ellen didn't have her meal until after Clea was in bed." When Michael didn't seem to pick up on the meaning of what I'd said, I prompted him. "Which means she didn't die as early as you thought, right? So Benno couldn't have killed her, right?"

"The word of a child, especially after the fact and from the daughter of the accused, isn't worth much, but I'll mention it to Peretti. It's not my case anymore, remember?" Michael put a sympathetic hand on my shoulder.

I backed away. "Clea also said Ellen was on the phone for a long time, and it sounded like she was mad at the person she was talking to. Didn't you pry into our phone records along with the bills?"

Michael started to say something but bit it back and took a pad out of his inside jacket pocket. "Look, Anita, I just wanted you to know that I got them to hold off as long as possible before they took Benno in, but it was out of my hands."

"Is that what you came to tell me?"

"No, I'm here because I got your message, one. Two, I told you before, I have my own doubts that Benno's our man."

"That's big of you." It came out more bitter than I intended.

"Don't thank me yet." Michael made a half-turn away from me to study the painted workers on the green window. "I went out for dinner last night, little Italian place down in the Village—Donato's?"

I must have flinched. "Donato's?"

Michael jerked his head around to stare at me. "Yeah, that's the place."

"The owner's from the same northern Italian town as Benno's mother. The food is wonderful, but it's a little pricey, so we only go on special occasions. How did you hear about it?"

"A credit card bill I saw somewhere recommended it. I don't suppose you're going to tell me you were there with your husband, the last weekend in April?"

"The last weekend in April?" Clea and I had spent the weekend in Philly, visiting my favorite of Benno's numerous cousins, who'd just had a baby. Benno was finishing a big job and had begged off. Not that I was about to say anything about it to Michael. "Why?"

"Because your husband was there, with a very attractive young black woman. Seems they were having a conversation that involved a lot of hand-holding. The waiter ID'd the woman from a photo as our Ellen, although Mr. Donato himself swore Benno was alone that night."

I was shocked, and it must have showed.

"Yeah, I thought you might not've known about that little tête-à-tête." He pronounced *tête* like the Asian holiday Tet.

"If Benno brought Ellen there, I'm sure there's an innocent explanation. Donato's is like family; it's the last place he'd take someone if he was having an affair!" I did my best to cover my feelings, but inside, I wasn't so sure. If it was a friendly meal, why hadn't Benno told me about it?

And Donato's would be the perfect place for an older man to take a younger woman he wanted to impress with his Italian. Plus I had no doubt that Donato would lie for Benno; it's one of those cultural-differences things. His wife was the genius in the kitchen, but Donato always managed to have a little something younger and slimmer on the side. According to Benno, it didn't bother Mrs. Donato as long as he was discreet and she didn't have to cook for the woman.

"Yeah, well, you ask him about it," Michael challenged me.

"Do you always go to memorial services for your murder victims?" When in trouble, change the subject.

"I try to. Gives me a chance to see how the grieving friends and family members are holding up. Seems your Ellen was a popular lady, but I didn't notice any relatives bothered to show."

"They're having a funeral at their church in Brooklyn."

"I hear you paid a visit to the father's grieving ex this morning." Michael changed the topic himself. "I don't know what's with you, Social Worker. You can't leave things alone, can you?"

"Is there a rule that says I can't pay a condolence call to Ellen's father when I'm in the neighborhood? Who told you, anyway?" Who knew, other than Marsha Ginsberg? Duh.

"I went over there myself. It occurred to me, in spite of what you think about my intelligence, that Mr. Chapman might not have had the whole story about that frame. Which you already know."

"So did you tell Peretti about that?"

"Not yet." Michael kept his patience. "But I will, unless you'd like to do it for me?" Barely. It must have been an attempt to make some allowance for my emotional state of mind.

"No." I hesitated, then decided what the hell. "So I was thinking, if Ellen didn't die when the medical examiner thought she did, because she ate her last meal later, then what if she was still alive when Marsha went to see her early Sunday morning?"

To my surprise, Michael didn't bite my head off. "It's a long shot, Anita. Even if it occurs to Peretti, I don't know as he'll do much to follow up on it. He's pretty satisfied with Benno as the killer. It makes a nice, neat, closed case."

I would have preferred annoyance to the apologetic, condescending tone he used.

"What about you? What do you think?"

"It doesn't matter what I think, it's not my case."

"So how come you're here, again?" I couldn't help pushing; Michael had to have some doubts of his own, to still be poking around.

"If the big boys from homicide don't have enough sense to show up, that's their problem. You got anything else for me, Social Worker, or shall we go check out the grieving friends?"

Michael's sensitivity didn't last long. I was a grieving friend myself. But—"Yes, one more thing. Marsha Ginsberg said she thought Ellen had a photo of Arthur Nessim in her room, that maybe Ellen had a crush on him? Do you know if it was there?"

"Jeez, Social Worker, there you go with the theories again! So which is it, the future stepmother or the boss? Pick a perp, any perp!"

"I'm just pointing out that there might be other people with reasons to want Ellen out of the way."

"You're a piece of work, you know that?" Michael shoved the

notepad back in his pocket without adding anything. "You go on ahead to the party, and I'll be in in a minute. Don't want it to seem like you're consorting with incompetents."

That was what I appreciated about Michael, his occasional fits of tact.

13

ETTING through the pleasantries after the service was not as bad as I'd feared. My mother had more than risen to the occasion and was the center of a knot of chatting students. Arthur Nessim seemed to have gotten himself back in hand and graciously introduced his twelve-year-old daughter to Clea, which helped no end. There's nothing more impressive to an almost-eight-year-old than a "big girl" who will deign to talk to her, and besides, Vera Nessim was a beauty. She had her father's honey skin and long, straight hair just a shade darker. What really hooked Clea, though, was her outfit—a broom-pleated skirt in pale blue with what I thought was a very skimpy tank top to match, and the latest in preteen jewelry, a choker of glittery beads and matching bracelet.

I was about to ask Arthur if his wife was also there, but when Michael approached us, I drifted off toward Jamie. He and Vlad were deep into something. I picked up a cup of juice and tried to eavesdrop unobtrusively.

No such luck. "Did you enjoy the service, Anita?" Jamie said to my back.

I turned to face him. Vlad walked away, face averted.

"*Enjoy* isn't exactly the word I'd use," I said. "It was very moving. You're a wonderful speaker."

"Thank you. It runs in the family. My father was a minister."

"But you didn't follow in his footsteps?"

"No, I chose to serve in a more practical way. I enlisted in the marines and got to see some of the world."

"Really?" My surprise was genuine. Jamie didn't look like he'd ever been the military type. Then I remembered the tattoo I'd seen peeking out from his shirt, and the sinewy canvas of his arm muscles.

"Excuse me, there's someone I need to speak with."

So much for a nice long chat. I'd intended to ask Jamie if he knew why Nafissa had dropped out of school, and how I could find her. When he walked away, however, it gave me a moment to reflect. He had no reason to share any information with me. If it came out at the school that he was involved with a student—well, he might have gotten by having an affair with Ellen as a fellow staff member, but students were different, and if Ellen and Nafissa had been arguing about him . . .

I looked around for Talile. She was pouring out juice at one end of a table loaded with platters of grapes, strawberries, and cut-up melon. It looked like the institute had gone all-out for the reception. Guilt on Nessim's part, or the homage of a lover?

I noticed Michael shaking hands with Arthur by the door before ducking out. I went over to Talile, who had just handed a cup of juice to Clea.

"How you doing, Bops?" I stroked her hair.

"Fine," Clea said, her usual chatty self. But then she graced me with a quick hug before bringing a strawberry over to Nessim's daughter.

Talile offered me a cup. "Is that your daughter?"

The inevitable question. I put a smile into my answer. "Yes."

"She is very beautiful."

"Thank you." She was. "Do you have children?"

Talile laughed. "My children are very big!"

"They're already taller than you are?" I gestured above my head to indicate height.

"Taller? Oh, more tall! Yes, more tall, and all grown up. I follow my daughter to America. She is twenty-sex. Twenty-*six*. My one son is twenty-four, and the other is teenage, eighteen."

"Wow." She looked to be in her twenties, tall and slender in a red silk blouse over a long flowered skirt.

"I married when I was young. Fourteen when my daughter is born." Talile glowed with pleasure at my amazement.

Different cultures, different worlds. "Your daughter came here first?"

"Four, no it is five years a gone. Then my husband dies, and I come too for a new life. It is a good country!"

"Is it a good country for Nafissa, too?"

The animation went out of Talile's face. "Nafissa—" She flung her hands up in a graceful question, then turned to refill the cup held out to her by a Chinese man.

I didn't know how to interpret the gesture. Someone flying away? Dreams taking wing? Her own inability to find words for Nafissa's situation?

More cups were held out and refilled. The fruit platters were almost empty. Arthur Nessim was coming toward the table.

"Talile, if you see Nafissa, I'd like to talk to her. Tell her it's not anything to do with the police." I got a card out of my purse, wrote my home phone number on the back of it, and handed it to her. "Will you ask her to call me? Please?"

She tucked the card into her skirt pocket. "Tomorrow I cook at the Red Sea restaurant. On Amsterdam. You bring your daughter?"

I nodded. "Yes, that would be nice."

Nessim came up on Talile's other side and put a hand on her waist. "Talile, thank you for your help." His face was closed, serious; he didn't even glance at me. "It's time to start clearing up now."

"It was a lovely service," I told his shoulder.

Then he turned to me and smiled. It was like I was seeing a whole different person. "Thank you."

We made complimentary small talk about our daughters, who were chatting together in an armchair by the window. Talile circled the room, picking up cups and napkins and putting them in a trash bag. I wondered about the proprietary way Arthur had touched her, and his peremptory, commanding tone. Was Talile another of his conquests? Or was it cultural differences? I had no idea where he was from. Maybe he was revealing his true attitudes toward women, attitudes I hadn't yet been on the receiving end of—and, as a white woman, might never feel directed at me? So hard to know!

It was time for us to go. I would have had difficulty separating Clea from Vera, but Arthur got there ahead of me and claimed his gorgeous daughter. I took Clea's hand and went to extricate my mother from her admirers.

We spun around in the big wooden door and were spit out onto the steps leading to Riverside Drive. The air was pregnant with humidity, the sky the sickly yellow that precedes a thunderstorm. A group of people were smoking on the sidewalk.

Vlad detached himself and came over to us. "Excuse me, I'm sorry, Anita, you will talk to me?"

"Of course." What I really wanted was to bum a smoke. "You'd better head home, Mom, before it rains." I bent to kiss Clea.

"Is your douter?" Vlad asked.

"Yes. She's adopted."

He frowned and repeated it. "Adopeted. Ah, yes, I understand. You are mother but she is not born from you!" A smile replaced the frown.

I asked for, and got, a cigarette. There was a flash of light, followed several moments later by a grumble of thunder.

"I don't keep you," Vlad said. "Only I must to tell you again, what I said before. Jamie and Nafissa, they are not the item. Jamie and Ellen, yes, before, but he is not with Nafissa."

"Oh?" Oh, indeed.

Vlad leaned a little too close to me. I could smell the sweat coming through his black polyester shirt. "No, Jamie, Nafissa is student. Professional relationship only. You understand?"

Yes, I understood. There was a warning in his voice. Vlad

was giving me the party line, protecting his fellow student, Jamie, the school.

"I'm not trying to make trouble. I just want to know what happened that night, if any of you saw anything—the police think my husband might be responsible for Ellen's death, and I want to find out the truth." Whatever it may be? a voice nagged inside my head. But I had other fish to fry. I kept up my pretense of innocent curiosity. "What about Mr. Nessim? Did he and Ellen have more than a professional relationship?"

Vlad reared back, surprised at the question. "Who is telling you that?"

At the sound of his raised voice, a young woman with light brown hair detached herself from the group and came to stand beside him. Natalya, the other person who'd been out with them?

"I just wondered." I shrugged. "Ellen—" But I didn't know for sure that Nessim's picture had been in Ellen's room, and I didn't need to be starting any rumors.

Vlad and the woman exchanged a few sentences in urgent Russian.

I held out my hand. "Hi, my name is Anita Servi. Are you Natalya?"

Her nod was tentative. The hand she allowed me to take was limp, the bones like those of a small fish.

"I was just saying to Vlad that Mr. Nessim seemed very upset about Ellen's death."

"We all is *upset*." Vlad spat the word back at me. "We all want police not bothering us. You too, not bothering with us!"

"Is terrible thing for us. We think America is safe place, but is true, anything can happen. We go to club, drink beer outside, go sing carry-you-okay—" Natalya shot me a quick glance, her eyes timid and proud at the same time.

Carry you okay? Then I got it, Japanese to English via Russian—karaoke, a specialty at the West End on Saturday nights.

"Did either of you see Ellen that night?" I persisted. "On the street, or—"

"No! Ellen always make trouble for Nafissa. No more now!"

He put his arm across Natalya's shoulder and steered her back to their friends.

The look Natalya gave me this time was frightened.

Damn the language difficulties! What did Vlad mean, Ellen made trouble for Nafissa? Had she told Nessim about a possible affair between Nafissa and Jamie? Or had Ellen caused trouble for Nafissa accidentally, by dying when she did and possibly bringing Nafissa's night out with Jamie to the attention of not only her brother but also the police? I stood there smoking, thinking about it.

The group drifted off in the other direction. A bolt of lightning cracked down over New Jersey. I counted six oh-shits until the thunder followed. I dropped the cigarette butt and started walking.

That picture nagged at me. If Marsha Ginsberg was right, had it been there when I found Ellen's body? It wouldn't have meant anything to me at the time, but if it hadn't been there . . . where was it? Did Ellen put it away, or did Nessim take it—after he'd plunged a screwdriver into her chest?

It was a theory. Michael might not be interested, but I had other ways to find out. Maybe Miranda would remember. I didn't have her phone number, but I certainly knew where she lived. I cut across Riverside, headed up the hill of 113th Street.

Okay, I'll admit it, I also had an ulterior motive. My mother wasn't going to stay forever, and although I wouldn't need a regular sitter once Clea started day camp, it was good to have someone for the occasional weekend or evening . . . which reminded me where Benno was and stabbed me back to the seriousness of the situation.

They'd added a university security guard to the building, sitting behind a long table in the lobby. He was a lot more on his toes than the doorman at Lincoln Towers; this time my confident, middle-aged white woman walk didn't do the trick, and he made me call up on the intercom. Miranda didn't answer, so I had to content myself with leaving a note for the guard to deliver. I didn't have much faith that he'd actually give it to her, but it was the best I could do.

The first big drops of rain had just splatted down on Broadway. I ran for home, blissfully unaware of the welcoming committee waiting for me in front of my building.

14

I T was the first time I'd ever been truly grateful for Howard Orton, occupant of the first-floor front apartment, known to the neighborhood as the Mayor of 111th Street because he took note of everything that went down on the block.

When he saw me approaching the knot of strangers jostling each other by the stoop, Howard elbowed his way through them and took my arm. "Let the lady pass!" he ordered, and miraculously, they stepped back.

But not without shouting a barrage of questions at me. "Do you know Benno Servi?" "Are you his wife?" "How do you feel about living in the same building as a cold-blooded killer?"

There were several bright flashes, too close for lightning. By then I'd figured out who they were and had my head tucked into the protective bulk of Howard's shoulder. The press. I should have been expecting it, but I was totally blindsided.

"Clea and your mother got in okay, Anita," he whispered to me. "Don't pay them any mind. I've made sure they don't ring anyone's bell, and no one's spoken to them or let any of them into the building. Vultures!"

"Thank you, Howard," I said. I meant it. He might have been a busybody, but at least he was my busybody, and his proprietary attitude toward the building and its occupants was working in my favor.

There was a loud clap of thunder. Howard smiled. "Rain! That'll teach them!"

✦

My mother met me at the door with a shell-shocked expression.

"Clea's watching a video. I hope you don't mind, Anita, but after the gauntlet out front, and there were seventeen messages on the machine—I thought it would be a good idea to distract her while I played them back. All the major papers, New York One news, Fox news, and a handful of hang-ups. They didn't recognize you downstairs, did they?"

I shook my head. "I don't think so. Howard escorted me in."

"I never thought I'd have a reason to appreciate that nosy little man!" Her laugh was uncharacteristically shaky. "I've turned off the ringer on the phone and the volume on the answering machine, so we won't hear anything. You can listen to whatever comes in later, in case it's actually a friend calling."

"I probably don't have any friends left," I muttered. I was suddenly too exhausted to care.

A barrage of rain splattered in through the open living room windows, and I could hardly muster the energy to slam them down. My mother installed me on the couch with Clea, who promptly climbed into my lap and stuck her thumb in her mouth. I didn't care about that, either.

The rain blew sheets of water against the windows. The lightning and thunder blasted so loudly that it distracted Clea from her video, and she whimpered in my arms. I stroked her head, rocked her in my arms. The only good thought I could focus on was that the storm would have drenched the reporters and sent them scurrying home.

My mother made a pot of spaghetti, opened a jar of sauce, and cut cucumber spears for a vegetable. We ate in front of the television. I left the dishes for her, too, and crawled into bed as soon as I'd tucked Clea in. After only four hours of sleep the night before, the occasional strobe of lightning that flashed into my room wasn't going to bother me.

✦

Sunday morning, I woke up with the dawn. It was one of those spring mornings after a rain, the air so sharp you could cut yourself on the shards of early-morning sun reflected off the buildings across the river in Jersey. I lay there staring out the window, not thinking about anything specific, letting Ellen roll around in my mind, her friends at the institute, the changes she'd been going through in her last year at school. I'd read Ellen's paper, which was written for an oral history class, about Nafissa N'doye. The experiences of new immigrants from Africa were quite different from the experiences of African Americans, and yet there were enough similarities to provide a different perspective on being black in the United States.

Black people are on the receiving end of ingrained American thinking about race, apt to be stopped by the police for DWB— driving while black—or even walking while black; last to be hired, first to be fired; given the shittiest jobs, the lowest pay. Yet the African immigrants, like all the tired, hungry, poor, who came to our wealthy shores, were here by choice, and brought the immigrant ethic of hard work along with the belief that it would be rewarded. And work hard they did. Ellen had interviewed Nafissa in the wake of the trial of the four white police officers who'd been acquitted for the murder of an unarmed black man, Amadou Diallo, in the foyer of his building. Diallo had been a street vendor, as Nafissa's brother was before he moved on up to a permanent stall at the Harlem Market.

Although Nafissa's life hadn't intersected with the random searches of the Street Crimes Unit that had been sowing discontent in the primarily black neighborhoods of Brooklyn and Queens, her brother had been radicalized by the protests in the aftermath of the shooting.

Both East and West Africans were having a growing impact on the city, finding niches in professional as well as service-oriented jobs and filling them. Protective Services for Adults, the city agency of last resort for my elderly clients, was staffed largely by men from Nigeria. The cashiers at West Side Market were primarily women from Ethiopia.

The immigrants Ellen met at the institute were likely to be

on the poor end of the scale, more likely to need to hustle, less formally educated—although they were often fluent in three or four languages. Vendors from the English-speaking countries, Gambia, Mali, Liberia, had added color to the streets of Brooklyn as well as Harlem.

The restaurant on Amsterdam where Talile worked was one of a growing crowd offering Ethiopian food not only to other immigrants but to New Yorkers always ready for a new cuisine and willing to try eating with their fingers. Clea loved those places, tearing off pieces of *injera*, the spongy pancakes served with steaming, spicy stews. Rolling the *injera* around a bit of meat, a sweet potato, was kid heaven—license to eat with your hands.

Thinking about all the ways the African cultures were making inroads into our lives brought me back to the Harlem Market, relocated by our obstreperous mayor from the bustle of 125th Street to a lot on 116th between Lenox and Fifth Avenues, where they could set up semipermanent, proper stalls. Of course, that was where I could find Nafissa! According to Ellen's paper, her brother sold fabric there, and Nafissa had a sewing machine in his stall where she made African-style outfits. Yes, and she'd told Anne that was where her dress had come from—although she hadn't acknowledged that she'd made it herself.

Never take a coincidence for granted. If it wasn't one of my mother's mottoes, it should have been. Didn't Clea need a yard of African print fabric, the brighter the better, to make a *lapa*, a wrap skirt, for her African dance class performance? I could take care of two errands with one stop, visit Nafissa at work and buy a *lapa* for Clea.

It would be good to make a purchase while talking to Nafissa; "you scratch my back, I'll scratch yours" is one of those human grooming behaviors that transcends cultural differences. People are always more willing to help if they're getting something in return, and it isn't only American culture where the customer rules.

Bringing Clea along would help, too. A child goes a long way toward easing suspicion. Nor did I discount the impact of Clea's color.

I've found that black people tend to treat me differently when Clea's with me. We do draw the occasional hostile comment, but notwithstanding the official opinion of the NABSW—National Association of Black Social Workers—which is that it's a form of cultural genocide to allow black children to be adopted into white families, I've found that black people are more than willing to give me credit for being somewhat less racist than the average person of my pigmentation.

Like the woman in a crowded elevator in Bloomie's, when I had six-month-old Clea in a snuggly on my chest. She'd asked the usual question—"Is that your baby?" I nodded. The woman leaned over and said, directly to Clea, who was way too small to understand a word, "Never you mind that she's white, honey, she's one of the good ones." The whole elevator broke up laughing.

On that optimistic memory, I decided to get up and go out for the Sunday paper. It was only seven o'clock; with any luck, the press would not yet have resumed their assault on the front stoop. I took a quick shower and pulled on a pair of jeans and my favorite purple sweatshirt.

Opening the apartment door carefully, so as not to wake my mother or Clea, I bent to pick up the pieces of paper that had been slid under the door. Surprisingly, none of them were Chinese take-out menus. Waiting for the elevator, I unfolded a note from Barbara. "Anita—I left a message on your machine, but I figure you're not listening. If you have to hole up inside all day to avoid the buzzards out front, give me a call or come on down. I've got some ribs marinating, so we can fire up the grill and have a party. Not that you'll be celebrating, but might as well make lemonade!"

There was a sealed envelope with my name written in the formal script of my neighbors, the Wilcox sisters. I slit the flap and took out a flowered card. It read, "Dear Anita, You and Benno will be in our prayers this morning. If there is any assistance we can provide, please don't hesitate to call on us. Catherine and Elizabeth."

God bless them, I guess I did still have some friends.

✦

No luck, but at least I was prepared for the horde on the stoop. I'd put on sunglasses and the attitude of a running back going for yardage. I put my head down, bulled my way through, and sprinted up to the corner with no one in pursuit.

After I picked up the *Times* at the newsstand on 110th and Broadway, I headed to the Hungarian Pastry Shop for cappuccino and croissant. I sat in the back, with the smokers, where I'd be hidden from anyone I knew who happened to stop in. I held my hands around the cup, sipped the hot, foamy brew, and flipped though the paper for the Metro section, looking for whatever they'd written about Benno's arrest.

We'd made it above the fold, a banner head across the middle: "Suspect Arrested in Barnard Slaying." There was no photo of Benno, thank goodness, but he was identified as Ellen's employer and as living on 111th Street. The story went on to detail the alleged affair, along with the statement that the wife of the accused—that would be me—had found Ellen's body.

The words doubled up on themselves and blurred into nonsense on the page. It was as if seeing it in black-and-white newsprint made the whole situation not more real, but less. My family on the front page of the *New York Times* Metro section; it had to be a nightmare.

Benno accused of murder, of infidelity.

I closed the paper and shoved it aside. The croissant tasted like paste. The cappuccino had gone cold and bitter.

I reached for the paper again and opened it to where the story continued inside. There was a brief mention of Benno's occupation, and that the screwdriver Ellen had been stabbed with had been a gift from him. I'd always thought it was just a figure of speech, but my whole body felt numb. Only my eyes seemed capable of movement, finishing the story, which was padded with quotes from "incredulous neighbors," like Barbara, who'd told the reporter, "I've known Benno Servi for eight years, and he had nothing to do with Ellen Chapman's death." They'd gotten to Catherine Wilcox, too, who told them, "Ellen was a lovely young woman. Mr. Servi is a fine man, and he would never have harmed her, or anyone else."

A tingle of pleasure at their words gave me the strength to read the boxed inset, with a picture of Ellen in cap and gown, that briefly described her life, the promise of an honor student cut off in full bloom, quotes from friends—including Miranda, the girl across the hall, and Arthur Nessim, praising her as a gifted young woman with the ability to bond with new immigrants and make them feel at home in their new country.

I put the paper down on the table and took another sip of cold coffee. My lips felt swollen, like after a shot of Novocain from the dentist. How could we go on after this? For all their brave words, how long would our friends stand by us? And what about the neighbors and colleagues who wouldn't be so staunch in Benno's defense? Nightmare didn't begin to describe what this experience was turning into.

And underneath it all, the fear for Clea's placement. What if the agency . . . they would see the article. They had the legal authority, Wertheim's reassurances notwithstanding, to take her away. Instantly.

My first thought was to get home and call Joel Rheingold, our attorney for the adoption. Maybe he could preempt them, file for a stay or a restraining order or whatever. There had to be something we could do.

"Anita, what's wrong?"

I'd taken a quick look through the open French doors at the Murphy bed, where Clea was ensconced in front of the tube, watching *Arthur* with my mother and eating dry cereal from a bowl. She barely looked up at me, engrossed in the program, but my mother was not so easily distracted.

I faded back from the doorway, and my mother threw off the covers and followed me into the bedroom. I sat on the edge of my bed and handed her the newspaper. While she read, I got the phone and Joel's card from the Rolodex.

Fortunately, I had his home number; we'd had a bad patch a few years ago, when one of Clea's aunts had briefly flirted with seeking custody. When Catholic Children's tried to evaluate her home, she refused to let them in. Then, after the first weekly visit scheduled at the agency, she failed to show up again.

The next we heard from her was in a lawsuit, naming Benno and me along with Catholic Children's and Child Welfare, accusing us of depriving her of "the company of said child." She asked for $10 million and treble punitive damages. The suit had been thrown out, but not before causing a lot of misery and extended phone conversations with Joel.

My mother finished the article and looked up, her expression as shocked as mine.

"I'm calling the lawyer," I told her.

Joel Rheingold was home; he'd seen the story; he'd spoken with Wertheim the day before, and they'd agreed that, with Benno out of the house and safely tucked away in jail, the agency might have cause for increased oversight but not to remove Clea from her home.

"But what if they do anyway? What if they show up at the door wanting to take her?"

"They won't, Anita. Catholic Children's is one of the better agencies. Their director, Rita Velarde? She knows you, doesn't she?"

Rita, a fellow graduate of Columbia's social work school, had been an ace during the aunt's lawsuit, but I was not reassured.

"But what about Child Welfare? What if they send someone to get her at school?"

"Look, whatever they do, they'll call first to be sure you're home. If you hear from anyone, just call me." He gave me his cell phone number.

In the theater of New York City politics, where scandal lurked in the wings, forces bigger than a director of social services could easily steal the scene. Catholic Children's might be reasonable; Child Welfare, the city agency with ultimate responsibility for children in foster care, was another story. Like all bureaucracies, it was more concerned with safeguarding its image than protecting the children in its custody. The story was major news, and the city might find it hard to resist a poster case for the new Adoption and Safe Families law.

Joel let me run through all my worst-case scenarios and possible responses, ranging from immediate flight to Canada—which he strongly discouraged—to alerting the administration at Clea's school and arming them with his number as well. Before he hung up, Joel also suggested that I should listen to my messages—he'd actually called me before I called him. "There might be something important on there. And since you don't have a cell phone, there's no other way for me to reach you."

He had a point, but I really did not want to wade through the cacophony of imploring, seductive voices of the media.

"Just fast-forward those, Anita. If you do hear from Rita, or in the unlikely event Child Welfare, you need to know. Forewarned is forearmed," Joel insisted.

I was not much relieved when I hung up the phone. Neither was my mother.

15

THE answering machine had accumulated another eleven messages, a majority of them from reporters, as I'd feared. Also Barbara, Joel himself, Anne Reisen with an offer of support, and the most recent, Rita Velarde.

It wasn't exactly good news, but as Joel had predicted, Catholic Children's wasn't going to do anything rash. At least not until Rita talked to their lawyers on Monday, who would then have to talk to the city's lawyers, and have a high old time figuring out whose ass needed covering and how. The one thing I knew was, Clea wouldn't be their primary concern.

Rita's message started out innocuously enough—she'd heard and read the news reports; as long as Benno was not in the home, she saw no reason at this time to change the placement. Emphasis on "at this time." Then came the kicker.

"Also, Anita, I should alert you that I will need to send someone to visit your home. Don't worry, it's just routine."

I swore at the three beeps that followed Rita's voice. Routine, my ass. That's what they always say; "someone to visit your home" could mean anything from our caseworker of the month to a Child Welfare worker with a court order and a cop to enforce it, and Rita could sleep at night knowing she hadn't lied to me. And I noticed there hadn't been any "when" attached to this visit. The workers with the legal authority to remove a child they deem to be in imminent danger are on call twenty-four/seven. I didn't like it, not one little bit.

My mother, reiterating her promise to discuss the options

with Aaron Wertheim, put on the same outfit she'd worn yesterday to the memorial and flowed out for her brunch date.
Better for us to be out of the house as well. I still intended to head over to the market, maybe treat Clea to lunch at Talile's restaurant afterward, so I called Barbara to say we'd be glad to come down in the late afternoon, but right now could she sneak us through the side exit from the basement?

The crowd of reporters had thinned somewhat, and none of them were watching the alleyway along the side. Clea and I ducked out, crossed the street, and headed up 111th to Broadway for the bus. Sunday morning the M4 doesn't run all that often; no one's commuting to work on the East Side, and other than work or museums, Westsiders don't cross town much. We got lucky; I bought Clea a papaya juice from Mike's, and the bus came just as she finished it.

Clea was unusually quiet on the ride. When we got off the bus at Lenox Avenue, she took my hand. We headed north to 116th, past old row houses and blocks of modern low-rise projects to the market.

"I came here one time with Ellen," she finally said.

"You did? What did she buy?"

"She wanted some cloth, but the man wouldn't let her touch anything. She was going to buy me a hairband, too, but then she got mad back at the man, so she said we'd go somewhere else, but we didn't. Will you buy it for me, Mama?"

Trust Clea to play her cards right. "If we find a hairband that you like, Bops, we'll get it. Do you know who the man was?"

Clea shook her head. "Ellen tried to be nice to him. How come he didn't want her to have the cloth, Mama? It's for sale to anybody, right?"

"Well, it's supposed to be," I agreed. "I don't understand why he wouldn't want to make some money. Did he have nice fabric?"

"It was pretty good. I want purple for my *lapa*."

I hoped the man would be more receptive to me making a

purchase than he'd evidently been to Ellen. In her paper, Ellen noted that the subject's brother had declined an interview. Assuming it was Nafissa's brother she'd been talking to, was he mad because of what Ellen wrote? Did he even know about it?

The streets were already crowded with people out to enjoy the Sunday sunshine. A pair of Hispanic men with neat white mustaches and wearing straw hats played a game of dominoes on a card table while a handful of *kibitzers* watched. Three women in linen suits with matching hats and heels—pistachio, peach, lemon meringue pie—stood outside Bayou.

The market is in the middle of the block, east of Lenox, between 115th and 116th. We turned down 115th, approaching the curvy, minaret-shaped signs that gave the place its official name, the Malcolm Shabazz Harlem Market, written in bulbous, cartoon letters in green, orange, and yellow.

Many of the vendors here got their starts on 125th Street, setting up tables along the sidewalks and giving the neighborhood the feel of a West African city bustling with merchants and traders. But Mayor Giuliani decided to listen to the shopkeepers who complained that the vendors had an unfair competitive advantage, not having rent to pay, and that they blocked the sidewalks, clogging up traffic. Although a few protesting voices charged that the mayor's ulterior agenda was to speed the flow of traffic through Harlem to the Triborough Bridge, many in the neighborhood had come to view the vendors as more nuisance than convenience. After all, how many cheap CDs and knockoff sunglasses does a person need?

So the vendors were given a site on 116th, where they originally set up their stalls under a makeshift variety of canvas, wood, and sheet-metal roofs. When the randomness of the place in its turn offended the mayor, the city relocated them again, to this site in the next block, and provided four rows of six-by-six sheet-metal booths, rather like storage sheds, with an arched roof of corrugated fiberglass over the three aisles.

Harlem is a churchgoing part of town, and the market wasn't yet crowded, although most of the stalls had their sliding glass doors open, and the goods inside had spilled over onto tables set out in the aisles. Clea and I cruised up the right side, past displays of leather goods, Coach bags, plastic *tchotchkes* with African themes, real African crafts like carved giraffes, malachite elephants, dolls in beads and turbans, displays of jewelry, stacks of thick mud cloth with its dramatic patterning, bright cottons with prints adapted from kente cloth and gold traceries, T-shirts, small electronics, sunglasses, and CDs. I would have paused to check out each booth that had fabric displayed out front, but Clea was intent on her headband, which meant the exact same booth she'd been to with Ellen. That was my ultimate goal, too, so I let her tug me along.

We went around a corner and down another aisle to the central area where a cluster of round tables were set out in front of a coffee stand with a sign that read YEHUDA DAUGHTERS BAKE SHOP above a Jewish star. Three willowy, dark-skinned women served doughnuts and coffee to a short line. Ethiopian Jews? Truly, New York is the center of the world; every ethnicity, religion, nationality, comes here eventually.

I read the signs as we entered the far left aisle. Jeneba Tawati, over a clothing stall; N'DIAMBOUR AFRICAN ARTS; KOREA IMPORTS; GUATEMALA, over a store with a different kind of woven fabrics, bright striped bolts of cloth, and leather sandals. Clea pulled me along until we got to a stall whose sign read simply AFRICAN IMPORTERS.

The wall separating two booths had been taken down, making a double-sized space. Only one of the sliding doors was open. In front of the closed door was a rack of garments, dresses of a stiff, batiked fabric that held their shape like tents, outfits of thin cotton with long tunics over baggy pants that tapered at the ankles, large dashikis for men, mud cloth pants. Behind the glass I could see an industrial-type sewing machine. Presumably, this was where Nafissa worked.

The proprietor, a dark man with a crocheted skullcap on his head, was involved in a laughing exchange with a petite red-haired woman in tight jeans and a chartreuse tank top. She had a pile of maybe a dozen bolts of cotton on a table out in front of the stall. She'd obviously asked for a yard of each, which he was cutting while they negotiated prices. It was also clear that she was a regular customer; he was giving her consideration, five dollars a yard for what usually went for seven. In return she promised to bring the quilts she made, next time she came.

In the center of the booth was a square table, covered by indigo mud cloth in a diamond batik pattern that hung to the floor, piled with thick, folded rectangles of mud cloth in blue and black, and brown patterned in an earthy green. Four rows of shelves circled the inside walls, filled with bolts of cloth in no discernible order. All bright, crisp cotton, the colors jumbled together, red, blue, orange, black, purple, green; some had designs in gold, some in black; there were multicolored imitations of kente cloth next to solid colors next to swirling prints.

There was a break in the shelves by the door, where a low table held a calculator, some order books and pens, scissors, and two tape measures. I also noticed a scattering of business cards, so I picked one up. It gave the booth address in the upper left corner; the lower right read KAWSU N'DOYE, above a 718 number. At least now I knew his name, and possibly had a home number for Nafissa.

On the shelfless wall above the supply table was a display of necklaces, silver amulets strung on leather cords, that caught Clea's attention. Mr. N'doye paused to smile and tell her they were from Mali, and meant for protection.

I was overwhelmed by all the fabrics. Purple, Clea said, but there were so many different patterns. I pulled out a bolt with a design of gold arabesques, and another with the big five African animals—elephant, lion, giraffe, rhino, and some kind of antelope—marching across it in a design of black and green. I held them in my arms, waiting for the red-haired woman to finish. She pulled a wad of bills out of her pocket and peeled off five twenties. A hundred dollars' worth of fabric! I was impressed. Twenty yards, those must be some quilts.

Before she picked up her two full bags, the woman leaned over and gave the proprietor a huge hug. I got a glimpse of his startled face over her shoulder, and I had to smile. Reticent man from Senegal meets effusive New York Jewish woman? He looked rather like a friendly lioness had him in her grip, but he laughed and patted her shoulder.

Well, it looked like Mr. N'doye was in a good mood after the big sale. When she left, he turned to Clea, explaining with a grave dignity what the designs on the amulets meant. "This one is for pride. This means faith in God, and that one is courage. With that one, you could be brave enough to run away fast if an elephant chases you!"

He laughed, and so did I. I'd decided on the direct approach. I held out my hand. "My name is Anita Servi, and this is my daughter Clea."

Mr. N'doye shook my hand, but his eyes went quiet, as if my name meant something to him, something unpleasant he didn't want to discuss.

I laid the bolts of cloth on the table. "My daughter needs a yard of material for a *lapa*. She takes African dance classes."

"You like purple?" His voice was wary, as if he knew I had come to him for more than a small purchase.

I had. "I saw your sister, Nafissa, at Riverside Church yesterday, but I didn't have a chance to talk with her. I was hoping she'd be here today?"

He shook his head, and his expression got a shade less friendly. "She is not working today."

I looked down, not wanting to make improper eye contact with a man whose culture I didn't know. "I guess she didn't work yesterday, either, since she was at the memorial service for Ellen Chapman—the young woman who was killed?" I glanced up. He nodded, once, waited for what I had to say next.

"Was that you with her?"

"No. It is a busy day for me. My countryman escorted Nafissa." Mr. N'doye stepped into the booth, lifted another bolt of purple cloth from the wall, one of the swirly ones with blue, green, and white mixed in, and held it out to Clea. "How do you like this one?"

Her face lit up. "That one is good!"

"Ellen baby-sat for my daughter." I put a hand on Clea's shoulder. "The police arrested my husband because they think he killed Ellen."

I glanced up at him. He rested one hand on a corner of the table and stared out of the stall at the people cruising the aisles. No one stopped by the booth.

"I am sorry for you," he said finally.

Clea leaned against my side. She had the pendant for pride clutched in one hand, along with a stretchy headband in a blue-and-yellow fabric. Mr. N'doye looked down at her. "You like that?"

Clea nodded. "And can I have the pretty cloth, Mama? That one?" She poked a finger at the bolt he'd selected.

"Yes, that's fine. And one yard of the material, please."

While Mr. N'doye cut the cloth, I asked if Nafissa would be back in class at the ESL Institute on Monday. He seemed to ignore my question, so I pushed on, told him how much Mabel Johnson, the older woman Nafissa was helping, missed her.

Without responding to me, he put the fabric in a plastic bag, and handed it to Clea.

"How much do I owe you?" I gave up on the conversation.

"Five dollars for the necklace, seven dollars for cloth. Twelve dollars."

I reached for my wallet. "And the headband?"

He shook his head. "For her hair, it is a gift for the little girl."

"Thank you." I bumped Clea with my hip, and she said "Thank you" in a small voice.

I believe that some things transcend culture, nationality, upbringing; how we feel about our children is chief among those universal human emotions. So is fear for the safety of our loved ones.

"I wouldn't do anything to endanger Nafissa, or involve the police in any way. She came to see me a few days ago, but we didn't really have a chance to talk. I'm sure she's upset by Ellen's death, and if there's anything I can do—" I got a card out of my bag, wrote my number on the back, and handed it to him along with the money. "Please give this to Nafissa. She can call me anytime."

He folded the card and the money into a pouch at his waist without comment.

I put the pendant over Clea's head and adjusted the knot in the back so it was at the right length for her. I couldn't resist pushing my luck. "Will she be here later this afternoon? We could come back, if that's a better time?"

He stepped out of the doorway to stand in front of his booth to smile at the people passing by, inviting them in, and shrugged. "She does not work here today."

A group of Japanese tourists paused in the aisle. Two of them raised cameras to their faces. Mr. N'doye smiled for them and gestured at his wares.

A man in a pink polo shirt held one of the dashikis from the rack up to his chest. Nafissa's brother moved away from us to help him.

I took Clea's hand, and we wandered down the rest of the aisle and up the other side. I noticed the redheaded woman in a jewelry booth, holding up a necklace of cowrie shells. Their transaction also involved laughter, but no hug for this vendor. I wished I had her life, buying as much fabric as I wanted on a Sunday afternoon, amusing vendors from foreign countries, sewing rainbow quilts.

I sighed. "Feel like some lunch, Bopster?"

Clea beamed up at me. The bright headband framed her beautiful face, like gilding on a lily. I knew I wouldn't trade my life for anything.

16

THE atmosphere when we walked into the dim interior of the Red Sea was not exactly welcoming. The tables were empty except for one, where a pair of young women, their heads wrapped in dark fabric turbans, were inserting sheets of paper into a stack of plastic sleeves. They barely glanced up at our entrance, then turned their attention back to their work. A man in a guayabera shirt stood to the side of a swinging door with a diamond-shaped window cut into it. He made no move to help us, either.

In spite of my profession, which requires me to ask the most personal questions of people I barely know, I'm not very good at talking to strangers. The unfriendly vibe was almost more than I could bear, and I realized that pressuring Mr. N'doye had taken more effort than I'd thought.

Clea, sensitive to the mood, tugged at my hand. I ignored her.

"Mama!" she insisted.

At her voice, the young women seemed to register our presence for the first time. One of them stood and took a few steps toward us. "Yes?" she said.

"Are you open?" I asked.

"Yes?"

Was she asking or answering? "We'd like to get lunch, please." I hesitated, then added, "Does Talile work here?"

"Yes." This time it was definitely an affirmative. She turned back to the other woman at the table, who handed her two of the menus, then gestured us to sit wherever we wanted.

Clea headed for a table by the window. The woman put the menus down and disappeared through the swinging door. The man in the white shirt still stood without moving or looking at us. What was the deal? I wondered.

Then Talile emerged from the kitchen, wrapped in a white apron, beaming at us, and the air in the Red Sea changed as quickly as if a switch had been thrown. Two bottles of soda appeared on the table. Talile scanned the menu over my shoulder, pointed to two or three items, and disappeared.

I was relieved. I'd been worried that Talile would have seen the papers and connected me as the wife of Ellen's accused killer, and would refuse to talk to me.

Clea explained to me what I had to do to make the *lapa*, which amounted to tearing off two strips from one edge and sewing them on at the corners, like an apron, to make ties. "Real *lapas* are a piece of cloth that you knot on the side, but Miss Dele says we're just girls and we don't have any hips, so to make sure they stay on she wants us to have strings."

Whatever Miss Dele told the class was law, I knew. I loved listening to Clea explain things; she sounded just like me, laying out the world for her.

Talile brought our food out herself, a large platter of steaming *injera*, then three bowls of mysterious stews that smelled wonderful. With a deft movement of her hand, she emptied the bowls in three piles around the edges of the *injera*, identifying them as *azifa*—lentils, my favorite in any cuisine; *shuro fit fit*, chickpeas; and *doro wat*, a stew with the chicken and the egg.

I asked her to join us while we ate, to share our food, but she ducked her head and went back to the kitchen. The *doro wat* was too spicy for Clea, so she stuck to the lentils and ate more *injera* than anything else. We asked one of the now-friendly young women to wrap the rest up to take home for Gamma Rho, and Talile came back out with a bowl of vanilla ice cream for Clea.

"In my country, we don't eat sweet. In United States, all

children like ice cream. I keep this for my grandchildren. You like it?"

I left Clea licking slow bites from the spoon and went to talk to Talile in her sanctuary, the kitchen. My lavish praise for her cooking was interrupted when the man who'd been standing by the door stuck his head in. Talile said something to him in a musical Amharic and he left us alone.

I figured I'd better get to it, and asked if she knew whether Nafissa would be coming back to the school.

Talile shook her head. "I call her. Her brother makes excuse, she went to store. I give my phone number, but Nafissa is not calling me."

The door swung open again. This time it was Clea. She let the door swing shut behind her and came over to put an arm around my waist without saying anything.

Talile smiled down at her. "How do you like my *injera*?"

"It's very good, thank you." Clea trotted out manners I didn't know she had. "How do you make it?"

Kids can surprise you, rising to the occasion with strangers.

Talile was pleased, too. She showed Clea the batter, pantomimed pouring it on the large, flat grill. "I give you some to take home?"

"Yes, please. Then my grandma can have a taste."

I shooed Clea out while Talile rolled and wrapped two of the white pancakes.

I didn't quite know how to bring up the subject of Arthur Nessim, but if anyone was going to tell me, it would be Talile. I stuck my toe in the waters, hoping not to bring trouble where there was none.

"Talile, do you know if there was anything special going on between Mr. Nessim and Ellen?"

She paid careful attention to tucking the wax paper around the *injera*, not meeting my eyes. First Vlad, now Talile; the subject of Nessim definitely evoked evasive responses.

"I won't say anything about it to anyone," I promised. "They're both grown-ups."

Talile wiped her hands on her apron. Her face was serious,

guarded. "Mr. Nessim is a good friend to the students. With Ellen, it doesn't matter now."

"What doesn't matter?"

Before she could answer, Clea was back. This time she left her manners behind. "Come on, Mama, it's time to go now!"

"Tabitha, Tabitha!" Clea favored the skinny waist of Barbara's youngest daughter with one of her patented two-second hugs. "Where's Malik?"

"Waiting for you in the backyard." Tabitha ran a hand over Clea's cornrows. "Nice pattern. Your mom do it?" Her own hair was straightened and smoothed back into a twist, setting off the slenderness of her face and high cheekbones.

Clea stepped away from Tabitha. "My baby-sitter did these. Now she's dead."

Tabitha looked to me for a cue on how to respond to Clea's fierceness. I shrugged at her to let it go and started down the street.

She stopped me. "My mom sent me up to meet you. There's still a few reporters hanging around out front, so she thought it'd be better for us to go around the block and come up to the side door from Riverside." There was relief in her voice. "I'm glad I caught you!"

"Thanks, Tabitha, that was really nice of you. I hope you weren't waiting too long?"

"Maybe half an hour. It's no problem. My mom was just worried, you know, with all that's going on?"

I nodded. Yeah, I knew. "Do you know if my mother's home yet?"

"I haven't seen her." Tabitha stopped at the southeast corner of 111th and Riverside. "Anita, maybe you should let me unlock the gate and then you come up. The guys saw me before, and they know I won't talk to them."

"Okay." I used my shoulder to point at Clea and gestured with my chin that she should go with Tabitha, who nodded her agreement. The reporters would naturally assume Clea was her child, not mine, and leave them alone.

"Clea, you go ahead with Tabitha. I'll be right there." Clea was going to give me an argument, until Tabitha whispered something in her ear and she scampered off.

Two white men in khaki slacks and polo shirts with IDs on chains around their necks were lounging on the stoop. A honey-skinned woman with two cameras slung around her neck leaned against a parked car. They looked up as Tabitha and Clea approached, but when they saw who it was, they went right back to their conversation. I strolled casually up the street and was in the open door before my presence registered.

There were about a half-dozen people in the backyard. My neighbors, the elderly Wilcox sisters; Malik's father, Bobby; Louis, Barbara's current beau, busy at the grill. Malik, in orange neon jams, made a beeline for Clea, dragging her by the hand to a wading pool that had more water around than in it.

Catherine and Elizabeth started talking at me simultaneously. I couldn't understand a word of their worried babble. Barbara handed me a beer and a piece of paper. The Wilcoxes went mercifully quiet while I read.

It was a notice from the Department of Child Welfare, DCW, saying that a worker had been by the house on "a routine check," and would I call as soon as I got this message to set up an appointment for her to return.

"They rang the Super's buzzer when you weren't home," Barbara answered before I could ask. "Two women. I told them they could leave that paper, but I couldn't let them wait in the hall. They knocked on the Wilcoxes' door—"

"Oh, Anita, I'm so sorry, I thought they were Jehovah's. They rang our buzzer from downstairs too and of course I didn't let them in, so when I heard the knock, I only opened the door to tell them to go away, but when I realized what they wanted it was too late!" Catherine, at eighty-one the younger of the sisters, still had the musical trill of a professional singer in her voice. "They asked the most awful questions. She wanted to know if Benno beat you! If we ever saw bruises on Clea or heard her crying! Can you imagine the nerve?"

Elizabeth banged her cane on the concrete. " 'Just doing our job' is what she said. That's what the clerks and bouncers used to say when they wouldn't let us into the hotels or white clubs when Catherine was on the road, 'Just doing our jobs.' Protecting children, my foot. Benno adores that child! He wouldn't harm a hair on her precious head, and I told them so."

"Miss Elizabeth, you're the best." I bent to kiss her cheek, brown and wrinkled as a walnut. "I'm so sorry they bothered you."

"I let that woman know I was ashamed to have my tax dollars paying the salary of people like her, harassing a good couple who took in a little baby and raised her as their own!" Elizabeth chuckled at her own audacity.

Catherine scowled at her. "I don't know how you can laugh about it, sister. It was a very unpleasant experience."

"Yes, and if Barbara hadn't been there, I don't know how I would have stopped you from inviting the two of them to park their be-hinds on our sofa to wait for Anita." Elizabeth glared right back at her.

"I was simply trying to be polite!" Catherine ran a hand over her head, smoothing the hair that her performer's vanity kept straightened and colored black. "I mean, all children cry sometimes, you know, and I didn't want them to think Anita had anything to hide."

Barbara rolled her eyes. Catherine is not known for thinking things through.

I patted her shoulder. "Thank you for sticking up for us, Miss Catherine. I'm sure this whole thing will be sorted out soon, and Benno will be cleared."

"Everyone has so many questions," Catherine complained. "Each one is worse than the next. First the police wanting to know about Benno embracing Ellen, then the reporters—"

"Catherine!" Elizabeth hissed.

"What about Benno and Ellen?" I asked.

Catherine's creamy skin flushed. "I didn't mean—it wasn't like that! They weren't doing anything wrong, I didn't mean to imply they were, I simply saw them on the street. Benno had his arm around her shoulders, and that policeman, he twisted my words so it sounded like—" She realized she'd gone too far.

"Anita, you hungry?" Louis threw me a lifeline from the grill.

I wasn't, but I grabbed on and pulled myself away from Catherine before I lost it. Let Elizabeth lecture her, I didn't need to hear anymore.

"Friends like that, no need for enemies." Louis bent over the grill and forked a sausage onto a plate for Tabitha.

"She means well, Anita, don't let her get to you," Tabitha sympathized.

"Yeah, I know." I stuck the DCW paper in my back pocket and followed Barbara over the windowsill into her apartment.

"How bad was it?" I asked.

"Don't worry, Anita. Elizabeth kept Catherine pretty well muzzled up while those women were there, and I made sure they didn't hang around inside. Tabitha said they'd gone by the time I sent her out to intercept you. I didn't want you walking into an ambush. Catherine's right about one thing, those reporters are bad enough."

"My mother hasn't shown up, has she?"

"No. She making you crazy, too?"

"I'm actually glad she's here, she's been a big help with Clea. I was hoping she'd be back early enough so I could do the laundry."

"You go ahead, just leave Clea with us. DCW comes back, we'll pretend she's Malik's sister!" Barbara offered.

We both laughed, but it wasn't all that funny. "If you don't mind, I guess I will," I said. "Might as well get something done today." One thing about school uniforms, it meant I had to wash every weekend. Clea's got exactly one navy sweater, five white polo shirts, two pairs of khaki pants, and one skirt; a week's worth.

Tabitha went up first, to make sure no social workers were lurking on the landing. I checked the answering machine: three reporters; no mother and no Benno; a long message from Joel Rheingold. He'd spoken to both Aaron Wertheim and Rita

Velarde; the good news was, Rita herself would make the home visit on behalf of Catholic Children's, probably late Monday afternoon, by which time he'd have a restraining order and be present to ensure that she didn't take Clea. The bad news was, Rita had warned him that DCW might act sooner. Joel, after consulting with Aaron, advised me to do exactly as I had been: not to be home when DCW came calling. He also suggested, in delicate lawyerese, that I might want not to send Clea to school tomorrow, although it would be a good idea for me to be reachable at work so no one would get the idea that I'd abducted Clea.

Well, it gave me something to think about, while I pretended I wasn't ticked off at my mother for not being there. I could've used another head to help me figure out what to do. I left a note on the table, telling her we were in the backyard.

I took my laundry down to the basement and loaded the washers, then went back outside. Clea and Malik had dug a huge hole in Barbara's garden and added enough water to make a wallow fit for a hippopotamus. Catherine redeemed herself by slicing into the peach pie she'd made, which was fabulous.

I put the wash in the dryers.

The Wilcoxes went back upstairs. I drank a second beer. Barbara sent Louis home with a plate of food. Tabitha and Bobby pried Malik away from the joys of mudville and hosed him off before heading for the subway. Clea looked like she was having a beauty treatment, with mud plastered on her arms, legs, and face. I made her do a preliminary rinse in the wading pool, then ran a bath for her in Barbara's tub. I was starting to be more worried about my mother than annoyed.

It was a good thing I had laundry to deal with, what my mother refers to as the meditation of mindless work. I balled socks and fretted. Why had Nafissa disappeared? Was her brother hiding her, or was she hiding from him? Was it because of her relationship with Jamie—if there was a relationship—or did she know something about Ellen's death? Was she somehow involved in it?

While I was folding the crease into Benno's jeans so I could put them on a hanger, the tears got me again. What if losing Benno was the only way I could keep Clea? What if losing him meant I'd lose her too?

I sat on Barbara's bed, stunned by the thought. I knew the system was perfectly capable of responding illogically to the whole situation. It wasn't bad enough Clea's baby-sitter was dead and her father in jail; in their infinite wisdom, they'd have no problem taking her away from her mother and her home to place her with strangers for her own protection. And even if, as Aaron and Joel said, I'd eventually be able to get her back, how would I ever be able to repair the damage to her sense of security, her trust in me, when I'd been so manifestly unable to protect her from being torn away from her family?

17

IT was after five when she turned up, and trust my mother, she
sailed in looking like she'd spent the day at a spa. I had to
wonder if Aaron's adolescent crush hadn't gotten more flattering with time; no lunch date with a ninety-something woman
leaves a person looking as young and as flushed as my mother
was.

But we had more pressing things to discuss, like, Where
were we going to spend the night?

We were just sitting down at Barbara's kitchen table to hash
it out when Clea came in, wrapped in a big pink towel, and
plunked herself down in Gamma Rho's lap.

I went to get her pajamas, a pair of red leggings and a big
San Francisco 49ers T-shirt my mother had brought her. I came
back just in time to hear Gamma Rho explaining to Clea that
she and I were about to have a sleep-over at the apartment of the
man who was going to get her dad out of jail.

It was news to me. "Aaron has plenty of room, Anita, and
he'd be more than happy to have you two. What do you think?"
My mother nuzzled Clea's neck and tried to kiss behind her ear.

Clea hunched her shoulder against my mother's lips and slid
out of her lap. "My dad should stay in jail." Clea scowled. "He
killed Ellen."

I was on my way out the door to get her pajamas. The words
stopped me cold.

"No, he didn't," Gamma Rho told her, firmly. "Your dad had
nothing to do with what happened to Ellen, honey."

"Then how come the police put him in jail?" Clea demanded.

I opened my mouth, then decided to let my mother handle it. My emotions were too scrambled; if Gamma Rho could be straightforward and emphatic in her belief in Benno's innocence, let her explain the flawed nature of our criminal justice system to a seven-year-old. It was more than I felt up to tackling.

Clea grabbed her pajamas and stalked back to the bathroom to put them on.

I raised my eyebrows at my mother. "Wertheim's apartment? Isn't that a little beyond the call of duty?"

"They've got a three-bedroom on Riverside and Seventy-seventh. His mother is in the late stages of Alzheimer's, so she's confined to bed. He has a full-time caregiver living there, in the maid's room, so you and Clea would have the guest room. Really, it's perfect, Anita."

"He lives with his mother?" The man had to be sixty, at least.

"He moved back in several years ago, after his divorce, to oversee his mother's care." My mother grinned. "And because she's still living in the same rent-controlled apartment he grew up in. At this point, when she dies, he'll be able to take over the lease. Although the apartment will probably fall under luxury decontrol soon—it's got to be worth more than $2,000 a month, in this market."

Real estate. The meat and potatoes Manhattan lives on. A rent-controlled apartment was something you hung on to for dear life; divorced couples have been known to continue living together because neither could afford a new place.

I thought it over. It made a certain sense. Where would we be safer than in a lawyer's house? No one would think to look for us there; none of my friends would inadvertently lead DCW to us; no reporters to dodge every time we went in or out.

"What about you?"

"Aaron felt it would be best if I stayed here to deal with the phone and any DCW worker who came to the door." Her tone was all business, but there was an unusual softness to my mother's eyes. Maybe the seeds of romance had been planted after all.

"Does he have a television?" Clea chose my lap this time.

"Yes, honey, he does."

"She wants to watch *Star Trek*," I explained. "It's our Sunday ritual. Benno cooks, and . . ."

"What time is it, Mama?"

"Almost six o'clock. We'd better get a move on. I have to go upstairs for a minute and pack some things for us. You put your sandals on, and I'll be right down."

With the help of Double A car service, we made it in time. My mother must have called ahead to alert Wertheim, because the first thing he did, after showing me where to put my overnight bag, was usher Clea into the living room and turn on the set. It was part of a totally modern wall unit, custom-made to hold a flashy digital sound system and retrograde turntable. The bottom shelves held records, with a rack of CDs up one side.

I'd hardly had time to look around the apartment, which I was dying to do. The walk from the tiled entry to the guest room gave me enough of a glimpse to realize that not only was the apartment a classic six, it had retained most of the original, prewar detailing.

I would have left Clea to watch the show by herself, but she latched on to my arm.

"You stay, Mama!"

The perfect host, Wertheim said he had some things to finish up in the study and left us alone. Clea's manners, on the other hand, seemed to have deserted her. She'd barely mumbled a hello, and I had to nudge her to say thank you to Aaron for the television.

Thumb in mouth, she settled herself half in my lap. The sofa we were nestled in was a slightly worn golden brown velour, with cushions soft enough to be real down. Two matching armchairs and an ottoman completed the set, with dark walnut end tables and sideboard. The walls were a soft cream, interrupted by tall bookcases; the wood floor was covered by a huge brown Turkish rug patterned in black, rust, and gold.

As I looked around, I realized we were in what must originally have been the dining room. There was a swinging door that I deduced led to the kitchen. Through an archway with open French doors, I could see Wertheim, with his back to us at his desk, in what was probably a living room converted to a study. The large window in that room faced west, and the apartment was on a high enough floor that it had an unobstructed view of the sunset, luminous pink clouds fading to orange.

I felt as if we'd landed in heaven, until I remembered where Benno was. Clea was totally engrossed in the program. I couldn't concentrate on the inner turmoil of B'lana Torres; I kept seeing Benno on a hard, narrow bunk with God only knew what kind of cellmate. Our alternate worlds seemed as unreal as the holodeck on *Voyager*.

I stroked Clea's shoulders, glad she was able to escape into the fantasy life of the idiot box. It was what she needed, to forget the grown-up problems seething above her head. At least on *Voyager*, there was always a happy ending.

When the program was over, she brushed her teeth without protest. Our room looked as if it had once belonged to a young woman. It had thick wall-to-wall carpeting in a deep rose. The headboard on the double bed we'd be sharing was gorgeous—it was marquetry, an intricate scene where a woman with long black hair strolled among deer and willow trees. This room also had a wall of bookshelves, in a light wood, and a framed print of a unicorn that I recognized as being from the tapestries at the Cloisters. Scanning the books gave me a sense of the former occupant's taste, which ran heavily to novels by women, from Jane Austen to early Toni Morrison.

"Mama, how come he has a picture of you?" Clea picked up a silver frame with a black-and-white portrait of a young woman in an academic robe, dark hair curling out from under the cap. Most of the pictures on the shelf were of a young woman with short, straight hair who bore a strong resemblance to Aaron—probably his daughter. The woman in the cap and gown had my kind of grin, wide enough to make her eyes squint. I could see how Clea, at first glance, had mistaken her for me.

"That's not me, Bops, but you're right, she does sort of smile like me. Let's remember to ask Aaron in the morning who it is."

I settled her into the bed and lay beside her to tell the day. Clea kept her eyes open until I ended with, "Now we're staying at Aaron's house so we won't be bothered by all those nasty reporters. Tomorrow Gamma Rho will take you to the zoo, because you're her favorite grandchild, and Dad will be home before you know it."

"Do you promise?"

"I promise." I kissed her cheek and waited until her breathing evened out. I left the door open a crack.

Aaron Wertheim stood in front of an art deco bar unit, pouring himself a drink. The woodwork was incredible, bird's-eye maple with ebony trim, a vintage piece Benno would have died for. It had doors that swung open to reveal slots for glasses and cocktail shakers, a collection of decanters and bottles, everything with its own special, built-in place.

"May I offer you a scotch?"

I hesitated, not wanting to be impolite. Lawyers; why did they all drink scotch?

"Or would you prefer bourbon? Cognac?"

I accepted a cognac. We made small talk about the bar, and the view from the bay window, which had a window seat with a pile of cushions covered in bright *marimeko* fabrics.

"Shall we sit?"

The glass of the bulbous snifter was so thin I was afraid it would shatter when I climbed onto the raised bench. I felt a little awkward, perched next to him; although the seat was the size of a twin bed, it was an intimate space for two people.

"I hope the statement I made to the media met with your approval?" Aaron swirled the ice in his glass. "I would have preferred to consult you first, but I thought it best to make our position unequivocally clear. I understand you were able to avoid talking to any journalists?"

I nodded.

He smiled. "Not an easy feat. So, how is your daughter handling things?"

We moved from chatting about Clea to the specifics of the case against Benno. I updated Aaron on my conversations with Marsha Ginsberg and Michael, adding that I was still trying to talk to Nafissa N'doye.

"That's good, very good. We will subpoena Ms. Ginsberg, which gives us a solid counterargument to one leg of the case the district attorney will present to the grand jury. His evidence is largely circumstantial, a house of cards. We should not have a problem with toppling such a flimsy edifice."

Aaron tilted his head, listening to a faint sound from the front of the apartment. "Ah, that will be Lavinia, my mother's aide. She was out for the evening." He put his glass on the sill and slid off the window seat. "Come, I'll introduce you."

I left my cognac with Aaron's scotch and followed him into the hall. According to my mother, Lavinia was a private pay aide Aaron had hired, five or six years ago, when his mother was diagnosed with Alzheimer's. I had a certain amount of professional curiosity in seeing Mrs. Wertheim. My mother had also told me the Alzheimer's had progressed to the point that she was all but comatose, unable to do more than swallow a few sips of Ensure. Without exception, the Alzheimer's patients I'd met in the course of my job had been sent to nursing homes long before they reached these final stages. But then, most people couldn't afford full-time care.

Lavinia was a dark-skinned woman, in her fifties maybe, a head taller than Aaron, with an island accent. She put her purse down on the hall table to shake my hand. Her grip was warm and firm. "Pleased to meet you."

"Shall we look in on Mother?" Aaron suggested.

"She been quiet tonight?" Lavinia asked.

"Yes. She managed a few sips of Ensure at eight."

At the other end of the hall was a half-open door. I heard the low hum of an air conditioner, felt the cooler air. Aaron stepped back to let Lavinia enter first. She walked around to the far side of the bed.

The woman who lay under a loosely woven white cotton blanket was curled on her side in a fetal position. Her limbs were pale, emaciated, her hair tufts of white fuzz sticking up like dandelion fluff.

Lavinia stood behind her and stroked her shoulder. "Ruth?" she murmured. "Ruth, I'm home now, and we brought you a visitor."

Mrs. Wertheim's eyes opened.

Aaron took his mother's hand. "Mother, this is Anita Servi, Rosemarie Gunther's daughter. You remember Rosemarie, she was here this afternoon to see you? She took care of Dad."

I said hello to the blank eyes. I had to admire Aaron. Watching someone succumb to Alzheimer's is incredibly hard, and yet he managed to treat his mother as though she were still present, a cognizant human being.

"I better change her now," Lavinia said. "You go on, Aaron, I'll rub her feet a bit before she sleeps again."

"Thank you, Lavinia." Aaron bent to kiss his mother's cheek, stroke the downy hair. "Good night, Mother."

"Good night, Mrs. Wertheim." I stepped up to the bed and touched the bony shoulder. Her eyes seemed to focus on me for a brief second before she closed them.

Back in the study, Aaron reached for the glasses on the windowsill. "Let me freshen our drinks."

The vertical lines between his eyebrows seemed to have deepened. I wished there was something I could say, but even sympathetic clichés were inadequate to the situation. Watching someone you love die physically is bad enough; with Alzheimer's, you must first watch all knowledge and memory be erased, back to infancy and beyond. Not to mention the fear that you yourself are carrying the genetic seeds of this particular dissolution in your own brain. I thought he might like a moment alone.

"I'll just check on my daughter," I said.

Clea was sleeping the sleep of the angels. I sat on the bed and put my arms over her little shoulders, rested my face on her back, thinking of all the perils life holds in store for children, all the things we parents are so helpless to shield them from. She barely stirred under my embrace.

On my way out of the room, I remembered the photograph in the silver frame. I picked it up and brought it out into the light.

18

OUR glasses with their two amber liquids glowed on the sill, but the room was empty. I settled myself with two pillows behind my back, sipped my drink, and appreciated the view. The sky was fully dark now, the lights from the Jersey side of the river more numerous by far than the few stars.

I had the photograph in my lap. As I contemplated the face of the woman with my grin, I got an odd, expectant tingling in my chest. It felt as if this woman might hold the answer to questions I'd lived with all my life. Could she be my real mother? Had Rosemarie done more for the Wertheim family than take care of their ailing father—adopted me and moved to California to protect them from the shame of an illegitimate child? My resemblance to the woman in the picture was stronger than my resemblance to Rosemarie.

When Aaron rejoined me, the tension in his face had eased. Seeing the silver frame, he smiled. I held it out to him.

"My sister." He shook his head and smiled wider. "I can't help wanting to laugh with her, although she died the summer after this was taken."

Aaron Wertheim looked up at me. I gave him my best version of his sister's smile and said, "I was born on December 8, 1957."

I watched him do the math.

He sat down and reached for his drink. I kept quiet, leaving him room to deny it if that was what he needed to do. I'd lived this long without knowing. If he didn't know, or didn't want to acknowledge who I was, I could still wring the truth out of my mother. I sipped at my cognac.

"Why didn't she tell me?" was what Aaron finally said. He looked stunned.

"I've been asking that question for decades," I told him. "You didn't know your sister'd had a child either?"

"What? My sister? You thought she was your mother?" Aaron took a gulp of scotch. "My dear, I'm afraid you've mistaken the parent in question. I believe I'm your father."

It was my turn to be stunned. Of course, it was the simple explanation, staring me in the face, and I hadn't seen it. The tops of the dark trees across the street shivered and swayed. I felt dizzy, swept up in a current of air. The one part of her story I'd always believed was that my father was dead.

Or so I'd convinced myself. Hearing Aaron acknowledge his paternity, I had the instant realization that in some irrational, internal world I'd also held the parallel belief that someday I'd meet the man who was responsible for the other half of my DNA. Not only that, but I'd instinctively know who he was as soon as I set eyes on him. But I hadn't.

Aaron was talking, almost to himself. I forced my attention to follow his words.

"My father died on March 31, 1957. I was home from Harvard for two weeks. The last time I saw Rosemarie was at the funeral. I wrote to her—the letters were sent back to me, unopened. I called—her mother hung up on me. I loved her. I couldn't understand what had happened." He spoke slowly, putting the pieces in place in his own mind as he thought out loud.

"When I came back to the city in June, I went to Rosemarie's apartment. Mrs. Gunther walked past me as if I didn't exist. One of the neighbors finally took pity on me and told me that Rosemarie had joined the army as a nurse. I tried to contact her, but they said there was no record of a Rosemarie Gunther ever having enlisted."

Here was something I could latch on to. "I tried to check up on that part of her story, too, and got the same result. She always told me my father was a GI who'd been killed before she even knew she was pregnant, and that when her condition became obvious, she'd been dishonorably discharged."

"Why didn't she tell me?" Aaron repeated. "I would have . . ." He stared into his scotch, then at me. "Why didn't she tell me when she asked me to represent—why didn't she at least tell me today?"

"I gave up on trying to figure out my mother's motives years ago," I offered. At that moment, it almost didn't matter to me that she'd been keeping this from me my whole life. Almost. "I'm sure she'll have an explanation."

I couldn't help laughing. The sound, to my own ears, was more dismayed than happy. I honestly didn't know how I felt. On top of everything else in a long, hard week, to find myself sitting next to my father . . .

"I'm sure she will. One thing hasn't changed about Rosemarie—she certainly spices things up." Aaron's tone was not exactly amused, either. He lifted his drink as if he were about to make a toast.

We clinked glasses, but then neither one of us knew what to say.

The silence felt enormous. I took the last sip of cognac.

Aaron got up to refill my glass. We looked into each other's eyes, then quickly away. In that glance, I had the sensation of a shared thought.

Aaron said what I was thinking. "It's a lot to take in. Perhaps we each need think things through before we discuss matters any further?"

He put it a lot more formally than I would have. I nodded, grateful for the respite.

"Good. Well, then, if you'd like to write your husband a letter, I'll be glad to deliver it tomorrow, along with the clean clothing. I'm sure he'd be delighted to hear from you."

He provided me with a yellow legal pad and a pen. There was an awkward moment before he left the room, neither of us knowing how exactly to say good night. In view of our new relationship, a kiss or a hug might have been appropriate, but we weren't there yet. We settled for little bows of the head, and I was left alone in the window seat.

"Dear Benno," I wrote, then stopped to look out over the Hudson and across the continent to California. Dear, dear, Benno—you are so dear to me, please let this not be true. I tore the page off, folded it into quarters, and tucked it under my thigh to throw away when I got up.

What I wrote instead was about Clea's dance class, buying the *lapa* for her recital, the barbecue at Barbara's. In the end, I added a paragraph telling him that Aaron Wertheim was my father. I kept it simple; the knowledge alone was enough, like having a compass tucked in my pocket.

I felt oddly peaceful, falling into sleep, but I had a restless night. Coolness from the air conditioner subliminally altered the room until I thought I was in Benno's cell as Aaron had described it, a chill coming off the tiled walls, the bed hard as a two-inch pallet. I finally got up and turned the damn thing off, opened the window to let in the humid night air.

Finding myself at work at nine-fifteen Monday morning was the most disconcerting thing that had happened to me in days. After the jolt of finding Ellen's body, nothing had been normal. Now here I was, cappuccino and croissant in front of me, pink message slips in my hands, Anne in the doorway of my cube.

"So how was your weekend?" she asked.

Well, let's see, my husband was arrested and jailed for murder, I went to a memorial service for my daughter's babysitter, tried and failed to find a woman who might be able to clear my husband, ducked visits from a DCW worker who wanted to take my child away, and oh yeah, I almost forgot, I found out who my father is. How could I even begin?

"Fine" is what I said. "Considering."

At seven-thirty that same morning, I'd left Clea sleeping in Aaron's guest bed and followed the smell of coffee into the kitchen. I'd been disappointed to find that Aaron had already gone to work, leaving a note on the table for me. "Dear Anita

and Clea, Help yourselves to whatever you find. If you need anything, ask Lavinia. I'll be in touch later in the day." It was signed
with a simple, informal capital A.

I'd just poured myself a mug and was on my way to shower
when my mother appeared at Aaron's front door. I hadn't been
ready to talk to her, either, but the look in her eye told me there
was no way we weren't going to confront the issue.

"I had a long talk with Aaron after you went to bed last
night."

I couldn't believe I was blushing. Of course she knew, she'd
known all along. It was brand-new to me, though, and I needed
it to be mine.

There was another new feeling in there, too—parents discussing me behind my back. I wasn't sure I liked that sensation.
"He called you?"

"Yes." She put a hand on my arm. "There's more to it than
you know, Anita. We have to talk."

"No, we don't." I pulled away. "Besides, it sounds like you
two have already talked. I need to get in the shower."

"There are things you should know."

She'd had forty years and more to tell me. Whatever it was
now, it could wait until I was ready. I had enough to deal with.

"There's coffee in the kitchen." I brushed past her to the
bathroom.

When I emerged, wrapped in a pine green towel, Gamma
Rho was laughing on the bed and Clea was pouting.

"Mama, did you tell me I was born in the Bronx Zoo?"

It took all the control I could muster to correct her without
laughing myself. "No, Bops, not in the zoo. You were born in the
Bronx, in a hospital."

"You didn't say that!" Clea accused.

"Well, I'm saying it now. Is Gamma Rho taking you to the
zoo?"

My mother had tried to take me aside, but it was my turn to
be the one who wouldn't engage in conversation. Let her mari-
nate in her own juices for a while, served her right.

I kissed Clea and left without breakfast.

✦

And there I was, faced with Anne.

"I saw the papers, so don't 'fine' me, Anita Servi! I know the cop mentality, but I can't understand how that rat-assed bastard Michael could have gone along with them and arrested Benno!" Anne slapped the *Times* down on her desk.

"That damn job, excuse me, *job*." She emphasized it the way cops do, referring to themselves as being "on the job." "I should've known going from a uniform to a suit wasn't going to change his mind-set. 'Arrest the bad guys, that's what I do.' "

"It wasn't exactly up to him, you know." So now I was defending Michael? "Besides, aren't you the one who told me all men are capable of infidelity?"

"Okay, so I think men are dogs when it comes to other women, but honestly, where are Michael's brains? Go for the boyfriend, it's such a cliché. He should know better than to think Benno's a cold-blooded killer!"

Talk about clichés. I didn't much care for the subtext, either. "So it's okay for you to assume Benno was fooling around with Ellen, but not for Michael to take it a step further? Anne, do you know something I don't?"

"No, of course not. I'm sorry, Anita, I didn't mean it to sound like that. The point is, Michael doesn't know anything either. He told me last week he didn't think Benno—he said he was working around that detective, Peretti, and the next thing I know—" She whacked the paper with the back of her hand.

"Ladies?" Emma chose that moment to stop in the doorway of my cube.

"Pardon my French, Emma, but my *former* lover, Detective Michael Dougherty, just put Anita's husband in jail for murder." Despair was not in Anne's vocabulary, but it was in her voice.

That made two relationships on shaky ground in the aftermath of Ellen's death.

I gave them an abbreviated version of the situation, heavy on the reassuring note of Aaron Wertheim, defender of the unjustly accused, light on the subject of DCW and Clea. Anne's face seemed to shrink in on itself as I spoke, her anger evaporating to leave despair in its wake. She'd trusted Michael as much as she could, and now he seemed to have blown his chances.

"If there's anything I can do, Anita—character witness, help raising bail, anything, you just ask," Emma offered.

"Absolutely!" Anne chimed in. "Anything at all, just let me know."

"Thank you. Mostly what I'd like is to catch up on these messages." What I also asked for, and got, was the afternoon off. I didn't know what I'd do with it, but I had to do something, and concentrating on the needs of my clients seemed overwhelmingly impossible.

I did, however, have to make an attempt to take care of some of the people I'd been neglecting all week. Mabel Johnson was at the top of my list; she'd already called once this morning, and three times on Friday, wanting to know where Nafissa was. I listened to her diatribe, letting her vent, until the word "shiftless" made its way into her stream of complaints, and I put a stop to it.

"Nafissa had a family emergency, Ms. Johnson, and it's my fault that I didn't call to let you know on Friday. I'm sorry, I know you wanted to go to the movies this afternoon. Let me call you back in an hour, and I'll try to find you another volunteer."

I knew it was hopeless; on such sort notice, finding someone strong enough to push Mabel's wheelchair was virtually impossible. Miracle of miracles, the problem was solved for me. I'd just struck out on my third call when Mabel herself called to say her neighbor's son had offered to take her!

I took it as a good omen and went to work on the message slips. I bawled out a Meals-on-Wheels worker who hadn't made a visit he was supposed to and got him to approve service for my client starting tomorrow, even if he hadn't seen her in person. I left messages for the St. Luke's hospital social worker about two clients. I made calls to several homebound clients, just to touch base.

Then I checked my answering machine at home, hoping for a message from Benno. My luck held past a few persistent reporters to Rita Velarde from Catholic Charities with the welcome news that she'd have to put off her home visit until Tuesday. I should have known my luck was running out when there was no word from Benno, but I decided to push on and call Arthur Nessim. I wanted to ask him some direct questions about Nafissa's whereabouts; surely the school would know why she'd dropped out, and where she was?

Nessim wasn't in, wasn't expected at all today. Jamie was teaching a class and so was unavailable. The man answering the phone had no idea whether or not Nafissa was back in attendance at the school.

There hadn't been a call back from Miranda, either; I realized I hadn't really expected her to call me—once the news about Benno's arrest was out, why should she? I drew vines on my notepad and thought about Arthur Nessim.

By then it was almost one. I decided to get a sandwich and head over to Riverside Church. I didn't have a session with the students scheduled until Tuesday, but it was lunch hour. If I pressed Talile about Nessim, reassured her that he couldn't retaliate against her by contacting immigration, maybe she'd tell me more. I had to do something.

The gods were a bit more helpful when I got to Riverside Church. I ran into Talile on her way into the cafeteria, but she wasn't happy to see me. In fact, she ducked back into the dining room, pretending not to have noticed me.

The news must be out, and I was persona non grata. "Talile!" I walked after her.

"You didn't tell me it was your husband!" she accused. "Jamie says we should not talk to you."

"I'm sorry," I said. "You have to believe me, my husband had nothing to do with Ellen's death."

She tried to go past me. I didn't let her get away with it, though.

"Please, listen to me." I stood in front of her, blocking her way to the lobby and the elevators. She held a tray with a tuna sandwich and a Coke. "Can we sit down?"

Talile searched the dining area, a high-ceilinged room paneled in dark wood, as if she were looking for a way out. A handful of people, none of them familiar to me, or to Talile either from the panicky look on her face, sat scattered among a dozen large round tables. It was a nice room, although it didn't seem an inviting place to dine.

I followed her to a table in the exact center of the room. Two elderly white women were just finishing their lunches. As soon as Talile put her tray down, they gathered their plates and left us alone.

"You met my daughter; do you think I'd do anything to hurt her? I'm not trying to make trouble for anyone here, either, I just need to know the truth so my daughter's father can come home."

Talile fidgeted with the plastic wrap on her sandwich, but she heard me out while I went through the whole situation, what the police thought about Benno and Ellen.

"It is so important to you, to see Nafissa? You tell me why."

"She knew Ellen better than anyone else. They both went out with Jamie, and there's something I don't understand—"

Talile glanced around at the other tables, making sure no one could hear us. She leaned close to me. "Nafissa is afraid of her brother. If he knows she is—" She held out two fingers together, the middle over the index, indicating intimacy. "On the night when Ellen died, Nafissa was together with Jamie."

"Nafissa was sleeping with Jamie?" I wanted to be sure I understood the gesture.

"No, no!" Talile was almost as horrified as Nafissa's brother might have been. "No, not sleeping! In the bar. With Vlad and Natalya. A date. When brother knows, he will marry Nafissa quick, quick, before his countryman is changing his mind!"

"I know she was with them, but I would never say anything to her brother about it."

Jamie walked past the door, on his way to the food counter. He looked over and frowned in our direction.

Talile followed Jamie with nervous eyes.

I asked the question I'd wanted to ask yesterday. "What's

going on at the school, Talile? Are the teachers getting involved with the students? Jamie and Nafissa, Mr. Nessim and Ellen—if Nafissa's scared to talk about it, if she's worried that the institute will make trouble for her with immigration, I can help her."

"Yesterday night, I go to Nafissa's apartment after my work. Brother tell me she stays with a friend from her country." Talile hesitated. "I know this woman. Tonight I will call her."

"Tonight? Why not now? Do you have her address? I could go over there myself—"

Talile ventured a smile at my eagerness, but when I stopped talking, her face got serious. "I don't know where she lives, only telephone number, and she is no answer."

Jamie stalked across the dining room toward our table. He carried a clear plastic container of chef's salad.

"Excuse me, Ms. Servi, I don't think you should be here." He glared at Talile.

She turned her wrist to read her watch. "Oh, I'm sorry, I am late!" and she was off.

Jamie turned his headlights on me. "I don't know why you'd even want to be here."

"My husband didn't kill Ellen." I was denying it so routinely, you'd think I believed it wholeheartedly. If wishes were horses . . .

To my surprise, Jamie sat down in Talile's place. "Okay, what is it you want to know so badly you're bothering my students on Sundays at their jobs?" So Talile had told him I'd been to the restaurant. "Go ahead, ask me anything. Maybe I can spare us all some awkwardness." The overhead light glinted off his round glasses, making it impossible for me to read his expression. He popped the lid on the salad, speared a chunk of iceberg lettuce, and studied me while he chewed.

I was so disarmed by his show of openness, I couldn't think what to ask. But there was the tip of a barb in his voice, and I reminded myself that whatever his motives, they were as opaque to me as if he'd framed them in Russian or Amharic.

He swallowed. "Cat got your tongue?"

"No." If he wanted it, I'd give it to him; but how exactly to phrase the question? Is there a major case of sexual harassment going on at the ESL Institute? Are you *schtupping* a student? Is Arthur putting the moves on a staff member thirty years younger than he is?

I settled for the innocent routine. "I was just trying to find out what's happened to Nafissa N'doye. She was volunteering with one of my Senior Services clients, who really misses her."

"Uh-huh." He grunted it with a "yeah, right" intonation. "Well, Nafissa has a very strict Muslim brother. He doesn't approve of some of the American ideas she's learned here. Eventually he'll realize that we're not corrupting her, and what she really needs to help him in the market is to speak fluent English."

"What if he decides what she really needs is to marry a good Muslim man and spend her time raising children instead of working?"

Jamie chased down a slice of ham and stabbed it with the plastic fork. "What is it you're really after, Ms. Servi? All this concern for a woman you hardly know?"

Okay, he asked for it. "I'm wondering if there isn't a problem with sexual harassment at the institute." Direct, but I didn't want to antagonize him. "Was Arthur Nessim having an affair with Ellen?"

I thought he was going to choke on a tomato. He coughed and pounded his chest.

Reaction, the question always got a reaction.

"Look, you're female. You've met guys like Arthur before, haven't you? He likes women." Jamie sat back. "But that's as far as it goes. Ellen knew that. The man's a flirt. No big deal."

"Uh-huh." My turn to be skeptical. "If you had feelings for Ellen, I'd think you'd want to know what really happened."

"Feelings?" Jamie leaned close to me. His breath smelled like hard-boiled egg. "I saw them together, your husband and Ellen, and it sure looked like a case of feelings to me."

That shut me up.

The container of salad was almost empty. He clicked it shut.

"This arrangement with Senior Services is starting to seem like a bad idea, at least with you as the liaison. If I were you, I'd stay home and leave the people here alone. They've had hard enough lives without this tragedy, and you stirring things up doesn't make it any easier for anyone to get on with what they need to do to be successful in this country—learn English."

"Maybe what the students need is the opportunity to study English in a school where the staff doesn't take advantage of their ignorance about American laws!" My heart raced with the audacity of what I'd said. I pushed my chair back, hoping he'd let it go.

"You know what I think? I think you're desperate to believe anything except the truth about your husband."

Jamie was halfway across the room by the time I got my mouth open.

"I'm not going to let it rest!"

The high ceiling seemed to swallow my words. Jamie didn't turn around, and no one else seemed interested in who'd dared to speak so loudly.

19

WHICH left me with unanswered questions, vague suspicions, nowhere to go, nothing to do. I took myself across the lobby and into the nave. I slid into a pew toward the back and bowed my head. A spicy, charred scent lingered in the air. From a distance, the intricate scenes on the stained-glass windows were like a child's kaleidoscope of deep blue flecked with red and yellow. I let them tumble and blur, and filled my mind with the high, empty space of the vault.

What came to me in my meditative state was the calming realization that Michael was the right person to be looking into Arthur Nessim, and furthermore, if there was some funny business going on at the institute, into that as well. I'd started out thinking that Ellen was having some kind of consensual relationship with Nessim, and things had gone very wrong. Now a new idea was forming. What if Ellen had been about to blow the whistle on a sex scandal of some sort, and Nessim had silenced her to protect his job, his reputation, the institute?

I stared into the stone ribs of the ceiling and chased my thoughts around the filigreed circles of light at the ends of their long chains. Who among the students did I know well enough to ask? Talile, although aware of something going on, might not realize how unethical it was; in any case, she hadn't been willing to say. Vlad was not about to rat out the school. Natalya—I didn't know her at all, and besides, she seemed to be attached to Vlad; nothing wrong with a romance between fellow students. So I was back to Nafissa.

What had she wanted to tell me when she'd come to my office that morning? In the wake of Ellen's death, had she intended to carry through with exposing Nessim? How did Jamie fit into all this? What exactly was his relationship with Nafissa?

The air in the nave brightened briefly as the sun burned its way through the overcast, then dimmed again. What sitting still had made me realize, more than anything else, was that I was tired down to the bone. I'd been going on grief and adrenaline; in the quiet, the effects of Friday night's lack of sleep had ambushed me.

I thought about walking home, checking out the reporter situation, and seeing if I could swoop in to pick up the mail, but I was too beat. It was all I could do to drag myself out to Riverside Drive to catch the M5 and ride in air-conditioned comfort down to Aaron's apartment.

It's not the heat, it's the humidity. The day's low gray sky matched my mood: heavy, oppressive. My reflection in the polished brass of Aaron's elevator showed a woman in a blue dress, rippled and blurred. Her eyes were dark smudges. I closed mine so I wouldn't see how sad she looked.

The apartment was quiet. I didn't see Lavinia, although I assumed she was there somewhere. I tried to reach Michael at the precinct; he wasn't in, so I left a message with Wertheim's number for him to call me.

I was grateful to be alone, to be able to turn the air conditioner on low, put on my nightgown, and climb into the soft bed. I felt like one of my clients, a woman in her nineties who got up in the morning and dressed in bra and girdle, stockings and tailored dress, put on earrings and brooch, and went out to do her marketing. After lunch, she'd change into a flowered nightie and take a two-hour nap.

"She's sleeping!" Clea's voice announced.

A solid little body thumped into me. No, I wasn't, not anymore. They were back, and so was consciousness.

Aaron had left a message saying he wouldn't be back until

eight. I called Barbara, who said a reporter and a photographer from the *Post* were still camped out on the stoop. We ordered Chinese delivered and made a nice meal of it, with Lavinia to keep the conversation from getting too heavy.

At seven, I let Clea watch an hour of television. My mother made free with Aaron's wine, pouring us each a second glass and settling me down in the window seat for a talk. By then I was curious, and awake enough to listen.

"You didn't say anything to Clea, did you?" I started.

"Of course not, Anita! And I hope you'll give me the benefit of your discretion, too. There's something you need to know, something I haven't told Aaron, and I don't intend to."

"Come on, Mom. Don't you think this has gone on long enough? Aaron has a right to know everything, as much as I do, and I'm not going to keep any secrets for you!" After all this time, anything less than full disclosure was not acceptable. Besides, I'd watched my soap opera, *As The Voild Toins Ovah*, as Benno's immigrant aunt Rose calls it, long enough to have learned that the root of all plot complications is truth withheld. For the good of the person who is being deceived, of course, but it inevitably backfires.

"You might change your mind after you hear me out."

We watched a fuzzy orange sun head for the New Jersey horizon while she explained to me that Aaron's mother had picked up on the feelings between the two of them. After her husband's funeral, when Aaron was back at college, Mrs. Wertheim had taken her aside and offered her money to stay away from Aaron. Her reasoning was that Aaron had a promising career as an attorney, but not if he were married to—"an uneducated *shiksa*" was how my mother put it, although with a disclaimer that Mrs. Wertheim had phrased it more diplomatically.

"At that time, it would have been almost impossible for a Jewish lawyer to join a white-shoe law firm, and while you might think a gentile wife would be an asset, not one of my class, and not a Catholic; to marry for success, Aaron would need a blue-blooded WASP."

If my mother was good enough to change Wertheim bedpans but not to marry a Wertheim son, she didn't want any part of the family. She turned Mrs. Wertheim down and went off in a snit to join the army as a nurse. At the preinduction physical, however, the pregnancy test turned up positive: I was on the way.

At that point my mother had two choices: telling Aaron or having a back-alley abortion, which was morally unacceptable to her. "I cared enough about Aaron to realize what saddling him with a wife and child, when he was still in school—not to mention adding the disapproval of his mother—would do to his future. So I swallowed my pride and went back to Mrs. Wertheim to say I'd reconsidered. She gave me $20,000, which, in case you've ever wondered, is how I bought the house in Berkeley."

I raised my eyebrows at that one. I'd lived with my mother's personality long enough to intuit that what she'd really been after was a ticket to California and a stake to start a new life as far from her parents as she could get. If she made it sound like she'd taken the moral high road out of concern for Aaron, well, rationalization has always been my mother's strong suit.

I also knew better than to argue with her professed past motivations. I'm no stranger to rationalization, myself. There was, however, the present to consider.

"Okay, so what would be your reason for not telling Aaron now? What harm could it do, with Mrs. Wertheim on her deathbed?"

She looked at me like I was being deliberately dense. "That's the whole point, Anita. She's not able to explain herself, and knowing what she did could change Aaron's feelings about his mother. Why not let sleeping dogs lie instead of opening up a can of worms for him to think his mother ruined his whole life?"

"Jeez, Mom, you sound like the farmer's almanac! Besides, what makes you think his whole life was a waste? Seems to me he came out of it pretty well, and so did you. Wasn't that the whole reason for your self-sacrificing acceptance of the Wertheim hush money? And who knows what would have happened if you two had gotten married?"

Actually, the thought gave me pause. Youthful attraction

was one thing, but my mother with someone as buttoned-down as a lawyer, even a rich liberal lawyer? I don't know.

My mother swirled her wine in Aaron's goblet and declined to respond. The oldest trick in her arsenal: if you don't like the question, ignore it. It depressed me. She'd finally been forced into admitting the truth about my father, but she still wasn't taking questions.

"Fine." I said the word with the same sulky spin Clea gave it, a child yielding to the authority of an inscrutable parent. "Anything else you need to get off your chest?"

"Just promise me you won't say anything to Aaron?"

"No." I wasn't seven, and I didn't need to let my mother off the hook so easily. "You should tell him yourself."

"Don't be like that, Anita. I know you're mad at me, and you have every right to be, but I did what I thought was best at the time. For all of us. That's what I'm still doing."

"Yeah, right." I heard it in my own voice, the years of resentment.

My mother bowed her head.

She was my mother, but I wasn't going to relent. "I won't lie for you."

For the first time in my adult life, my mother gave an inch. "Okay, if he asks you, you do what you think best, but could you please not volunteer the information?"

My mother, self-serving as usual. Although it was the closest I'd ever heard her get to humble, and I confess I took advantage. "Maybe you'd head back to my apartment before Aaron gets home? Let me have a little time alone with my father?"

She hesitated. Rosemarie Gunther hates to be left out of the action.

I gave her a dignified way to exit the scene. "Mom. What Aaron and I really have to talk about is Benno's case. He's my priority right now."

Aaron came in while I was putting Clea to bed. She was telling me the day, for a change, complete with lions and tigers and bears, heavy on the flamingos, which had made the biggest impression on her. Aaron told us the joke about why flamingos stand on one leg—if they picked up the other one, they'd fall down—and we both groaned.

When I joined him in the kitchen, he was making notes in an illegible scrawl on a yellow pad and finishing off the cold sesame noodles.

"You've already eaten?" he asked.

I nodded. "But I'll keep you company, if you're ready to tell me how Benno's doing?"

He wiped his mouth with a paper napkin and sat back. "I find myself in an unusual position. I had no idea, when I agreed to represent Benno, that he was my son-in-law."

"Is that a problem?" It hadn't occurred to me.

"Not necessarily. As long as he's aware of the relationship, and I'm on guard against any possible conflict of interest on my part. It was perceptive of you to have written him about the situation, otherwise I would have had to inform him myself."

"Without asking me?" It seemed a little presumptuous of him, but then, he was a lawyer.

Aaron's expression was bland; his words weren't. "I don't allow personal feelings to interfere with my representation of a client."

I felt like a rebuked child. If that was how he wanted to play it, okay, just the facts, ma'am. "What's happening with his case?"

"The grand jury is scheduled for Wednesday afternoon. Benno and I had a full and open discussion of the evidence, and he's given me permission to discuss the substance of our conversation with you. Some of the issues that arose are rather personal, and while this would not present a problem if you were simply the wife of a client, I must admit I feel rather awkward discussing them with my daughter."

"Maybe we could let that ride, right now? Until we've both had some time to let it sink in?" It was beginning to occur to me that having a father might not be all it was cracked up to be.

We looked at each other for less than a second before his

gaze slid away, glad to let the subject drop. Not exactly the decisive confronting of issues I'd expected.

"Well, then, to get down to Benno's narrative account of what happened the night Ms. Chapman was killed. As Benno described it, and I'm inclined to believe him—he had no reason to lie to me—after he finished stabilizing the bookcase, Ellen hugged him, in the way of saying thank you, and they exchanged a kiss."

I sucked in air. This is how the world ends, across a kitchen table strewn with half-empty containers of Chinese take-out.

Aaron raised a sardonic eyebrow. "It was only a kiss."

"If that's all it was, why the hell didn't he tell me about it?" But I knew the answer. Although Benno's as honest as they come, one of his beliefs about marriage is that it's often better not to tell your partner everything you're thinking. Or doing, evidently.

"Admitting to a peck on another woman's lips on one's anniversary is not the action of a prudent man. He might perhaps have been foolish enough to assuage his guilt by mentioning it some while after the fact; once Ellen's body was found, however, and with the police suspecting him—" Aaron cleared his throat, like I was supposed to understand the delicacy of Benno's position.

Like hell, I thought. The fierce expression on my face got me the arched eyebrow treatment again.

"Benno mentioned that you'd been looking at him as if he *were* a criminal. Can you understand at all how embarrassed he was?"

"Embarrassed? For Pete's fucking sake!" The man was in jail for murder—talk about embarrassing! "That's all there was to it? He had a guilty conscience over a kiss?"

Aaron had moved on to the Lamb Szechuan Style, a good excuse to let the question pass.

I thought about how it might have happened. If Benno were attracted to Ellen, if he'd decided not to act on it, but then the circumstances . . . Wait just a damn minute. "What about that little chemise? What about the dinner at Donato's?" I demanded.

"Yes, the anniversary gift. An innocent mistake. After taking his purchase home, Benno compared it with a similar item in your wardrobe. Realizing his error, he intended to exchange it for the proper size." He cleared his throat. "In my younger days, I was guilty of the same faux pas myself. Unlike Benno, however, I did not realize what I'd done until the lady opened the box. And in my case, the item in question was too large." I could've sworn the great Wertheim was blushing.

He lowered his head to consult his notes, flipped back a page, and said, "As to the meal at Donato's, the sequence of events seems to be as follows. On Saturday morning, April sixth, Ellen left a message on your answering machine. You were out of town, with Clea, in Philadelphia?"

I nodded.

"Retrieving the messages, Benno returned her call. She initially stated that the matter could wait until Monday. He was concerned about her, however, and invited her to dinner. During the meal, Ellen confided that the administrator at the English as a Second Language Institute, where she was currently a volunteer, had offered her a summer job. Apparently he was also making approaches of a more personal nature, which were not exactly unreciprocated."

This time I did the raised eyebrows bit. "Nessim's married."

"Yes. Ellen appreciated that fact and had no intention of pursuing a relationship with him. She also very much wanted the job and didn't know how to accept the position while rejecting the man. Benno provided a male perspective on how to handle the situation gracefully, to, as he phrased it, put Mr. Nessim off without putting him off."

It fit what I'd been thinking about the institute like a dovetail joint. Aaron started on a new page of notes as he listened to my theory, but his only comment was a muttered "interesting."

"I wonder why Ellen never said anything to me about a situation with Nessim?"

"Actually, I was curious about that myself. I asked Benno if she had." His tone was amused. "Evidently the two of them concluded that you would take a hard-line, feminist position, and counsel her not to accept the job. They apparently felt the situation required a more nuanced interpretation of political correctness."

"Benno never told me about it, either." I made it a statement. The question I didn't dare ask out loud was, Why didn't he mention taking Ellen to Donato's, if nothing had happened between the two of them?

"Ellen asked him not to, and he kept her confidence." Aaron paused, as if listening to my unspoken question, and went on to answer it. "Anita, I'm no psychologist, but I am a man. Given what I know about human behavior, I'd say your husband probably did feel some—slight attraction—to Ellen, and along with feeling guilty, he didn't want you to overreact. I gather that Ellen was somewhat of a member of the family, and my impression is that Benno didn't want to jeopardize the relationship between you and Ellen, and more importantly, between Ellen and Clea."

I got up and started clearing away the Chinese food cartons. I didn't know what else to say. My husband's an idiot?

"I'm just going to say good night to Mother, then we'll have a cognac, shall we?"

I was in more of a margarita mood, but the unreasonableness of tequila was probably not what I needed. "Sure," I said.

The window seat seemed to be the spot. I was staring out at the orange glow of the city reflected off the low, dark sky when Aaron handed me a snifter.

"You look as if you'd lost your last friend."

"That's about how I feel," I said. Like I'd eaten a double helping of Mournful Oatmeal.

He laughed, but give the man credit, he picked up on my mood.

"Anita, please forgive me. I did not intend to make light of the situation. It does, however, give us something to work with, an alternative, and innocent, explanation for some of the events the state's case is based on. Benno may feel as guilty as

Judas Iscariot, but it was not such a serious kiss."

I hadn't thought I was making that big a mountain out of Benno's molehill, but I guess I was feeling pretty betrayed. Why hadn't he just *told* me? I took a sip of cognac to cover my embarrassment. It went down like smooth fire.

"There is in law what's known as the concept of mens rea, evil mind, or more commonly, guilty mind. Mens rea refers to intent, as differentiated from motivation. That is, intent is one of the criteria used to determine if an act can be deemed criminal. If I burn down your house deliberately, that is arson. If I fall asleep with a lit cigarette, which subsequently starts a fire, it's an accident. So, if your husband had no intention of kissing Ms. Chapman, if it was merely a matter of proximity, an impulse of the moment, almost, you might say, an accident . . ."

"You don't just kiss someone by accident!" Men.

"Well, perhaps you do. A kiss can certainly be unpremeditated, can it not?"

In my opinion, that was stretching it—what Benno himself would call an elastic concept. As far as I was concerned, he had every right to feel guilty.

"In any case, Anita, that occurrence is between you and Benno, a matter of marriage rather than of law. We will not mention it to the police. The dinner, yes, I'll have my investigator reinterview the waiter as well as Mr. Donato and get more specifics as to what they witnessed. Now, shall we run through your observations of the situation at the institute again?"

"Yes." I infinitely preferred concentrating on the case to discussing my marriage.

Aaron asked questions, fleshed out his notes, muttered "interesting" a few more times. I was the one who refilled our glasses as he outlined a credible alternate scenario.

Both Arthur Nessim and Jamie Westlake stood to lose if there was a flap at the institute. Either of them could have been the person who'd argued with Ellen over the phone while she was baby-sitting; either or both of them could have known Benno would be walking her home and set him up.

I played devil's advocate and tried to poke holes. "But

Nessim couldn't have known Benno would go upstairs with Ellen; he didn't usually. Doesn't that seem like an awfully coincidental piece of luck?"

"Perhaps." Aaron didn't seem at all bothered. "That's not ours to worry about, it's the district attorney's. Have you spoken with the detective today?"

"I left a message, but he never called me back."

"Good. There's no need to tip our hand as to a potential defense. First thing tomorrow, I'll have my investigator look into the situation."

I wasn't so sure that was a good idea, and I told him so. It was hard enough to get the students to talk to me; I could only imagine that a stranger asking questions would drive them deeper into silence. And as for anyone being willing to testify in court . . .

Aaron waved away my objections. "Not the students, Anita; he'll speak to the support staff. Trust me, John's very good. The institute does have secretaries? People who do the clerical work?"

"There's a roomful of computers, and people who answer the phones—I guess I always thought it was students, doing a form of work-study. I don't think Arthur Nessim has his own personal secretary, though."

"Perhaps not, but there will be someone who keeps track of the enrollment, does the bookkeeping and other routine matters. Your point about the students is well taken, however. It would be best for you to let the matter drop with them as well."

I don't like being told what to do, by anyone, and I would've argued the point if Clea hadn't been wailing, "Mama, Mama!" She'd gotten the bedroom door open. Standing there in her oversize T-shirt with her thumb in her mouth, she was a pathetic sight.

I calmed her down somewhat, but she'd had a bad dream, and what she wanted was to be home in her own bed. After calling my mother, who looked out the window to determine that no reporters were still lurking, I packed up our things, and Aaron called a car service for us.

A light fog had rolled in. The midnight ride up Broadway felt like we were traveling through a phantom city, all soft edges with silent figures drifting along the sidewalks. Clea curled against my side, her eyes open, the streetlights flashing yellow reflections from her dark pupils.

20

BENNO would have been turning over in his cell if he'd known what I was doing, but the quickest route to the Harlem Market lay through Morningside Park. The city had done a lot of work on it in the past few years—rebuilt the steps down the steep hill from the heights, dredged the pond, resurfaced the ball fields. It wasn't an overgrown jungle occupied by dealers and crack smokers anymore.

Still, I paused at the entrance on 113th and studied the prospect. A misty rain was falling, shrouding the tops of the trees. Below, the asphalt steps were swept and the hedges trimmed, sturdy yellow and orange marigolds flowering at their feet. There didn't seem to be any people around, not surprising on such a drizzly afternoon.

A poem I'd seen on the subways, nestled among ads for blemish removal by Dr. Zizmore like a pearl in a pigsty, came into my head.

> Western wind when wilt thou blow
> the small rain down can rain
> Christ if my love were in my arms
> and I in my bed again

Some anonymous author, five hundred years ago, got the moment and my mood perfectly. I put on my woman-with-a-purpose attitude and started down. Any mugger operating on a Tuesday after lunch, the least cosmic time of the week, probably deserved my twenty bucks for his work ethic alone.

A black man in running shorts with a blue hooded sweatshirt pulled over his head trotted up the stairs, punching the air with his fists. I made an effort not to be reflexively scared. The man, who was paying absolutely no attention to me, had well-developed thigh muscles, and was clearly in training. I kept going. He made it to the top, turned around, and passed me again, not even breathing hard.

Near the bottom, I could see a cluster of kids, junior high age maybe. A gym class practicing on the ball fields? There were girls as well as boys clustered around a man in sweats. Thank the goddess for Title 9—get those girls out and moving, teach them how to throw, catch, run. Equal access, and more important, equal seriousness of purpose when it came to sports, gave girls a kind of physical confidence I wish I'd learned at an early age.

I zigged east and north to 116th, crossing streets as I hit Walk lights. This part of Harlem is in transition—West African restaurants mingled with Dominican groceries, every fourth storefront shuttered, check-cashing places and Laundromats, apartment buildings with boarded-up windows, others with flower boxes of geraniums splashing their stoops with lipstick red and hot pink. I passed a jittery man with an orange nylon do-rag wrapped around his head; an elderly, coffee-skinned man in a brown suit; two heavy women in cotton housedresses and cardigans, talking in Spanish, with shopping bags on their arms; a reddish-brown woman, in lavender leggings that left too little to the imagination, pushing a stroller. It was a neighborhood, like mine or any other.

Walking the streets of Harlem with drops of precipitation curling my hair, I went over the things I still had to do with my day, starting with what I'd already accomplished. My mother and I had decided to keep Clea out of school another day, so they'd gone off to the Museum of Natural History. I'd spoken to her teacher and arranged to pick up her homework assignments. Yes, homework in second grade; school in New York is serious business.

The rest of the morning I spent doing paperwork and making phone calls, which culminated in a home visit to Virginia Campbell, one of my favorite clients, a retired nurse who lived in a shabby apartment in one of the glorious old apartment houses on Morningside Drive.

Virginia was always a pleasure. A woman with skin so pale you could see the blue veins in her cheeks, she knew what she needed and didn't hesitate to ask for it. In this case, a grab bar for her tub. In a storeroom in the cathedral's basement, crowded with so many donated canes, walkers, and commodes that we referred to it as "Lourdes," I'd found exactly what she needed. It would've taken Benno twenty minutes to install . . . but Benno wasn't available to play handyman for my clients, and Virginia would have to pay her Super to do it. So I delivered the bar and stayed for a cup of tea. We sat at the kitchen table, by a window overlooking Morningside Park. The view had inspired the idea of visiting the Harlem Market to see if Nafissa was working.

I'd felt virtuous enough, leaving Virginia's, that a trip to the market seemed like merely a slight detour. I took a page from my mother's playbook and rationalized tracking down Nafissa as tying up a loose end for Mabel Johnson; if her volunteer had really dropped out of the picture, then I'd have to find her someone else. In the back of my mind, curiosity about Nafissa's earlier visit to Senior Services still nagged at me. The social worker radar had picked up the vibes of someone in need, and it was that as much as any more reasonable explanation that drew me down the hill.

Armed with that explanation, I stopped at a pay phone to call Anne and let her know I wouldn't be coming back to work. It was already after two; I'd have to head straight home from the market to be on time for Rita Velarde's visit. Worrying about that ordeal, and how much I'd be able to keep Clea from understanding, dragged at my heels.

I must have paused a bit too long outside the open gate to the market, because when I looked up the security guard, nursing a cup of coffee in a booth just inside the Cyclone fence, was checking me out. I had on a blue-flowered rayon skirt and white linen crop-top, with a tailored shirt over it for a jacket, so he couldn't have seen much of my figure. It must have been enough, though; he hitched his pants up and came down the steps.

"Can I help you, miss?" The man looked like he went to the same school of style as the guards at the courthouse—polished mahogany dome of shaved head, two gold staple rings in his right earlobe.

I explained that I'd come to buy fabric, and I was trying to remember which aisle the merchant I was looking for was in.

"Not too many vendors here this afternoon. Shouldn't be too hard to find, if he's open." A cell phone chirped in his shirt pocket. "Hang on a second, now, and I'll walk around with you." The phone looked ridiculous in his big hand. He took it into the booth and turned his back to me for privacy.

I didn't need an armed guard. I crossed my fingers, hoping Nafissa would be at her machine, and hustled myself down the aisle toward the N'doyes' stall. At first I thought I'd struck out; the sliding glass doors, curtained with a light green fabric patterned in gold, appeared to be closed. I hesitated, about to knock, when I heard voices from inside.

"Nafissa?" I knocked on the glass.

The silence was profound. Overhead, a plane pulled noise along behind it on the way to La Guardia. I knocked again, gave it a few seconds before I pulled on the handle. The door bumped open an inch, then stopped. I put my nose to the crack.

It was too dark to see anything. "Nafissa, it's Anita Servi, from Senior Services at the cathedral? Nafissa?"

I stepped back and waited. The guard came around the corner.

"That the place you wanted? Doesn't look like anyone's around, but there's plenty of others sell fabric. Come on, I'll show you."

"No, this place has exactly what I want. I was here the other day." I gestured at the door. "Besides, I think someone's inside but they're not answering."

"Oh?" He knocked on the glass himself, loudly, with authority. "Hello? Anyone there?"

We listened to car horns dueling in the intersection.

"I'm sure I heard voices."

"Yeah, well, maybe the people don't want your business." He tucked his hand under my arm and started walking me down the aisle.

I wasn't the only one who judged people by context rather than stereotypes; I had to admit that what I was doing, trying to get into a poorly locked shop, could seem suspicious.

I dug in my heels, but leather-soled sandals don't grip very well on asphalt, and the guard gently tugged me along. I tried to jerk my arm away, which stopped him.

"Look, miss, I don't want no trouble. I'm just doing my job. You want to buy something from these people, fine, you come back another time." He started moving me along again.

"Do you know Nafissa N'doye or her brother? Did you see either of them come in today?" By that time we were at the gate, and I realized I was being escorted off the premises.

He let go of my arm. I got a card out of my bag. "I'm a social worker. Nafissa was helping one of my clients, and she didn't show up today. I just want to be sure she's all right."

I actually fluttered my eyelashes at him. It got me a shade more friendly of an answer.

"Yeah, she was here. Came in a few hours ago, but if she's not answering, either she left or she don't want to see you. Sorry, miss, but that's all I can tell you."

"Can we just go back and look? Don't you have keys or something?" I did the eyelash bit again, put a hand on his arm. "I'm positive I heard voices. What if someone's in there with her? We have to at least make sure she's okay."

He shook his head, impervious to my middle-aged charms.

" 'We' don't have to do no such thing. You'd better head on home now." He had me on the sidewalk, and he stood with his arms folded, barring the way back in.

"Okay, then let me look somewhere else for fabric. I really do need a yard of cotton."

He didn't budge.

"Come on, this is a public place. It's a market, and I want to shop." I stared back at him, then looked down. "I won't cause any trouble."

I stepped around him and headed down a different aisle. I scanned the shops on either side, hoping none of them sold fabric. A glance back over my shoulder told me the security guard wasn't following me.

I cut across the center of the market. The booths of the food court were closed, shuttered with metal gates. The N'doye shop was in the far aisle, and I headed for it again.

The door was still open a crack. I knocked on the glass again. There was no answer. I put both hands on the sliding door and pushed.

This time it slid open about a foot, and Nafissa stood in the opening. She was wearing a long, loose dress in a swirly pattern of rust, ocher, black, with a matching head wrap. Her features looked blurry, swollen. Her mouth smiled, but there was something else in her eyes—fear, defiance, a warning.

I kept one hand on the metal edge of the door so she couldn't slide it closed in my face. "Hi, Nafissa, it's Anita. I just came to see if—"

A quick jerk of her chin stopped me. "We are closed." Her lips formed two silent words after she spoke aloud.

Help me?

I tried to pick up her cue. "Oh, that's okay, I won't take but a minute. I only need a yard of cotton. I was here on Sunday, and I saw what I wanted—maybe you could just cut it for me?"

The whole time I was talking, Nafissa's face was working. Although I couldn't make out the exact words, her desperation was clear. Where was that security guard when I needed him?

"My brother is not here. You come back, one hour, two hour, he be back. Please, lady, we are closed now."

I kept up my insistent-customer routine. Nafissa's expression went blank, and she stopped the silent conversation. I noticed that her arms were not in view. I couldn't see anything in back of her in the dark booth.

Then she seemed to tilt toward the open door, and looked at

my hand. I asked a question with my eyebrows and got the slightest nod in agreement.

"Please, won't you let me in for just a minute? You're here now, and I have to get back to work. All I need is a single yard, for my daughter—you could cut it right now." While I spoke, I held up one, two, three fingers.

On three, I put both hands on the door-frame. Nafissa leaned her weight against the opening, and together we slid the door wide.

Nafissa kept on sliding and hit the floor sideways. I stepped over her, into the stall, and into Jamie. I shoved him backward. Unfortunately, he landed on the sewing machine table instead of on his ass.

I opened my mouth to holler for help. In the second it took me to think what word I should yell, Jamie was back on his feet. Metal flashed in his hand. "Knife" appeared in my brain. Instinct took over, and the start of pure sound came out of me.

Jamie smacked my face with his other hand, and I shut up. He lurched for the door. It shuddered on the track and slid closed.

Still on my feet, I dropped down and wrapped my arms around my knees.

In the sudden absence of light, sound was all I had. A solid thud and a moan—Jamie kicking Nafissa, still on the floor. She rolled against my shins. I reached out involuntarily to steady myself and realized her feet were bound together.

Then a bump against the glass and a sliding sound, wood. I made out the diagonal silhouette of a brace, holding the door closed from inside.

My fingers were busy at the cloth around Nafissa's ankles. I didn't get nearly far enough before Jamie kicked at her head again on his way to me.

He yanked me up by my hair. I squealed at the pain, bit it back when I felt the knife at my throat. A sinewy arm wrapped itself around my waist.

The security guard was knocking on the glass. "Hey, anybody in there? Hello? Hello?"

Jamie didn't need to tell me to be quiet.

We waited about a week while the man muttered to himself and tried to rock the door. The stick Jamie had used to lock it held. "Yeah, no one's in there. Told that woman not to bother. Now, where the hell'd she get off to?" On and on.

My eyes adjusted, but there was nothing to see.

The knife scraped against my windpipe when I swallowed. I felt the sharp nick of a shaving cut. My hand rose to touch it. Jamie pressed harder, and I let the hand fall.

I prayed for the guard to stay, to keep Jamie at bay while— while I did what, exactly?

I tried to look down at Nafissa, moving only my eyes.

A thin line of light lay along the bottom of the door, curved up over Nafissa's cheek, took a break for her nose pressed up against the glass, and disappeared into the cloth wrapped around her head.

There was a sharper, metallic sound when the man outside rapped again on the glass. A moment of silence, followed by a dim spot of light, like the idiot was trying to see through the curtain with a flashlight.

Look down, look down, I told him. Look at the face pressed against the glass.

The light stopped flitting around the back wall. Two beats of silence. Then his voice, casual. "Yeah, okay, like I said, no one here, door's locked like it should be. No problem."

A final tap at the glass, then silence. I counted ten oh-shits, twenty. The tension in Jamie's muscles eased to where I couldn't feel his heart beating against my back. He let the knife drop about an inch, giving me room to breathe.

I swallowed. My tongue felt glued to the roof of my mouth. I glanced down at the floor again.

Darkness. Jamie hadn't noticed what Nafissa was doing, but had the guard seen her signal?

I felt for her feet with mine.

"Stay still!" Jamie hissed.

I did. Another one of those hour-long minutes went by.

"What are you going to do?" I whispered.

Jamie's answer was a thin line of pain at the base of my throat.

So he didn't know either. Good, that gave us time. Nafissa had had a plan; now it was my turn. I didn't think Jamie was going to slit my throat right then and there; too messy.

Words, I had to use my words.

"My legs don't feel so good. I think I might pass out." I let go of the rigid grip I'd held on my muscles and let myself tremble. My teeth chattered, and then I was afraid I wouldn't be able to stop.

"Lie down." He took the knife away.

I curled on my side around Nafissa. My hands went instantly for the binding around her wrists.

Fabric ripped above me. I wasn't going to have enough time to undo these knots, either.

Sirens wailed somewhere far, far away. Footsteps scraped on cement, inches from where we lay. A woman laughed in a language I wouldn't have understood even if it had been English.

Jamie dropped on top of me, his knee pushing my hip into the floor, my right arm pinned under me.

Instead of pulling my arms back, however, he went for my face. I tried to think if it was better to be gagged with my mouth open or closed. Either way, it was a losing situation.

I pressed my cheek to the floor, making it harder for him to get the cloth around my head. He rolled me back onto my side, and the pressure of his knee eased.

I went back to Nafissa's wrists.

Open or closed was a moot point. Jamie stuffed a wad of material into my mouth, then took a couple turns around my head. It was all I could do not to gag.

Don't vomit, don't vomit. Breathe through your nose and whatever you do, don't vomit. I thought it like a mantra.

One knot came undone, but I couldn't find the next one. Nafissa wiggled her fingers.

I'd just realized the fabric was twisted in a figure eight when Jamie grabbed my arms and flopped me over on my belly.

Fine particles of damp, dusty grit from the straw matting got into my nostrils. I banged my legs up against Jamie's back, a weak gesture of protest. I was helpless as a fish, unable to get enough oxygen, to move my body the way it was supposed to move.

Physical resistance was futile. Think, Anita. My options were severely limited, but so were Jamie's. If I were him, I'd leave us here to die.

He moved down to my feet. An infinity sign of fabric wound its way around my ankles.

No, if I were him, I'd kill us and leave our bodies here. End of the day; if Nafissa's brother didn't come until tomorrow morning, if no one had seen Jamie come in or could identify him, who would ever know?

Simple.

A huge cracking sound exploded above our heads. Once, twice, three blows, a billow of light as the curtain was pushed back. Men's feet stepped over the shattered door.

Someone fell to his knees on my back. Men's voices, shouting.

Jamie rolled off me, then another body landed on the pile pressing me into the floor.

The chaos sorted itself out to blue uniforms grappling with Jamie, hauling Nafissa and me out like bundles of laundry. Hands worked at the gag around my mouth.

I couldn't get enough air through my nose. Panic rose in my throat. Fingers felt for the hunk of cloth filling my mouth.

A spurt of bile surged out with the gag. I coughed and choked, retched up the rest of my lunch. A hand with a paper towel wiped at my mouth. New York's Finest had been replaced by New York's Bravest—the fire department's paramedics.

Sirens were wailing everywhere. I wished they'd shut up so I could start thinking again. The paramedic wrapped a blanket around my shoulders and tried to lay me down. The embrace of the blanket and the hands trying to ease me horizontal were too much like the imprisonment Jamie had forced on me. I battled back and got to my feet.

My knees went wobbly. A chair materialized in the nick of

time. I couldn't stop shaking. Shock, my brain said. You're in shock. The cool, damp air settled into my bones like a Berkeley fog.

I looked down at the green liquid that had joined the blood on my white blouse. Kiss that garment good-bye, I thought.

21

I T rained all the rest of that afternoon and on into the night, a slow steady rain that did nothing to wash out the memory of how helpless I'd been in Jamie's hands.

It had started as a delicate tattoo on the arched fiberglass roof between the stalls. They'd kept me wrapped up in the chair while a slight man with a black mustache, wearing a suit with a somber tie, made the rounds. He asked me if I was okay, then went on to Nafissa and finished up with the security guard. I assumed the guy was Peretti, the detective from Homicide North, although he didn't bother to introduce himself on that first pass.

The sound of the guard's voice enraged me. Okay, he'd come through in the end, but if he hadn't stopped me the first time—yeah, Anita, if he hadn't stopped you, he wouldn't have been suspicious enough to follow up, to notice Nafissa's face at the bottom of the booth, to respond to her silent distress signal. If he hadn't been doing his job, you and Nafissa might both have been killed in there.

I forced my attention to the woman who wanted to get an IV started on me.

"I don't want that." I kept my arms under the blanket. She gave me an argument about needing fluids. I asked for something to drink, then, to take the taste of vomit out of my mouth.

Nafissa was on a stretcher, a square of gauze taped to one

temple. I met her gaze, and a shudder took over my body. If the guard hadn't seen her!

They'd put us in the same ambulance, Nafissa lying down, me seat-belted to the narrow wheeled chair. In the warm bright interior, the rain audible as a background patter now that the sirens had stopped, I reached out for her hand. She gripped back. We rode to St. Luke's like that, survivors with a lifeline to each other.

With a police escort, we were wheeled right into a curtained cubicle in the emergency room, where I allowed myself to lie down on a bed. Nurses came and went, checking our vital signs. One of them swabbed the shallow cuts on my throat, coated them with ointment, and taped a piece of gauze over the area. Another one wanted me to exchange my stained clothes for a hospital gown, but I refused. There was no way I was being admitted!

A doctor—at least, I assumed he was a doctor—shone a penlight in my eyes and told the nurse I could have something to drink. Nafissa was wheeled away, and a uniform came in to guard me. I lay back and tried to close my eyes to make him go away, but the room swam.

Staring at the striped curtains was no better. Every time someone walked by, they swayed, and I got dizzy. I rolled onto my side. It was an improvement, but then my thoughts started up.

How could I have been so stupid, charging into a situation I hadn't anticipated in the least little bit? All the time I'd had Nessim on the brain, not Jamie. I'd jumped to a conclusion, based on what? Nessim liked women, had maybe liked Ellen a little too much. He ran a school where faculty mixed a little too freely with the students. No, it wasn't like a university, where the students depended on teachers for grades and recommendations, but a female student who wouldn't put out, or a male student who objected, could still be intimidated. With the new Immigration and Naturalization Act, even legal immigrants were afraid of being deported for the slightest violation of the law.

It was Jamie who'd brought immigration up with the students, ostensibly so they could protect themselves, yes. And Jamie who'd seen Benno with Ellen shortly before she was killed. Jamie who'd been having an affair with a student, not Nessim. Jamie who'd definitely had a relationship with Ellen, and been spurned. Why hadn't anyone seriously considered Jamie?

Because he had an alibi.

Suspecting the boyfriend may have been a cliché to Anne, but there was a grain of truth embedded in it. I spun through the same loop two or three times until the thought of what it all meant for Benno finally derailed the train: if he wasn't Ellen's lover, then he wasn't Ellen's murderer.

I sat up.

"Please don't do that, ma'am." The cop stood up, alarmed. "I'll get the nurse."

He stuck his head out, looked both ways down the corridor, waved at someone. A Filipina nurse brushed past him with a cup of sugary, lukewarm tea. I took it in small sips that sat well with my stomach. The nurse went over my pulse and blood pressure again, asked if I needed anything else.

What I needed was my lawyer. Then I remembered the visit from Catholic Charities I was supposed to be home for. "What time is it?"

"Ten to six."

I hopped off the bed. The petite nurse hopped me back on, with an assist from the uniform.

"Detective'll be here in a minute," he told me. "You're not going anywhere before he talks to you."

A phone, I had to get to a phone. God bless technology, he had a cellular. I called my mother, who was half frantic. Once she heard I was all right, however, she gave me the gist of Rita Velarde's visit.

According to my mother, things had gone smoothly in spite of my absence. She'd explained to them that I'd had a client emergency at work—which wasn't far from the truth, although she hadn't known it. Rita'd brought a very unpleasant woman from the Department of Child Welfare with her. My mother described the DCW woman like the wicked witch in *The Wizard of Oz*, all skin and bones and dressed in black, with a personality to match. The witch had tried to make nice to Clea, all the while looking for an excuse to snatch her away. Fortunately, Joel Rheingold had kept his word to be present for the visit and to make sure no one interfered with Clea's placement. My mother managed to hustle both social workers out before Clea snapped to the subtext of their visit.

Michael appeared through the curtain, pushing an empty wheelchair, and cut the conversation short. I couldn't have been happier to see him if he'd been Benno himself.

"Get me out of here!"

"Hop on, Social Worker. You look like you'll live, and we have to talk."

I was more than ready to go, but Michael didn't take me far. We turned a few corners and wound up in a cul-de-sac outside a door marked Radiology. Michael told a mini tape recorder his name and mine, the time, date, and where we were, then set the thing in my lap. I went through just the facts, ma'am, of what happened when this little social worker went to market.

Michael had clicked the machine off and started in on a lecture when I heard bigger trouble approaching: my mother. Having totally disregarded my request that she not come to St. Luke's, she was harassing the nurses as to where was I then, if I hadn't been discharged?

"I don't mean to give a statement and run, but that's my mother, and if I don't appear, she'll turn the place inside out looking for me." I abandoned the wheelchair and followed her voice.

"I have *never* seen such inefficiency! You're hardly busy in here. Police are crawling around the place like lice, so you tell me how a patient simply walked out!"

The nurse couldn't get a word in edgewise, and she was trying.

The rapid change in my mother's expression when I came around the corner, from annoyance to dismay, gave me an idea of how I must have looked. Blood and vomit stains on my rumpled white shirt, my hair loosed from its bun and wild around my face, the red marks on my cheeks from the gag, the gauze on my throat—I was a mess.

She put her arms around me, and to my shame I started crying. She hushed me into the wheelchair Michael had pushed after me. It took her all of five minutes to locate my purse, badger a doctor into parting with a sample pack of Ativan, and cow Michael into letting me go.

She would have walked out with the wheelchair, too, and pushed me home, but I insisted on walking. The rain had let up, and it was only four blocks. The cool night air and the physical exertion, mild as it was, gave me time to regain my composure and walk off the helpless feeling.

The familiarity of Broadway was comforting. College students buying six-packs of beer and pints of Ben & Jerry's in Mama Joy's, Leon shaking his cup out front; the fluorescent glow from Tom's washing the sidewalk; the metal shutters over Bank Street Books, Lechter's, Samad's Deli; in the larger world of my neighborhood, all was as it always was. Hearing that my mother had also had the presence of mind to let Aaron Wertheim know what was going on so he could get started on Benno's release helped too.

By the time we got back to the apartment, Barbara had Clea tucked into bed. She didn't stir when I went in to kiss her. The soft, perfect skin of her little face got me crying again.

My mother's solution this time was to put me in a tub of Epsom salts, which in my opinion was a mistake; it gave me the opportunity to beat myself up. What would have happened to Clea if I'd died? With Benno in jail, would they have let my mother keep her? Against my will, I had an image of Clea among strangers, the only mother she'd ever known dead, her father in jail for killing her baby-sitter, her grandmother unable to see her.

I dunked my head, merging my tears with the hot, salty bathwater. Don't go there, Anita. It didn't happen, don't even go there. It's a worst-case scenario, and it didn't happen.

My mother rinsed my hair under the tap, dried me off like I was a baby, and got me into a flannel nightie. She'd boiled a bag of Tabatchnick's frozen chicken soup with matzo balls, and I managed to eat half of it.

I didn't want the Ativan, but she insisted. It would've been a good thing if it had worked. Alone in our bed, Benno's absence lay heavy beside me.

Wertheim's concept of guilty mind clung to me like lint. Benno's attraction to Ellen was almost the least of it. What was harder for me to admit was that I'd entertained, seriously, the possibility that my husband had not only been unfaithful but was also a killer. The kind of person who could plunge a screwdriver into his mistress's chest, then come home and make passionate love to his wife.

How would I be able to look at him . . . or he at me, knowing what I'd thought?

When the red numbers blinked their way to 11:11, I gave it up and crawled into the sofa bed with my mother. She curled an arm around me and sang the old union songs that had been my lullabies as a child. I fell asleep to the image of Joe Hill accompanying the Union Maid on a picket line around the courthouse, demanding Benno's release.

Morning came clear blue and cool, with the smell of coffee. Clea was already in her school uniform, sitting at the counter with Gamma Rho. It was almost as if the past few days had never happened.

My body, when I got out of bed, told me otherwise. I was

stiff all over, with the first flush of purple bruises on the backs of my wrists and around my ankles. Mercifully, the red marks on my cheeks disappeared with a light dust of face powder.

Clea managed a good whine about not having her homework and being behind in class. I cooled her jets by leaving her at the early drop-off program before school and promising to talk to her teacher. After hearing a highly edited version of the story, Ms. Sheehan had no problem agreeing to let Clea make up the work during the morning recess.

I had almost as easy a time clearing things at my job, where I gave Anne and Emma a slightly less edited rendition of the previous afternoon's exploits. It amazed me how calm I felt, knowing it was all over and Benno was in the clear. I wasn't quite ready to take on anyone else's problems, though, so I kept to paperwork and off the phone, except for a call to the ESL Institute.

I needed to touch base with Nessim; I was concerned about how the students would react to the news about Jamie. I'd decided to offer to set up a kind of conversation/counseling session if he thought it would help them express their feelings. But I got the receptionist, who told me Nessim was in a meeting with the police, so I left a message.

Updating the stack of files on my desk brought me to Mabel Johnson, and her complaint about Nafissa not showing up. Nafissa had been heavy on my mind anyway. I called St. Luke's and found out she'd been discharged that morning. There was no answer at the 718 number on the card I'd picked up at her brother's booth on Sunday. Even if Nafissa went back to school at the institute, which I hoped she would, I decided I'd find another volunteer for Mabel. Nafissa had been through enough at the hands of white Americans.

I closed my eyes and let the scene from last night play itself out again in my mind. I knew I'd have to do this over and over, repeating the trauma until the fear leached out of it, and my memory could let it go.

✦

Just before noon, Michael put in an appearance. I could see Anne stifling her curiosity; she wouldn't allow herself to give Michael the satisfaction of her asking. He played it cool, making it clear he'd come to see me on official business.

Before I could get any questions of my own out, Michael cut to the chase and told me they were still processing papers downtown to get Benno released.

"Pays to get a good lawyer. Come on, Social Worker, I'll take you to lunch. I gotta tell you, I'm glad Peretti's the one who'll take the heat for a wrong arrest."

Michael made me wait until we got to Le Monde before he parted with any information. We were the first of the lunch crowd, so we got a table outside with no one around us. Michael ordered a steak sandwich and fries. I opted for the onion soup; my nerves weren't up to red meat.

Jamie had invoked his right to counsel, and they hadn't gotten a word out of him. What the police knew, they'd put together from Nafissa's story, and Michael gave me the gist of it. Yes, she'd been with Jamie, Vlad, and Natalya that Saturday night, sitting outside at the West End, when they saw Ellen, with Benno and the bookcase. Nafissa hadn't noticed when or if Benno left, but she thought that Jamie had been somewhat distracted, looking toward Ellen's building. Seated where they were, they'd had a clear view of the door.

Vlad and Natalya had taken off first. Jamie was supposed to escort Nafissa home on the subway, but he sent her off on her own. At the time she'd been relieved; she'd decided to tell him she couldn't date him anymore, in part because of her brother but more because she'd figured out he still cared about Ellen. It was only later that Nafissa had realized Jamie'd abandoned her at the 110th Street station because he intended to go back and see Ellen.

"Some things transcend culture," I said. Never date a man on the rebound.

"Seems Ellen warned her Jamie was a sick puppy as far as liking dark-skinned women, but she didn't know the half of it. Private Westlake had a little problem, stationed in Somalia. We got a fax of his service record this morning, complete with a couple rape accusations—unsubstantiated, of course, but at least the military wrote 'em down."

Our food came. Michael fed french fries into his mouth and kept on talking around them.

"No sign of forced entry, so either Ellen let him in or she opened the door thinking it was Benno come back for some reason. Then they argued, he picked up the screwdriver . . ."

When she heard about Ellen's death and the cops came to the institute, Nafissa panicked. "Hard to tell which she thought was worse, far as her brother was concerned—having been out with a white infidel or talking to the blue-uniformed devils. Either way, when Jamie told her to go home, that he and the other two wouldn't tell the cops that she'd been with them, she accepted it and split. Course, that allowed us to think Jamie had a solid alibi."

"Did she say why she came to see me at work the next morning?"

"Peretti was asking most of the questions, and I might've forgot to tell him that little detail. My guess, she was afraid Jamie was involved, worried about his behavior. She wanted to talk to someone, get a second opinion, like. You thought she had a reaction to my picture on Anne's desk? So maybe she changed her mind, figured you'd just tell her to tell it to me, and she was still trying to avoid any involvement with cops."

Michael went off on a riff about how much damage a few scared, inexperienced cops could do to the whole force when they over-reacted to a situation any veteran would know how to handle without drawing his gun.

"Yeah, yeah, but what next? How come she dropped out of school? What was Jamie doing at the market yesterday?"

"Whoa, Nellie. I told you, we didn't get particulars, so I'm guessing again, but if Nafissa wasn't at school, she wouldn't have to see Jamie. Who I already said I think she was afraid of. The story got a little garbled around the middle. Some woman from the school told her you were looking for her, your husband was arrested for Ellen's murder. That seemed to really shake Nafissa up. It came through loud and clear that her conscience was bothering her because she had a pretty good idea we had the wrong guy.

"I'm telling you, if she'd just come out with the whole story, it would've saved us a lot of grief. There we thought Westlake had an alibi, and all the while he had her terrified." Michael washed the bite in his mouth down with a sip of coffee. "What we figure is, with you stirring things up, Jamie went to the market looking to make sure Nafissa kept her mouth shut. Seems Tuesday is the brother's day to hit the wholesalers. If Jamie knew that—which he probably did—he also knew there was a good chance Nafissa'd be at the booth alone. Whether he meant to kill her, who knows? By the time his lawyer gets into it, Jamie'll come up with a nice, innocent story. But one thing we know, he didn't tie Nafissa up until after you came banging on the door."

"You mean if I hadn't come along, Nafissa would have been safe?" I was horrified at the thought that I'd almost gotten her killed.

"That's not what I said, Social Worker. Yeah, maybe Jamie'd've left her alone, but then you've got Benno being railroaded for a murder he didn't do. Don't even think about it. All's well that ends well, if you know what I mean."

His cell phone chirped. I sat through a string of "yeahs" that ended with an "I'll be right there."

He pulled a twenty out of his wallet and put it on the table. "I hate to eat and run, but—do me a favor, Anita?"

I guessed I owed him one, for what I wasn't exactly sure.

"Talk to Anne for me? I know how she feels about the job, I can't change that, but could you just remind her how I feel about her?" He put his hand over mine. "Okay, she's had some bad experiences with men, but maybe you could tell her that we're not all two-timing pond scum?"

Michael was gone before I could lash out at him with what was on the tip of my tongue—"You mean, like Benno?"

I added some money for the waitress and went inside to pay. Of course, that wasn't what he meant.

I stood on the sidewalk, debating whether to go home or back to work. The sun burned its way through the low cloud cover and poured a sticky heat into the city. In light of Michael's request, I decided on work.

When I got onto the cathedral grounds, though, I didn't feel quite ready to go back inside. I walked past Senior Services to the Biblical Garden and sat on a stone bench in the far corner. A sage plant was blooming, bright blue flowers on tall stalks. I watched the bees humming around, taking care of business. The air was hot, still, heavy with humidity.

What I regretted most was the way Ellen's dying had altered my image of her. She'd been attracted to an older, married man, and she'd chosen to confide in Benno, not me. And then the ultimate betrayal: she'd kissed my husband. No matter how unpremeditated, how innocent, a kiss was a kiss. If she'd lived, where would that kiss have taken them?

Would Benno, like Jimmy Carter if you believed his story, have been content to leave the lust in his heart and not act on it? I sat there long enough for the bees to buzz some sense into me. Benno was a good man, secure in who he was, in love with me. Okay, he wasn't blind. Ellen had a lot going for her, but ultimately she was a young woman with insecurities, looking to older men to help her figure out who she was.

Still and all, we'd been friends. What was she thinking, to have kissed my husband? I heard Marsha Ginsberg's words, "the little bitch." A bee dive-bombed my hair. I batted it away. What was I doing, thinking like that?

Grief has its stages; I'd watched for them in Clea, but ignored my own process. Denial, anger, acceptance. Clea had displaced her anger onto Benno, but mine was directed right at Ellen.

Then, finally, comes the ability to mourn. I didn't realize I was crying until I saw Anne wavering toward me. The light refracted from the water in my eyes, flashing sparklers around her hair.

In the end, when I'd finished sobbing and managed a thirdhand version of what had really happened, it was Anne who talked to me about Michael, Benno, men, and women.

"It doesn't matter what any of us think, Anita, it matters how we behave. Michael had to arrest Benno, but he didn't have to believe Benno was guilty; he did everything he could to prove Benno was innocent. So did you, Anita. Stop beating yourself up about it. Benno didn't have an affair with Ellen. That's just your fear talking. We all have temptations buried in our hearts, but they don't mean anything. They're phantoms, irrationalities that may rule the night, but when you let them out into the light of day, they evaporate."

She stood behind me and rubbed my shoulders. Anne might have phrased it in New Age vocabulary, but she was right. Actions are what count. I concentrated on breathing while she massaged the doubts out of my stiff neck. When she was finished, Anne rested her hands lightly on my shoulders before leaving me alone again.

A peacock dragged his folded tail through the open gate. My thoughts moved on from men as potential betrayers to men as fathers. I didn't have any real idea what having a father would mean for me, but I knew how important Benno was to Clea. Whatever insecurities I may have had about Benno as a husband, what I was having the hardest time forgiving myself for was questioning his dedication as a father. He knew Clea's whole future rested on our staying together until she was safely adopted. He might have abandoned me, but he would never have risked what a divorce would do to her life.

Which brought me to Ellen's father. I had no opinion on why Carl Chapman had left his wife, or gone back to her either.

What was all too clear, however, was the effect his choice had had on Ellen. I found myself feeling sorry for the man, surely the first step toward forgiveness.

A phone call home for messages had told me there'd been no word as to exactly when Benno would be released. My mother in her infinite wisdom had decided to take herself off to Aaron's so we could have our reunion as a family. I appreciated the gesture; I knew the last thing Benno would want was a welcoming committee that included any more people than absolutely necessary. I also smelled a rationalization—she had her own reasons for wanting to spend some time with the father of her child.

At three o'clock, I picked Clea up from school. Although Gamma Rho had already discussed Benno's homecoming with Clea, I went through it with her again while we swung our hands together and walked down 112th. Child of the media age, Clea related it to the story of *The Fugitive*—they'd been showing previews for a remake of the TV show, a program we'd never let her watch, but it provided a context she could handle for someone being wrongfully accused of a crime.

We stopped in at Sedutto's for ice creams—chocolate with chocolate sprinkles for Clea, espresso bean for me. We were on the stoop, crunching the last bites of cone, when Benno turned down the corner for home.

He looked odd without his knapsack, walking more slowly than his usual New-Yorker-on-the-move pace. As soon as she saw him, Clea bolted. Benno took her in his arms and carried her down the street toward me.

I tried to read Benno's face, which told me about what you'd expect: not much. He seemed pale, withdrawn, badly shaven. I put a smile on my face and all the years I'd loved him into my eyes.

A wind from the river carried the perfume of linden trees in full flower, erasing the exhaust fumes and sun-cooked concrete aroma of the city. Benno sniffed the air and spun Clea in a circle. The look in his eyes told me that although Ellen's death and too many things unsaid stood between us, our daughter was there also, and all the years ahead for our marriage to hold. I opened my arms to take them both in.

"Hi, honey, I'm home," Benno whispered into my hair.